W9-AZT-526

A KILLER CALLED "IT"

It glanced around after it shut off the tazer and slipped it back into its jacket pocket.

It rolled the little boy's body farther into the seat of the truck.

It shut the door.

It glanced around the pretty neighborhood as rain began falling.

It looked at the house, with its big picture window in front and its lawn, and the way the foothills rose behind the suburban property.

It went around and slid into the seat and started the truck up again.

It felt the Other One inside it.

It had a growl in its throat as it petted the boy's head, scruffing up his hair.

"Don't be afraid," it said.

Then it reached in the glove compartment and pulled out the duct tape and the box cutter. . . .

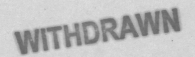
WITHDRAWN

Other *Leisure* books by Andrew Harper
writing as Douglas Clegg:

THE HOUR BEFORE DARK
THE INFINITE
NAOMI
MISCHIEF
YOU COME WHEN I CALL YOU
THE NIGHTMARE CHRONICLES
THE HALLOWEEN MAN

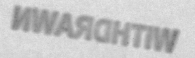
WITHDRAWN

ANDREW HARPER

RED ANGEL

LEISURE·BOOKS NEW YORK CITY

A LEISURE BOOK®

September 2003

Published by

Dorchester Publishing Co., Inc.
200 Madison Avenue
New York, NY 10016

If you purchased this book without a cover you should be aware that this book is stolen property. It was reported as "unsold and destroyed" to the publisher and neither the author nor the publisher has received any payment for this "stripped book."

Copyright © 2003 by Douglas Clegg

All rights reserved. No part of this book may be reproduced or transmitted in any form or by any electronic or mechanical means, including photocopying, recording or by any information storage and retrieval system, without the written permission of the publisher, except where permitted by law.

ISBN 0-8439-5275-X

The name "Leisure Books" and the stylized "L" with design are trademarks of Dorchester Publishing Co., Inc.

Printed in the United States of America.

Visit us on the web at www.dorchesterpub.com.

For Tommy Dreiling

With increasing thanks to Steve Park. Thanks to Raul Silva, Don D'Auria, Brooke Borneman, Tim DeYoung, Diane Stacy, and everybody at Leisure Books. Additional thanks to Dr. Katherine Ramsland, Tom Dugan, Matt Schwartz, C. A. Mobley, Shocklines.com, and others who know who they are who helped me with forensics, procedural matters, and the work and life at a state hospital for forensics patients.

For news of upcoming Andrew Harper novels, be sure to e-mail AndrewHarper@DardenState.com or visit www.DardenState.com on the Web.

RED ANGEL

NOTE TO READER

This is entirely a work of fiction, and although it is loosely set in actual locations, even these have been fictionalized to a great extent. Moon Lake, San Pascal, and Darden State do not exist as such. Neither do the characters in this novel. They are wholly fabrications of the author.

Then I saw an angel coming down from heaven, holding in his hand the key of the bottomless pit and a great chain.

—The Book of Revelations

Prologue

1

Night. Twenty-three triple-fenced acres. Bright lights created an unnatural glow of daylight around the facility. The low white institutional outposts of a state hospital.

THE DARDEN STATE HOSPITAL FOR CRIMINAL JUSTICE, on the engraved granite marker at the entry gate, flanked by a guard house and a parked police SUV.

Within, locked doors led to the quiet of long green corridors. Patients asleep. Restrained. Drugged. Muffled sounds as some within the rooms talked or even touched. Rules were broken when authority was removed.

A nurse set up meds for the after-midnight shift, counting pills, sorting them into cups.

The echoing rattle, squeak, slide of the wheels of a med cart as a psych tech and nurse moved down the hall, their voices low and nearly inaudible.

A doctor passed them, clipboard in hand,

flanked by two large men in white jackets and yellow shirts.

The sound of someone jogging down another hallway—a *tap, tap, tap* of shoes.

Doors were shut; the vending machine area was locked; the white light from the canteen cut a rectangle of brightness into the dim hall.

Ward D, at the end, another corridor closed off from the rest.

Twin red lights set above the emergency box interrupted the white and green of the hallway.

Two correctional officers stood guard in front of steel doors that each had a porthole window.

Above the doors a sign read: PROGRAM 28 | SPECIALIZED TREATMENT AND OBSERVATION. AUTHORIZED PERSONNEL | ACCESS LIMITED.

Through the porthole windows, the hall had a metallic, futuristic look.

Rooms to the left, observation area to the right.

Three psych techs sat at desks. Joking. Gossiping. Complaining. Voices low.

The rooms were dark, behind bars and glass.

Patients slept.

One of the forensics patients within Program 28 began to wail as if to wake the dead.

In seconds, a psychiatric technician unlocked the door, running to the patient's bedside.

The lights came up in the room with the cot.

Another psych tech stood in the doorway.

"What the hell," the psych tech said.

"Jesus H," said the other.

The patient, eyes closed as if he had been asleep the whole time and had not cried out, lay there, his prison-issue pajamas torn across his chest.

On his stomach were words, carved as if by sharp fingernails.

It was a long sentence and ran from just beneath his nipples to the small tufts of hair below his waistline.

The psych tech near the cot scratched his head, but didn't for a moment stop watching the patient on the cot.

His name was Michael Scoleri, but he called himself Abraxas, and he was known in the outside world, before he had been sentenced to life as an SVP and then reclassified as an SSPVS7, for carving this name on the bodies of the women he murdered.

Before he had entered Darden State, he believed he was God.

Now he was not so sure.

His restraints were torn at his wrists.

Blood all over his hands.

On his stomach, the words:

SUFFER THE CHILDREN TO COME UNTO ME.

In smaller cuts beneath this, along his thigh, when he was inspected, there were names, including LUCAS.

2

The stone angel stared with sightless eyes at the man.

3

In a stone room miles from Darden State, steam rose from a pool of water.

The man held a limp child in his arms, dipping the child's scalp back into the water.

3

Christmas was a week and a half away. The snow-topped mountains above the Inland Empire of Southern California attest to winter, although in the valley below, it was generally all palm trees and orange blossoms.

Two days earlier, in a ditch at the edge of an orange grove in Caldwell, California, a boy had been found dead, partially mutilated, with bird wings strung on a wire coat hanger wrapped around his neck.

Then another victim, again with the torn wings, this time in San Pascal County.

"Another angel," one of the cops had said, a young female investigator who was on the scene within two hours of the second body's discovery.

The lead investigator, a broad-faced man of fifty, had said to her, "Let's get some geography on this and the others."

"He puts them to sleep," she had said. "Then he kills them. Then this. What do you make of these marks?"

"Bites," the other detective had said. "They're his teeth."

Suburban hillside, adobe ranch house, modest but lovely, lights on the front porch and in the narrow garden courtyard. Sunday night. The usual TV routine: flipping around forty or so cable channels to find a minute or two of some show or documentary. The TV screen alternated between a story about ancient Egypt on the History Channel, CNN, and the local news show. Settled on the local news, but now and then Trey Campbell flicked back to CNN.

Trey Campbell sat up after he and his wife had put the kids to sleep. She was doing the *L.A. Times* crossword, wearing her reading glasses, with the bright lamp turned up. Occasionally she'd ask him a word. "What's a seven-letter name of someone who starred in old MGM Musicals?"

"The whole name?"

"Just the last name."

"Well . . . Astaire. Or Garland."

"Mr. Trivia."

"It's my brain. It's like I have the most expensive computer chip in my head, and all it remembers are MGM movies from the '30s and '40s. Or who starred in all the Dracula movies. Or the name of Henry the Eighth's fifth wife. Or which Wallace and Grommet episode involves sheep. Totally useless. If I could just apply it to solve the problems of the human condition . . . Hey, what about—" He was about to mention another name or two from the MGM musicals, but had flicked to the local news.

He kept the sound slightly low out of respect for his wife's crossword puzzle obsession.

"I don't think it's either of those. I think there has to be an 'r' as the second letter."

He'd been hoping to catch the news before going to bed the same night that the body was found. He'd heard from some buddies across town that there were some kids missing over in San Pascal County, and when the news piece flashed onscreen he turned the volume back up.

Just the tail end of the story. "—a man the *Inland Empire Daily* has dubbed the 'Red Angel'—" And then the news story ended. Trey had missed most of it.

" 'Red angel'?" his wife asked. "Is that what they call this guy?"

"Jesus," Trey said. "Somebody's killed kids in San Pascal. This must be the case Elise is being called in to consult on."

"Dr. Conroy?" Carly had a slight edge to her voice. Conroy was a beautiful woman on top of being an excellent forensic psychiatrist. Carly was rarely jealous of other women, but Conroy more often than not looked like a movie star along the lines of Sharon Stone—sexy and beautiful and smart and classy—and completely out of place at Darden State, where the rest of the staff looked like the most ordinary mortals in the world.

Whenever Carly mentioned Elise's name, it was always with a hint of annoyance that Trey might have to work in close proximity with her. They even joked about it, but he knew not to push that button with his wife.

"We talked Saturday night. She wouldn't tell me the specifics of the crime, just that some of the detectives had been bringing her in to try and work up a psychological profile of the killer. I just didn't think it was right here. This fast. I thought it was an old case."

They watched the rest of the news broadcast in silence, but other than the name the local media had just given the kidnapper and killer, not a lot of information was being let out.

When it was over, he said, "They don't have anything. They wouldn't put this on the news if they did. Not yet. They're trying to get someone to come forward, I'd guess. Awful. Awful. I guess this guy has a strange M.O. for them to call him the Red Angel."

"Terrible," Carly said. "Makes me want to double check the burglar alarm."

"What a nightmare for those parents. I can't even imagine," he said. He leaned over and kissed Carly on the forehead. "We're lucky."

She put the crossword down and leaned into him.

"Sure are."

"I don't know what I'd do if something . . . well, not that it will."

"I'm sure they'll catch the guy. Soon."

"You never know. Back East with that sniper a while back it took longer than anyone thought it would."

"This one," his wife said, "they'll catch."

"I wish I knew what this guy was thinking. I wish there were a way the cops could stay a step ahead of him."

"Don't start that stuff," she said. Sweetly, but firmly.

It raised its ugly head between them. The conflict.

How he could sometimes start to think like the psychopaths he worked around at Darden State.

About getting inside their heads.

It was a talent he hated, but he had it, and he had tried to accept it.

"I just don't know," he said. "When you're a kid, you think the world is one way. And then you get older, and you grow up, and you have kids of your own. And you know it's never always a good place to be. The world. For those kids. For their parents."

"I know. It's like we're still living in the jungle, and there's always someone out there ready to attack," she said. "It's the world. What was it you told me? The predatory nature of human beings."

"Yeah, but not like that."

"I don't know. Seems pretty much like that. That's a human monster. You work with them. You know."

"I work with them where it's safe. Out of their cages . . ." He didn't finish the thought.

The weather came up on the TV, "Lows in the 20s in the mountains. Good skiing up in Big Bear through the upcoming weekend. White Christmas up in Arrowhead. For those in the Valley, it looks like it will be mild on Monday with a high of 65 to 70, dropping slightly through the week. Chance of showers midmorning tomorrow, changing to clear skies by evening."

When he switched off the TV that night, Trey said a prayer for the dead kids, then another one for his own two children. He went around and double-checked the locks on the door, his nightly ritual for the past several months. He also triple-checked that the burglar alarm was on and working, its small yellow light flashing in its white plastic case.

He tried not to run through the killers he'd worked with most of his adult life, as if sifting through them would help him understand the mind of this new murderer who went after children.

The Red Angel, he thought. *Why do they call you that?*

Falling Angels

Chapter One

Moon Lake, California
the San Bernardino Mountain range
18 degrees, 3 A.M.

1

Outside, cold as hell. Chance of snow likely. Ice along the edges of the roads. Ice hanging from the trees beyond the stone walls of the sacred holy place.

The chapel of rock.

The Mad Place.

Steam and warmth within.

2

In the Mad Place, it moved frantically about its business.

The stench was unbearable. It was waking up

13

what was inside it. The odor of fresh death in its nostrils makes it gasp with desire.

It didn't want this to happen, but it was too late.

Bombs exploding in its head and the roar of the Other One obliterating its will, it pressed its face to the arm and bit.

Tongue dry. Breathing hard. Heart pounding too fast.

Teeth pressed into skin.

Biting.

Savagely.

Tearing.

Repeatedly.

Until there was nothing left on the body to bite.

The angel whispered a prayer of hellfire and brimstone as the steam came up against its face.

Then it cut off the bird's wings.

3

Afterward, inspired, it wrote in the notebook that it had titled *Revelations*.

AND SO I SAW THE GREAT BEAST ARISE AND TAKE WITH IT THE INNOCENT LAMB, TEARING ITS FLESH. BUT THE ANGEL OF THE LORD HAS COME AND SAVED THE INNOCENT ONE FROM THE FIRES OF PERDITION.

It tore out this page and crumpled it up and set it in the small hand.

It felt relief.

It felt heaven shining on it.

It knew it was alive, because it was covered with

sweat. It felt the warmth of a thousand suns upon its skin. It felt that all-encompassing love, that acceptance.

Transcendance itself.

It basked in the heat of the eternal as it sensed its own breathing, stomping, maddening life with wonder.

Ah. That was what it expressed. *Ah.*

Then, a second later, it felt the pounding in its head again.

The chill returned.

The lifeless, mutilated body of a child in its arms.

Sacrifice.

4

It hadn't slept in four days because the voice of the Other One didn't stop.

It came home at three A.M. It was weary, tired of resisting. Tired of what it must do.

It had to go out again in a few minutes. It had to make its run and find another one.

But it was hungry, and it needed to get in from the cold.

It needed its mother.

Its old dog, Jojo, looked up from beside the fireplace, a slight wag of the worn old tail, and then put his head down again on the little wool rug, back to doggy dreamland. The dog was better than people, it thought. Dogs were better because they didn't keep anything in cages. Dogs were better because they bit when they wanted. Dogs were better because they loved.

Music from the 1940s was playing on the old turntable: Glenn Miller. The place was all muted reds and browns and greens and yellows, between the fabric on the couch and chairs to the ceramic figurines over the mantel, above the glowing fire. The smells of stew coming in from the kitchen mingled with the faint but undeniable stink of urine and the heavy brown stench of old cigarette smoke that always hung in the cabin. Years of smoking in the little house had left their marks in stains on the green curtains. There were four rooms, all small. This was the only home it had ever known.

It stepped in and wandered first to the bathroom to relieve itself.

After this kind of night, it had to relieve the pressure of its bladder, which had been building up.

It looked at its face in the little square of mirror above the toilet and saw the scratches and raised welts that covered it. Like wax had melted over its skin.

The sound of the television came from the living room. Like shouting. It hated that kind of noise, but she liked the TV and music on when she was alone. She didn't like to think she was by herself, and it didn't like her to feel that way.

No one should be alone, it thought. The devil came out when you were alone.

It came through the door, snow in its hair. It tossed its coat over the back of the flower-print sofa and was about to go to the fridge for a Coke or a beer, but its mother called to it. It checked the windows for faces but saw none. Piles of clothes in a corner.

It wanted its supper, but it didn't want her to feel bad, so it went into her bedroom, where the piss smell was heavier but cloaked with perfume that smelled like orange blossoms. The bedroom had the dolls in the corner and her paperback books in piles near the window, which had been covered over with plastic sheeting and duct tape to keep the wind out. The tubes were there, and the bed, and it had to check her levels so she wouldn't have pain. Her pills were all lined up, and it put them in a small Dixie Cup and passed them to her. It got a glass of water, one of many on a nearby table, and watched as she drank it down.

It was weary from the previous night and keeping the Other One out of its head.

It sat beside its mother and stroked her hand because she liked it to do that. She was a smart woman. It had known that all its life, and she had cared for it when it was just a little boy, and it was grateful for that because it didn't think it would have lived. But it had the thing inside it already, the Other One, and she couldn't know about that. She couldn't know what it had to deal with to keep the Other One, the Real One, in its cage. She had simply loved it for who it was, and it had served her and wanted her to sleep peacefully at night.

It still loved her completely, and loved everyone because it was a loving being, and it only wanted what was best for those around it. It was the Other

One that was the monster, and it didn't even like thinking the name of the Other One for fear the cage would start rattling again.

"Where you been all night?" she asked.

It didn't want to tell her, just like it had never told her when it was a child that it lived in the darkness and watched what happened when the birds started flying and when its other half felt the scraping and cleaning and purifying. "I was callin' and callin'. That girl's been callin' too. You need to go get her at four, she says, or she's gonna just get a room down there, and I told her to get a room if she has to and never come back. I don't know how you put up with her. Don't give me that look. Yes, I know her name is Monica. Monica Monica Monica. I hear that name and it makes me want to spit. And I got a pain in my back." It told her to turn over slightly, and it began rubbing the middle of her back, because it was where she hurt the most and when the pain got to be the worst, it gave her a massage like this, and she felt better.

"Read to me," she said, reaching near her waist, feeling for the book she left there. "Read to me from this one."

It picked up the small paperback book with the yellowed pages. On the cover, a muscular young man with blazingly brilliant blond hair that luxuriously fell down his back, as if he was meant to be the princess rather than the prince, embraced a scantily clad woman whose breasts burst forth from her tunic. She was wrapping her arms around his bare waist, her head tossed back lightly. It was called *Gladiator's Conquest*.

It opened the book to the dog-eared page.

It began reading, its voice a ragged whisper.

"Louder," the old woman said. "I can't hear a god-blessed word."

It didn't notice what it was reading to her. It heard what it thought was a child mewling outside, and it panicked a little because the child couldn't run now.

The woman interrupted. "I think you need to rest up, baby. I think you've got to get out there in a few hours. You don't need to stay up like this. How about a little sleep? You're so good to me. But maybe you need a little sleep." Her voice was feeble and raspy, so it went to get her a glass of water.

"Here you go," it said, bringing the water to her.

"What is it?"

"Water."

"Just water?"

"That's it," it said, and sat back down beside her, holding the glass for her while her twisted hands gathered around its hands as it tipped the water up to her lips. After a sip or two, her throat cleared and she sounded better. "I think you need some sleep," she said.

It nodded. "I got too much to get done right now. I can sleep later. You might want to sleep."

"Read me some more. Please. Oh, please," she said, then took another sip from the glass, a sound in her throat as if she were greedy for water.

"Nurse's gonna be here in an a couple hours," it told her. "Sleep 'til then."

It felt the Other One, the one in the cage in its head, begin to snarl and snap like a mad dog, and it let go of its mother's hand, and checked the tubes to make sure they were clear. Then it told her that it needed to go finish some business. It read the book as loud as it could, but even with it nearly shouting out the story of the woman in the book as she felt the man's "throbbing pressed against her femaleness, she wanted the heat of him more than life itself," it heard the child.

A little bird chirping in the woods.

Its mother said, "I bet it's gonna snow today. It'd be nice to have more snow. It makes the world all clean and ready for Jesus at Christmastime. That'd be nice, wouldn't it? Pure, clean snow. Just like your daddy liked."

"If it snows," it said, "then Betty can't get here. You don't want that, do you? We love Betty."

"Well, you'll be here if she can't come," its mother said. "You are such a good son. Such a good boy. I don't like that damn nurse much anyway. Sticking me with her needles. Giving me those awful pills."

"They help with your pain." It couldn't bring itself to say the C word. It could barely use the word "hospice" without starting to feel like it wanted to go into the Mad Place and let the Other One out for good.

"You help with my pain," she said.

Its mother smiled, feebly, and it could tell she

was already drifting into sleep and peace, which was what she needed. It closed the paperback and set it back down on the bed.

It stood and felt the throbbing in its skull as the mad dog in its head rattled the cage and began howling.

It wondered if its mother could hear the howling, but it was working hard to keep its mask on, to keep the muzzle on, at least until it got out the door, out into the snowy night.

It had to stop the child from making noise. Little bird chirping.

The child kept crying.

It couldn't keep the Other One in the cage any longer.

The Devil wanted to come out and play.

Chapter Two

The Inland Empire Valley
68 degrees, 5:30 A.M.

1

There was a vastness to the area of Southern California called the Inland Empire. It was a sea of land that stretched beneath snow-topped mountains, a valley that led to the great desert beyond. Pock-marked and cratered by foothills and flatlands, endless tract houses near the freeway, beautiful homes and mansions up near the hills, it had once been home to one of the biggest citrus-growing industries in the world. The old towns, like San Pascal and Redlands and Riverside, were beautiful and somehow untouched since rising out of the orange groves in the early twentieth century.

Redlands, California, could be found approximately two hours' drive due east of Los Angeles, if the freeway traffic was bad. The town was atypical for the dry near-desert area. Its climate in the winter was warm and stable, with generally clear blue skies, although the rains and wind sometimes descended between November and January for a week at a time without much warning. The smog from Los Angeles, more than sixty miles to the west, cleared with the winds of autumn. The Santa Anas rushed like invisible fire down from the desert, cleaning the skies.

In winter, the air seemed crystal clear, and the mountains of Big Bear and San Gorgonio rose above the temperate landscape below, palm trees and the tan houses along the low hills and the flatlands of the orange groves among such towns as Mentone, Bannock, Yucaipa, San Pascal, Little Orange, and Redlands.

2

In his house in Redlands, Trey Campbell awoke in a cold sweat.

Unsure of where he was. Of who lay next to him. Another bad dream.

But it was only a dream.

A dream and a memory: He and his family had been attacked the previous summer by an escaped murderer named Agnes Hatcher. It was in the past now. He had been working through his fears. His family had been in many therapy sessions dealing with it.

It only was alive, still, in his dreams.

And in his work, to which he had to return after

23

months of an enforced sabbatical of sorts.

Today was D Day.

His work involved daily encounters with men and women who had committed the most unimaginable acts of violence and murder.

And he loved, and missed, his job.

But he dreaded it, too.

3

He tried to wipe it from his eyes, the last of the previous night's dream.

Everything was out of focus in his room.

The blur of purple light from the window.

He reached across to the bedside table, feeling around the small stack of paperback books, the clock radio, for his glasses. He had only begun wearing them since summer. He had been told that his vision problem might be a result of the trauma from the experience. He wasn't sure. He didn't like to think of himself as so psychologically weak. All he knew was that one morning he'd woken up and had not been able to see anything—it had all been a blur. Then he had seen some things in focus, but not everything. Then he could see better, but his vision was no longer twenty-twenty.

Then the psychiatric examination, then the glasses.

That's how it had affected him.

His vision.

His kids, they'd had nightmares, and his wife woke up sometimes fighting him as if for her life.

With him, it was dreams and lack of good vision.

Within three months, he was used to the glasses, wire-framed, round. His glasses on, he felt better, more secure. The night and its dream, were gone. Not just a dream.

A rerun of how I spent my summer vacation.

He was too old for this kind of silliness. Dreams. As if they were anything other than just the messed up innards of a guy who had spent most of his adult life working with the criminally insane.

Nearly thirty-seven years old, and he still had a fear of his own stupid nightmares. Jesus, he thought, you can be rational all your waking life, but in dreams, that damn irrational superstitious side comes out again.

You never feel safe again.

Not after he'd watched his family be threatened by a killer. He knew he'd never feel the same about people. About people near his wife and kids. Once that had happened, it changed everything.

Before the previous summer, Trey Campbell had not believed that evil had a human form. He had believed that the killers he encountered in his job were products of abuse. Many of them were; some of them were not. But whether they'd been abused or not, it didn't matter once they got power over someone.

All they needed was a feeling of power over someone.

He had learned that with Agnes Hatcher.

She's gone now. Put her out of your mind.

It was the problem of his job. It put him in proximity to killers and sociopaths constantly. Where he worked, they had no power.

But if they were on the outside, they might.

Then they were truly evil. It didn't matter to Trey about their past once they stepped over that line.

Nothing mattered but protecting his family when it came right down to it.

At a certain point in life, making the world safe for your own family, for your kids' futures, and for others', was the only thing worth doing.

He just wished sometimes that someone would tell him it would all be all right. The worries, the stress, the struggle, and tests that life put you through.

Trey Campbell was never quite sure that life would be all right.

Not anymore.

4

He turned over, seeing the dark hair of his peacefully sleeping wife. He smelled her hair—it had an herbal scent from some new shampoo. He kissed the back of her neck, not out of ardor but from the need to feel connected, to be away from the world of his nightmares and of the recent past.

In sleep, lost in a dream herself, Carly pulled away, turning onto her back. Her face, so relaxed. Watching her mouth open slightly to breathe in and then out . . . he wanted to wake her and hold her tightly to him, but he knew that she wouldn't appreciate it.

This wasn't the first time in the past several months he'd had this nightmare.

This would not have been the first time he'd awoken, wanting to hold her and press his face beneath her chin to find some comfort.

But as with those other times, he would let her sleep.

His side of the big California King bed was soaked with sweat. His left arm ached from sleeping on that side. The smell of impending rain outside the half-opened window—that sweet, almost flowery smell before the rain clouds would dust down across the hills. The fresh cool air of December. He could hear jays screeching in the garden. None of this was about insanity. None of this was about the people he'd worked with. Their faces.

Their eyes.

Eyes are the places where we live. That's what Agnes had told him once. Agnes Hatcher, of last summer, of his nightmares, of his children's nightmares.

That's over, he thought. Over.

Remember what the shrink said: You are enmeshed with the people you treat. Stop identifying with them.

Four and a half months of three times weekly sessions with a psychiatrist had not erased the nightmares. One of those sessions per week included the whole family. Even the kids seemed to have put their nightmarish vacation in some perspective. *But not you.* Maybe nothing could. *Not that you have a great history of respect for psychiatrists. . . .*

27

The light had not completely come up outside the bedroom window. He could see hazy shadows of the oleander hedge that bordered their property.

5

He sat up, sliding his feet to the edge of the bed. He wiped at his face, as if to iron out the last vestiges of the dream. He glanced over at Carly, who was snoring lightly. Her face had the slight crease of the pattern from the pillowcase she'd been sleeping on. They had barely made love since summer. It had been his fault. He was almost afraid to touch her at times, as if anything he came in contact with might be threatened.

Anyone he was close to might be touched by something far worse. . . .

He wanted to not feel so alone, even surrounded by his family. Even next to his wife.

Alone. Like having a secret you can't share with anyone because it will affect them too much.

So as not to wake her, Trey rose slowly and gently from the bed. He padded over to the chair by the dresser, grabbing the underwear he'd left there. He slipped into these. Caught a glimpse of himself in the mirror above the dresser. Christ. He combed his hands through his greasy brown hair. His eyes were puffy, and his stomach seemed to be a little too paunchy. Four months of therapy, classes, studying, and housekeeping—and not much else. Oh, except dwelling on all the bad things. The Nasties, as he had described it to his son. Not just what happened

28

to the four of them last summer. But what always happened at that place. Only Nasties.

For the first time in nearly six years, Trey thought of his father. It was the face. Trey was beginning to look more and more like his father.

Trey Campbell went out into the hallway. He shut the door lightly to the bedroom.

The sun was only just coming up.

He loved dawns. Loved them because they were peaceful. Nothing bad happened before the day started.

It was only the day itself that brought the Nasties with it.

Clouds gathered beyond the window.

Clouds gathered in his mind as well.

He dreaded going back to the job that had nearly cost his family their lives over the summer.

It was not going to be a good morning.

D Day.

Dreaded Day.

Doomsday.

Ward D Day.

29

Chapter Three

1

Before the sun rose over the mountain, the blue truck stopped abruptly, brakes squealing.

From within the truck, a girl cried out as if someone had struck her.

December, Southern California, a side road off the main highway up the San Bernardino Mountains toward Big Bear and Lake Arrowhead and Bluejay and Moon Lake and Green Mountain. Trucks lumbered up the main highway, groaning with gearshifts. Beams of purple light cut through the trees, bursting from the cloud cover like an escaped convict. The sun lurked. A dark kind of light came up. Melting snow along the rim of the road. Mud on boots as he walked away from the truck and the girl inside it.

Male, Caucasian, mid-forties, 5'10", stocky build, wearing chinos, a red flannel shirt, and a brown leather jacket over this. Brown, brown, with distinguishing marks, an unusual gait, as if he had a slight limp. Behind him, a woman. Female, late teens, dyed blond hair, 5'4", buxom, tanned. Breasts big and full, curvy hips.

She followed him, barely a woman, her white-blond hair pulled back and twisted, her brown-and-red-checked donut shop uniform still on from the night before, over which she wore a light beige jacket. She smelled of krullers and coffee and cigarettes. She pulled off the ear buds from her Sony Walkman as she went, and the distant, nearly indistinct tinny sound of a pop teen princess' hit mingled with the noise of distant trucks on the lower highway. The ear buds dangled from the Walkman, clutched in her fist.

The air was cold and clean.

At the roadside, on the slight dirt shoulder, the truck's engine idled. The passenger door was flung open.

"I said"—she had the thick accent of backwoods redneck even in a Southern California landscape— "get back in the truck, dammit! Do not do this to me. Don't run to your little hidey-hole and leave me to deal with you-know-who up there. Not that witch and her nastiness. You owe me. Big time. Now get back here right this minute. You don't take my car in the middle of my shift like that. You hear me? And that shitkicker truck, I hope I never see it again. You was gonna sell it. You told me we'd get the money for it. But you didn't. Didja? Nobody wants that goddamn truck. Nobody! Jesus! Jesus! Sometimes, I swear you are nuttier than a shithouse rat!"

He only slightly turned, grunted, and then continued on, slinging his backpack carelessly around as he went. She was mad enough to spit.

"Duane? Are you listening to me? Get your ass back here. Jesus. All I can say is you better be inside for supper, or I'm not gonna wait for you, and you best not give me that look, or I ain't gonna wait on you no more. Don't you go treatin' me like some flophouse maid, you goddamn . . . you don't talk trash to me like you did an' you may not be eatin' your supper, you may be wearin' it, and that dog of yours may just wind up with a bullet in its head, that's all I'm sayin'. I swear to God I will take down that huntin' rifle and put that poor dumb animal out of its misery!"

He stopped when he heard this. Turned to face her.

"You hear me, Duane?" She said the name Duane as if it had four syllables. Dew-ay-enn-ee. "That's right. I'm gonna take my daddy's gun and put that poor dumb animal out of its poor dumb misery. It can't even stand up to take a shit. You don't give me that look, Duane. You don't give me that look. That's your mama's look and I know just what it means." She talked fast and barely took a breath until she stopped. Then, one final string of shrillness: "Look, you owe me an explanation, that's all I'm sayin' and hell yes I'm pissed off for waiting for three hours. You could at least tell me something or use the damn phone instead of running off to your little hidey-hole every time you go all fetal on me."

32

"Leave me alone. Just go home, Monica. Leave me alone." His voice was soft, barely audible. "And don't you touch my rifle. *My* rifle. It ain't yours."

He turned back around, shaking his head, and continued into the woods.

The backpack around his shoulders was heavy. Something squirmed inside it.

"I did not move up to the backwoods to be treated the way I could've been treated if I stayed back in Palmdale!" she shouts, her voice becoming more twangy as it grew louder. "Maybe I shoulda run back to Palmdale and then where'd you be? You and the old witch."

2

Sun glinted off the edge of the mountain as the man she had called Duane entered the shadows of the woods on the side of the mountain.

3

The girl went back to the truck, tossed the Walkman onto the seat, shut the passenger door. She lit up a cigarette and leaned against the truck, shivering, puffing away for a minute, looking out over the valley below. She muttered something about families and men and love.

Then she tossed the cigarette, sashayed to the driver's side of the truck, and opened the door. "I hate this goddamn truck!" she said as if he could hear her. "I hooked a loser!" Using the truck's door, she raised herself up slightly, and slid onto the seat. "You hear me, Duane?" Tears began to leak from the corners of her eyes. She swiped at the first drops, as if trying to erase something that she didn't want to fully face. She glanced out the window, up the mountainside, to the turn in the road, the house that sat in the lightening darkness as the sun revealed itself through the mist to the east. The light was on at the front porch, and she thought she even heard the damn dog barking.

Adjusting the rearview mirror, she noticed that her lipstick was smeared.

She dabbed at the edge of her lips with her thumb, and glanced at her reflection. Unhappy with the result—more of a lipstick smear than before—she reached in the glove compartment. Felt around for some tissues. Pulled one out and wiped it across her lips.

She reached down and pressed her hand against her belly.

She couldn't feel the baby yet, but she knew it was there.

Chapter Four

1

It didn't like that whore Monica always yelling at it. It had messed up its head and messed up its night, and it had left her stranded down in the valley at her donut shop, but it had other things going on. It couldn't wait on that bitch hand and foot just because she was pregnant now.

Not when it had important work to do.

Holy work.

It was heavy in its arms, its backpack, its bundle, its gift.

In the haze of steam, soaking its entire body with sweat, it could make out the edges and curves of the rock wall. It stepped carefully along the perimeter of the cavern to avoid the bubbling water. It moved as swiftly as it could. Even so, it was almost positive it heard their footsteps close behind, could hear the gang of them whispering, knowing that they were closing in on their prey.

35

It almost slipped when it came to the drop.

It set the bundle down, then squatted beside it. It felt the smoothness where the now cooling waters flowed down the stones into the deeper chamber of the cavern.

The Chapel.

The Mad Place.

It sat down, grabbed the gift.

Something touched it from behind.

The feeling of warm breath on its neck.

It felt its heart go cold.

Something bad inside it took over.

It pushed hard down through the drop, feeling the water wash over it.

It went through into the stone room.

The lights were all on—outdoor garden lights that were strung around like Christmas tree lights.

Gave a sacred look to the Mad Place.

It was safe. That was all that mattered.

2

The little bird had woken. It got scared when that happened, because it wanted the bird to sleep right up until the time of the offering.

The bird cried out, a muffled scream.

NOW!

The Other One clawed at the cage.

The Other One would be out soon.

It unzipped the backpack to see the little bird's face.

Ripped off the duct tape.

It brought out the little pills and forced them into the little bird's mouth. Then it held the child's mouth shut, making it swallow.

"Good," it whispered.

Chapter Five

1

Rays of sunlight through a cloud hangover. The foothills of Redlands, green-brown in winter. The vast valley beyond. The snow-capped mountains. Palm trees between the valley and the sky. Parrots, gone wild years ago, squawk as they fly in a flock, tree to tree. Beyond the oleander hedge, a dog barking.

Trey Campbell fumbled through his morning routine.

Stepped outside to the flat pavement at the edge of the garden to do twenty push-ups, and twenty sit-ups.

The smell of impending rain in the air.

Back inside, feeling grumbly and not up to the day.

The house was an old adobe, one of only a handful in Redlands, which was a town known for its beautiful array of homes. It was laid out hacienda-style, so he had to pad across the cold stone floor of the hallway. Past the kids' rooms, through the living room (careful not to stub his toes on unseen furniture), before he could make it to the kitchen. Clear to the other side of the house. He opened the fridge, grabbed a carton of orange juice. He drank the last of it directly from the carton. Thought better of it, and went to get a glass. He checked the water cooler—half full. Two empty bottles beside the cooler on the red tile floor. His main drinking problem was water itself. He could not get enough. Poured out a glass or two of pure spring water "from the purest spring of California," so said the company's label. Drank it down.

Dehydrated. That's what you are. He scribbled out a reminder note for himself on the small chalk board next to the fridge: CALL WATER GUY. GET MORE AGUA.

Beneath this, he left a note for his wife that she would probably not see until his workday had begun: "I already miss you. Let's take the kids for pizza tonight. Chuck E. Cheese. Small celebration for Mark." His son had just lost another baby tooth, bravely, and the tooth fairy hadn't visited yet.

Then he sat down at the kitchen table, looking out at the dark garden. Slowly, the light came up. He sat and watched the sun's early light spray color across the bougainvillea that was still flowering pink and red across the garden wall. The clouds moved in swiftly from the west, dimming the sun's early brilliance.

He could not get his mind off the one thing he wished he didn't have to think about.

Work.

"You know?" he had said to his wife a few nights back. "Since I've worked there, I've seen twelve murder cases. On premises. Eight suicides. Three eyes taken out. One case of genitals being ripped off. Other assorted mutilation. It's really the Welcome Wagon to Hell, isn't it?"

And she had looked at him. That look of hers that was part surrender and part fire. She said, "But you're still going back there. I know you. Even though you know I hate that you do it. And you know what danger it put the kids in—no matter if that was a fluke. There's potential danger. You're still going."

"Here's what I believe. I believe that my work there does some good. That if I keep learning, keep observing and interacting with these kinds of killers, that I can build from it so that, in understanding them and how they operate, people can be protected. They're not monsters, even though they do monstrous things. I think they're throwbacks, at least the psychopaths. And they were okay at one point in their lives, until a switch got turned on. Something went wrong. Maybe it was abuse. Maybe it was just hormones. But something turned on. And if I can help the psychiatrists and others, be part of that team, to try and see where the switch is, maybe there's a way to turn it off."

His wife had seemed less sure. "I think you see

this as a mission. But it's not. There are other jobs you can do."

"That's why I'm going for my master's."

"Even with a master's degree, I know you," she said. Resigned. Not entirely happy. "You're still going to work with them."

He had to say it. It wasn't pleasant to sit with his wife and have an argument, even a calm one, about it. But he had to say it. "This is my life's work, Carly. I'm nearly forty. I am scared by this sometimes. But this is what I was meant to do. I know it's going to lead to the right place. I know it in my heart."

When he'd said this, she had leaned against him, her arms going around him. "All right. I'll try to understand. But if there's an opportunity to get out of there, if another job presents itself that puts you out of the line of fire of those criminals, I want you to consider it."

"I will," he had told her.

And this particular morning, he had to go back to that place. It wasn't like living in Redlands with a mortgage and kids in school and a flat tire on the way to the local supermarket.

It was a territory of madness.

2

When the phone rang, he let the machine pick it up. It would be Anderson calling to make sure Trey was ready to get back to the job.

Psychiatric Technician, Supervisor of D Ward at the maximum security hospital called Darden State.

Chapter Six

*It didn't like when the little birds, the angels, got out
of the tape and rope.*

The little bird had begun crawling through the
space between the stone rooms. The little bird
chirped a little, not even knowing that she chirped,
and it wanted to cup the bird in its hands and make
her all calm and quiet again.

It got down on its hands and knees. It sucked in
its gut, drawing its shirt over its head, the sweat
clinging to it even half-naked, like grease from an
old fryer. The stink rose up from the solid dirt. On
its elbows, crawling like a serpent, it went to where
the little bird crouched in a dark corner.

Flickering lights caught flashes of her face.

The little bird with the sad eyes and the dark hair.

It crawled toward the child, calling the little bird
by name, keeping the hypodermic needle hidden
in its left hand, the tip of the needle poking out
between its fingers.

From the mattress in the corner, it heard the

moans and whimpers, but it blocked them out. Ruthie is dead, it thought. *Dead. Gone to Hell. Ruthie was a whore. Ruthie was born of Satan. It's the voice of Hell coming up from the water.*

It calls to the little bird, "Don't be afraid, little bird. Don't be afraid."

Chapter Seven

In December the water flows high along the naturally formed ditches, or washes, coming down from the San Bernardino Mountains. The water, nearly ice cold, follows a trail of what had once been dry riverbed down to the larger Santa Ana Wash. There it creates a huge river in the winter from what had just been a shallow summer trickle. In the unincorporated area of the Santa Ana River, running between Riverside and an unincorporated area called Bannock, the Wash floods while stinging nettles and young jacaranda trees are covered beneath it. This onslaught of water continues west, until eventually it drains into the Pacific Ocean.

By May the rivers will begin drying again in the near-desert of the valley, until finally they will be nothing but a memory come June.

But in December, the Christmas season, the water is high and washes all kinds of debris with it along the banks, particularly after a sudden and unexpected rainfall.

Victor Robles and his sister Maria stood on the bank just above the rushing water. School would start in ten minutes, but they had some time to do their daily treasure hunting. The Wash sometimes produced beautiful garnets that they brought to their mother, and then, sometimes she put them into jewelry she made for Maria. The rain battered at them, but Victor enjoyed it, moving out from under the umbrella his sister carried. Despite that it was December, this was still Southern California, at the edge of the desert, and it was seventy-one degrees.

He had already found some pretty stones and one perfect garnet—an exciting find for the first heavy rain since October.

Usually he found old aluminum cans or occasionally a lone shoe. He shouted for Maria to try to grab the branch that jutted up from the rushing brown water. She either couldn't hear him or didn't want to help. She stood up the bank, the large umbrella down around her eyes.

"Your loss!" he cried out. There was something out in the water, hanging from branches. A nest? Too far for him to reach without falling in the water. He stepped onto a large stone. He felt the icy water wash across his Nikes but it put him closer to the branch. He tried to focus on it while the gray rain beat down, his glasses fogged, and he heard his sister cry out. He looked up to her and saw that she was pointing to the small island of ragged trees at the middle of the river.

There, among their scraggly branches, was something that looked like brightly colored cloth.

Victor took off his glasses, rubbing the fog away. He put them back on and squinted.

He thought he was seeing an angel. It had wings tinged red around its neck. The tips of its feet seemed to be just barely tip-toeing on water. But it was still a blur, and something in his young brain could not quite understand what he was seeing.

Its head seemed to hang down, and he thought it might be someone's idea of a joke: putting a dummy out there.

He almost fell into the river when he recognized what it was.

Later, he told the police that he thought the little girl was still alive because her legs seemed to move.

But that had probably been the water rushing over the victim's feet.

Victor Robles and his sister never saw the dead girl's face.

Chapter Eight

Town of San Pascal, San Pascal Valley
68 degrees, 5:55 A.M.

1

Jane Laymon awoke that morning with her boy-friend's head pressed down on her breasts.

She pushed him away. He rolled back on his side, his eyes lazily opening to the misty darkness. Then he drew back to her, kissing her shoulder. He was sort of cute, in a way that might normally arouse her, but not this early in the morning, and not when she had so much to get done. He had short dark hair and smelled like limes to her. It was the cologne he wore. It reminded her of islands and the beach. When she'd met him, it had been the first thing she noticed: his scent.

He rolled back toward her and murmured some-thing about "horny."

"No way. And not with that kind of breath." She

47

glanced at the clock. She'd had about six hours of sleep. She rolled onto her stomach, using her elbows to prop herself up. She glanced out the window over the bed. Outside it was still dark, but getting light. Noise and smell of traffic out on the freeway, just down the hill. Her apartment faced the smog most of the year, but in winter the air was clear.

She felt his hands rubbing her lower back.

"I love you, baby," he said. Here was the thing about Danny. He was too good looking for his own good. Or her good. She kept wondering if she really cared for him, or if, after her botched relationship with Rick Ramirez, she was just looking for a safe harbor that would not put her through the ringer. Danny was the polar opposite of Rick. He was clean-cut, her age, athletic, loved his job, loved kids, loved getting out and coaching the local Boy's Club basketball team, loved dropping the whole police thing for a fun day riding horses up in Holcomb Valley, or getting out to the beach in L.A. to windsurf. Just the kind of guy her mother wanted her to marry, or at least give her grandchildren by. Where Rick had come with his own baggage—a bitterness about women from his divorce, had been nearly thirty-eight, which meant they had very little in common other than mutual attraction—Danny had arrived with none of this. He had dated a few other women, but did not have the long list that Rick had trailing him.

So everything about Danny should've made her fall in love with him.

But she hadn't fallen in love yet.

She had fallen in like. And that was good enough for now.

"Let's play," Danny murmured, kissing her gently on the lips. He was aroused, and she knew that if she stayed in bed another minute, she might be also, but she had to remember that it was a work day. Not a play day.

"I'll see you tonight." She leaned back and looked at his sleepy face and half-lidded eyes. He had something between a snore and a smile on his face. "You can stay in bed for two more hours. I've got to get going."

Danny pressed his hands along her stomach and sides, and whispered something that was intended to be sweet but just meant to her that he was tired of the sexual cooling they'd had for the past few days. The relationship had progressed from hot and heavy over the months they'd known each other to a regular routine.

It wasn't quite as romantic or spontaneous as it had been in its first flush.

Some days he took second place to her work.

She liked Danny. A lot.

She even hoped they had more of a future together than just an on-again-off-again thing, like they'd had so far.

She liked nearly everything about him. Including the sex.

But she loved her work.

Loved it.

They were both cops. She was a newly minted

detective, and he was busting his chops over in San Bernardino.

"I can't slack off yet," she whispered to him, kissing him too lightly on the mouth. "You sleep some more. I need to hit the road."

"It's okay," he murmured. "I'll get up in a sec and make the coffee."

But even after her shower he was still in bed, facedown, catching the last of his sleep before the alarm on his watch would go off.

2

Naked, still dripping water, she went to the kitchen and set the coffeemaker going. She heard the baby crying in the apartment next to hers.

She went to the walk-in closet, the one luxury that her small apartment afforded, and grabbed her running shorts, sports bra, and oversized T-shirt for her morning run. She dressed quickly, tying her hair back in a ponytail to keep it from flying all over the place for her run.

In the bedroom, she slipped into her Nikes. Danny, in bed, was just snarfling awake. "You don't have to leave so early," he mumbled, rolling onto his back, stretching out like a cat with the canary in its mouth. "Just stay and . . . cuddle."

"I've got twenty-four hours to requalify," she said. "Easy for you to sleep in. You don't have a jerk like Fasteau on you making comments about how girls can't shoot."

"You're a perfectly good shot," he said. "Jesus, this discussion gets old."

"Not to Fasteau. Not to the department. Maybe you'd take it less lightly if some woman sat around telling you how lousy a shot you were all the time she looked at your balls."

"Keep talking dirty to me," he laughed.

"It's not funny. He's got this pissing contest going with me, and it's driving me nuts." Then, much against her intention, she started laughing, too. "Why is this driving me up a wall? Why?"

"Riddle me this, Cat Woman, what's going on with you on the target range?"

"I don't know. I guess I just tense up. I guess I think about Dad and how he never really wanted me to hold a gun. And, well, even if I try not to think about it, I do."

"You just need to relax when you shoot," he said. "It's easier to hit the targets when you don't think about it."

"You sound like Fasteau."

"And you sound unsure of yourself. He's a moron. You'll requalify. Don't worry."

"Tomorrow, I have to. If I don't get past firearm requalification procedures, I'm screwed. So today I need to get out and prepare. If I don't have this down by tomorrow, I'm screwed."

"Six months of getting up at some ungodly hour to go out and take shots at the range. You'd do better just to come back to bed and cuddle." He said it sweetly, but it was not what she wanted to hear.

Jane didn't want to say what she thought about this comment. She didn't want to explain to him that she had to be better than the rest of her team. That the men she worked with still, in the twenty-first century, didn't treat women coworkers as well as they treated other men. That she had to be smarter, faster, and even possess a better sense of humor than her bosses to move ahead in her investigative work.

Instead, she told him, "It's not the cuddling I'm worried about." Then she went to him and kissed him on the lips, and said, "I've just got to stay motivated. That's all. I'll see you tonight."

3

She was motivated as hell. She had to be. The San Pascal Special Investigations Unit was small, consisting of men (except for her, the trainee), and she knew she had to be better than any of the others to gain experience and get noticed. She was the lowest on the totem pole. But she intended to be the best.

At everything.

So far it had worked, but not to the extent she'd wanted.

And the one thing she truly sucked at was handling her gun. Hitting targets.

Worse, her partner, Fasteau, rode her ass for it, and made her feel as if her qualification the year before was a fluke.

Worst of all, she was afraid he was right.

Her morning began early, usually just before six A.M., with a three-mile run around the reservoir, followed by checking her e-mail for messages from Sykes, who was always one step ahead of her on the investigations, and who, along with Tryon over in Riverside, had taken her under their wing to try and get her more involved in ongoing investigations rather than the crib deaths she ended up having to spend time on. After her run and her e-mail check, she tried to put in at least an hour down at the firing range over in San Bernardino, and then the real workday began.

The weapons training range had been built by U.S. Marines just about the time that Jane had entered the police force, and it was primarily used for training San Bernardino County police in special tactical maneuvers. Jane loved the place. It had towers and barricades and an amazing target range. It made practice fun, although it never helped if Fasteau came out and jeered from one of the towers. She had been given a special dispensation to use the firing range to practice, although there was a perfectly good shooting range in her own county. But the San Bernardino facility was top notch. It gave her a heightened sense of what her job was: to stop the bad guys.

That was how she saw it.

She was still a little unsteady with her 9mm Glock 17.

But she was getting better.

4

She was a big woman, slender but imposing, from a race of giants (her father's side, Northern European, and from this she got height) although she was not quite six feet tall. Her jet-black straight hair and dark eyes were courtesy of the Cahuilla, a Native American tribe local to the San Bernardino area. She was not quite twenty-six years old. She looked like an amazon, and she knew it helped her in her investigative work because her height was the first thing that intimidated the other detectives and the cops and even the coroner at times. Second thing was her voice, a husky alto that her mother thought made her sound like a young Lauren Bacall, made huskier by a cigarette habit she'd had to kick by the age of eighteen because it slowed her down on the basketball court. But the voice remained husky and scratchy, and she used it when the men at the San Pascal County Sheriff's office began to treat her the way they treated the girls at the station. But she had one problem that was more a badge of honor about the Good Old Boys than anything else, since she didn't think she'd ever have to use it in the field: Jane Laymon was a lousy shot, and she knew it, although she kept covering her ass by getting over to the shooting range just after rising at least five days a week.

Her motto was, *If you go, go big or just don't go at all.*

She'd been taught it by her mother, even after

54

her father had tried to discourage her from getting into police work.

She intended to go big and make her mark in homicide investigations. She had wanted to do this ever since reading her first true crime book, ever since first studying forensics and criminal justice in college.

She had passed all the physical agility require-ments of the San Pascal County Sheriff's office and had advanced to working homicide, assisting mainly with cases as a liaison between Homicide and the CDRT (the Child Death Review Team), which generally had meant assessing, along with the coroner, Sudden Infant Death Syndrome cases and not much else. She had stepped up to this job because it was the only one available when she got into the department, but she soon discovered that it was halfway to social work and never quite as effective.

But the past week had become more active.

Someone was hunting.

Jane knew about hunters. Her brother had been a hunter. Not the kind with a rifle in the woods during deer season.

But the kind who hunted people.

In this case, the hunter wanted children.

Chapter Nine

1

Jane blotted out other thoughts while firing at the outline of a man's form on the paper sheets at the practice range. For a fleeting second, she imagined it was Fasteau.

She was sick of the desk aspect to her work and wanted to get involved more with homicide rather than the mountains of paperwork required of working on cases with the coroner and his assistants. As far as she was concerned, she was a glorified administrative assistant who now and then got called in on investigations when nobody else was available to get coffee or call potential witnesses.

She had been thrilled that Tryon and Sykes had called her in to do work with their team on a new manhunt that was just forming.

She would not be at the desk that day. She would not be checking fingerprints or brainstorming with detectives who liked using her for her brain but didn't want her stepping on their toes in the field.

It had to do with the kidnapping and murders of the children.

So far, two boys and a girl.

She had been on the scene for the victim found in the orange grove in Mentone, called in because of her work with the Child Death Task Force. She was the bone that San Pascal threw to the other counties whenever something happened that involved kids.

None of the other investigators liked the paperwork involved with those cases.

Or the fact that they'd have to work a lot of databases with CASMIRC, the FBI's Child Abduction and Serial Murder Investigative Resources Center.

Since she'd begun working on Child Death investigations, this had rarely been an issue. Usually it was a case of accidental death, murder in a family or with a specific neighbor. Kidnapping generally had not been the issue. Once it was, the Bureau stepped in.

But the county sheriffs of the tri-county area (including San Bernardino, Riverside, and San Pascal) liked their teams to catch these killers fast. It made things easier and kept the communities both safe and quiet.

Tryon, the Sheriff's Investigator from Riverside, had called her onto this one. Normally, a San Pascal County detective trainee wouldn't be called to cross county lines, but because of the body found in the San Pascal Canyon two days earlier, this was a special case, and Jane headed the task force on child death. She could be called in on cases of this nature in Riverside and San Bernardino Counties, if need be. Although she intended to move more into general homicide as her career advanced, she was currently the one called in most for child death cases.

Jane Laymon came off the firing range, her Glock holstered, her black T-shirt blotched with sweat, her arm sore from the constant firing.

The call, relayed to her by another trainee, had come from Tryon in the Riverside office, and it had carried with it a note of "urgent." She jogged through the lineup of trainees waiting their turn at the range and saw Fasteau leaning against his dusty old black and white Caprice Classic, a car that should've been retired several years before, out by the road. Fasteau saw himself as an old-fashioned gunslinger of a cop. She disliked him. She had to work with him. She couldn't wait for a change in partner.

The sun was just coming up across the white peaks in the distance. That was the thing with Southern California winters: snow on San Gorgonio while it was seventy degrees in the valley of the Inland Empire. The breath of the dry desert to the east came up with the sun.

"Nice wheels," she said.

"Best I could do," Fasteau said, an indecipherable look on his face. "How was practice?"

"Enlightening." She passed him, going over to the passenger side of the car. She opened the door and slid into the wide front seat.

"Hit the target this time?"

"Let's go," was all she said in response.

"Ready for this?"

"Well, if I can't shoot maybe I can just look at dead bodies."

He shot her a dark glance. "What the fuck." It was his favorite phrase, and she was fairly sure he used it whenever his small reptilian brain reached an impasse.

"Fasteau. Let's just go."

"No. I'm like what the fuck. Bam. Bam. Bam. We got kids falling out of the sky on us."

I'm stuck with a damn idiot cowboy instead of a cop.

When Fasteau pulled the car out the dusty drive, she asked, "Where did he kill?"

"We don't know. The body was moved. Between Caldwell and Bannock."

"The Santa Ana River," she said. "Right on the line. Down in the Wash. Our guy put him between counties. All the unincorporated areas. He's bright. Ice-cold water to try and screw up evidence. Three counties. Riverside, San Bernardino, San Pascal. The one on the other side of Caldwell was in water, too. An irrigation ditch. We need to get this guy," she said. "Do we have to draw straws to see who works this one?"

"It's a political nightmare," Fasteau said. "Kids getting killed. They've got some guys working on it, but it's stuck with us and Riverside. The boogeyman is loose. Once it hits the news, people start feeling like it's an epidemic."

"Hate to tell you, but it hit the news last night."

"Can't Tryon keep them out of it. Ever?"

"Maybe he wants a little media. Maybe it'll flush out a witness. The Bureau in on it yet?"

"Sure as the rain will fall."

"I know what Tryon wants. He wants to keep the Bureau out of this. He wants to get the guy fast. I wish we could get some of L.A.'s resources in on this."

"We got state coming in after three today to confer. All-out manhunt, that's what's on the agenda."

"Jesus," she said, glancing off in the distance as they merged onto the 10 freeway, "this is number three."

"One for each day," he said.

"Let's hope there's no number four," she said. "We're not getting this guy fast enough."

"I know. *What the fuck*. That's what I say."

"Clean up the language a little," Jane said.

"Can't help it. I was raised in a barn. Jesus, Jane, killing kids, dumping them, but taking the time to tie little wings on them. 'Hark the herald angels sing.' Like it's a Christmas pageant."

"I know," she said. "Makes you wish you could change the world. Just get rid of the predators."

"The way you shoot," he said, "it'll never happen."

2

Thirty-five minutes later, she stood over the crime scene: a rift in the white gravel of the Wash, the gray reeds and sprays of yellow grass rising up along the river bank. In the middle of the river, a clump of gray trees. At the edge of the riverbank, an orange inflatable raft. They'd already removed the victim from the trees. She glanced at the others.

Hard as hell to keep a crime scene clean in the middle of a river.

Tryon's probably already pissed off.

A couple of detectives stood together, talking, smoking their cigarettes. Mills and Walker, and they both were condescending assholes to her. They were from San Bernardino and Caldwell, out in Moreno Valley. Every county was pitching in on this one. The manhunt was gearing up fast.

The killer was gearing up, too.

Sykes and Tryon were at the river's edge. Tryon glanced back, waved.

She was the rookie. They were the experienced ones.

They treated her the way she suspected they treated all young women. Looked at her breasts, then assumed her brain was smaller than theirs.

She had to put up with it, to a point.

But she did her job, regardless.

It was what she had been born to do: investigate crimes. It had been her hobby, her interest, the way her brain was wired.

This case was a shot. It wouldn't be handed to her.

If she was going to crack it, it would be on her own.

The sun, nearly up in the sky. The grumbly sounds of traffic out toward Corona.

The day had begun.

Jane Laymon went over to where the victim lay on the sandy ground alongside the banks of the river.

Chapter Ten

1

Leaning over the body.

Caucasian, female, age eight, brown, brown.

Gina Parsons.

They already knew the name.

When rich white kids got taken, things happened fast. It was the underbelly of criminal investigation. Nobody in the department talked about it much, but it was there. Black, latino, Asian—it took longer to get those investigations going. Jane intended to change that. She intended to make things better. And it wasn't just because she was half-Native American or "Indio," as Fasteau often reminded her, annoyingly, when he nastily suggested once that she try a bow and arrow instead of a Glock.

It was because kidnapping kids, rich, poor, white, brown, every single one of them deserved the same resources.

But it was true: The richer the kid, the whiter the

kid, the more news got out and the more pressure came to bear on the investigation. Kids went missing all over, but it was when a white kid from an upper middle-class background went missing that the media was all over it and resources were marshalled to get that kid and get the kidnapper.

Gina Parsons was not lucky.

But the next kid might be if the manhunt kicked into gear as rapidly as it seemed to be going. The FBI would be on it; three counties would be on it; and the hardest part was going to be blocking the media so that law enforcement could get the job done with a minimum of interference.

2

She crouched down, careful not to touch anything. Not until they started bagging evidence.

The victim had been laid out on the river bank by the first cop on the scene. Mistake number one, she thought, but let it go. There had been no way to really secure the place where the killer had put the body.

She took a mental picture before too much got going: no blood on the corpse, but traces of red and pink around the white bird wings. *Some water bird. Duck. Goose. Swan. Seagull? No. Duck.*

Red angel, white wings with a touch of red.

Some violence to the corpse.

Features partially obliterated.

If this one is anything like the others, she was dead before you hurt her.

You put her to sleep first. So she wouldn't feel anything. So that she was already gone. Dead.

Then you made her this angel.

Jane closed her eyes for a second, wishing the world was not such a terrible place.

Trying not to imagine the last moments.

3

She pulled out of her thoughts when she heard the sound of an approaching vehicle.

Shouts already came from the cops out on the road.

She glanced up to the edge of the highway.

A white news van with Los Angeles–based call letters had arrived.

"Damn it." She stood up, but watched as Tryon barked at the cops to keep them out of the crime scene.

A camera man got out of the back of the van, and some reporter came around from the other side of it.

"What a job they got," she said under her breath.

Fasteau, coming up beside her, chuckled. "I like that one reporter. The blonde. She's hot."

Darden State

Chapter Eleven

1

IST, NGI, MDO, SVP.

These were the main categories of patients at Darden State.

Incompetent to Stand Trial. Not Guilty by reason of Insanity. Mentally Disordered Offender. Sexually Violent Predator.

IST, NGI, MDO, SVP.

The Darden State Hospital was officially called The Darden State Hospital for Criminal Justice.

The unofficial title: The Darden State Hospital for the Criminally Insane.

Those incarcerated there were termed by the state "forensics patients."

2

Darden State was surrounded by razor-wire double fencing, then a third electric sensor and electric shock fence in between those two. It further ensured its own security with redundant electronic detection systems, as well as an outside patrol from the Department of Corrections, 24/7. There had been at least one catastrophic escape from Darden in the past twelve months, and the hospital could not afford another such error.

Within the fences, its twenty-three acres were neatly manicured. A fruit and vegetable cooperative had been running successfully on six acres of land since 1972 when it was begun to provide a productive outlet for inmates. The mild Southern California winters allowed the crops of apples, lettuce, oranges, tomatoes, and melon to flourish year round. This was both a form of therapy for the patients and a source of pride. But as patients' rights had become stronger, other activities and pastimes were added. The in-house newspaper was begun, written and published by inmates.

Following this, briefly, a television production room was used for the inmates to broadcast their concerns within the gates of Darden. This was discontinued after three months when a riot occurred as a result of a broadcast. During the riot, in the spring of 1997, six men were killed, and three left in critical condition. No staff members were involved, as the rule on the wards was that once a riot broke, the staff immediately left the ward and the doors were locked down. When killing among inmates took place on the state hospital grounds, such as happened with the deaths during this particular riot, the investigation was minimal and charges were generally not filed. Darden State was, after all, a hospital that incarcerated sociopathic murderers, serial killers, and those few sane inmates unfortunate enough to have copped the insanity plea upon the heels of their very sane and well-thought-out murders.

Darden was nearly a city unto itself. It held upwards of eight hundred inmates, as well as five hundred staff members on three daily shifts. Staff included psychiatrists, nurses, aides, orderlies, cafeteria and laundry workers, recreational counselors, social workers, and a distinct breed of workers called psychiatric technicians or psych techs. These were generally well-educated staff, specifically trained to work with the category of patient at Darden. The psych tech came to understand the unpredictable nature of Darden State's criminally insane population in a way that the psychiatrist, who only saw the patient one hour a week, would never know.

There was occasionally a labile patient who required more than one staff member at a time for supervision. A labile patient was one who was slow moving, apparently slow thinking also; then, all at once, he or she turned into a tornado and became the greatest threat to the individual standing nearest. A labile patient was rare; oddly enough, most patients seemed fine. They seemed normal. In fact, they seemed extremely ordinary in this world of walls and fences and locked doors.

There was no one incarcerated at Darden State who had not murdered or, at the very least, been accused of murdering someone, but there were varying degrees of murders and murderers. The average term of incarceration was forty years, although several patients were released after fifteen based on the court-decreed criterion of whether they were threats to the outside world. Occasionally, a psychiatrist would deem a young recent arrival not a threat to the outside world, in spite of a murder. Such a patient might spend less than two years in Darden State. That is, if he or she was cleared by a panel of psychiatrists, mental health officials, and a presiding judge.

The size of an inmate's room was determined by both state and federal standards. There needed to be a locker, a bed, and a chair. The room was ten feet long by eight wide. It needed a two-inch fire door with a small porthole window for outside observers. There were also three-, four-, and six-man bedrooms. Clothes were all khaki for the men, and dark brown pants and khaki shirts for the women. Especially dangerous patients had wrist-to-waist restraints. Orange shirts and large ID tags were worn whenever the patients were working outisde on the grounds in a specially funded program called Living and Learning.

There was one new designation: a special dormitory with six rooms in it.

These were for the most violent of the human predators who entered Darden State.

These were the six forensics patients who had been labeled with a designation previously unused in the state of California. They had been transferred from each of the facilities in the state specifically to Darden, which had received special funds for their care.

It is called Program 28, so-named because it is the 28th such program to handle specific psychologically labeled patients in a controlled environment since the programs were first implemented at Darden State in 1966, neatly coinciding with the era in which Darden went from a place of shock treatments and rumored lobotomies to drug treatment and sedation. All previous twenty-seven programs had failed to some greater or lesser extent. Each was designed by a team of psychiatrists who brought in state and sometimes federal funding into the hospital. The positions at Darden State were as often political as they were medical and supervisory.

Program 28's patient designation was SSPVS7. Sexual Sadistic Predator Violent Sociopath, Level 7.

Each had been a high profile case, involving the most heinous murders, even among the general inmate population of Darden.

Restraints through the night were the norm in Program 28. Each patient in Program 28 had at least two psychiatric technicians with them on each shift.

Michael Scoleri was in a room by himself in Program 28.

Scoleri was an SSPVS7. Good-looking young man, small eyes slightly wide apart. Blond hair, cut short.

The rain outside his window was like pebbles thrown on glass.

Restraints on his wrists and around his ankles.

Michael Scoleri nodded to the voice he heard.

"Yeah," Scoleri said. "Sure. You needed that one. The little girl."

3

At Darden State, wake-up in Program 28 was at six A.M. in the patient dormitories. This was to get the six patients through their routines a good forty minutes before the other patients were roused, so as to keep the Program 28 patients separate from the rest. The first meds of the day arrived at eight. Between those two hours, the Program 28 patients showered, cleaned up their rooms, made their beds, and then got breakfast in the cafeteria.

In the showers twenty minutes later, Rob Fallon, a non-Program 28, counted the tiles as he washed, making sure to scrub the parts of his body his mother had labeled dirty twenty years earlier. Rob Fallon was an SVP, but often went with the Program 28s because of his recent attacks on staff members. It was either that, or he'd have been transferred north, and north didn't want him. Neither did Patton State. He didn't live in the pods of Program 28, but just outside them.

Because Rob didn't have the harsher designation of Program 28, he had a bit of free rein on the ward and in the dormitories, although he still had a one-on-one psych tech at all times to make sure he didn't go off and begin his systematic seduction of other inmates or staff.

It had been Rob's affair with a staff nurse named Howe the previous summer that had turned tragic. It was one of the problems of Darden State: If a sociopath was attractive and a staffer was messed up enough on the inside, bad things resulted. Staff members who had been at Darden more than a decade were now given routine psychological testing and subsequent counseling to ensure that they had not begun identifying too much with the patients.

4

The white bar of soap smelled like others who had used it before him, and he didn't like thinking about their filth, their dirty parts. He had no name for them, other than the ones he'd found out about in biology class in high school, but even then he couldn't say them aloud. The soap lather felt like a foam pillow rubbing him. The more he rubbed, the more it began to smell like clean bleach, like a white bottle of clean bleach poured over a wound. So damn nice. He rubbed the soap against his skin so much that his skin turned a raw pink color, and the soap disappeared into milky fragments. He liked getting clean, and he had no respect for some of the patients who were depressed and remained filthy most days. He liked shedding his hospital clothes and getting under the hot jets of spray.

It was a lot like high school gym class, and he'd

always enjoyed showering with others. He wished some of the guys would talk more, but they all went into their own little worlds in the shower. Watching the yellow tiles while he lathered up and rinsed off, spied on by the perv orderlies and psych techs just didn't do it for him anymore. He needed some entertainment. He hadn't had much entertainment for a long time.

It was his sixth year in Darden State, for what the media had called "the Adonis murders." They were right on the Adonis part, he knew. Just not the word "murder." He had been merely asserting himself, taking his rightful place.

When Rob thought about how they bled, sometimes he smiled.

Someone watched him (they always did, he knew it, he kept watch of them as they watched him), along with the four other men from D Ward. The man watching them, named Jim, was big and stupid and so used to nothing happening that anything could happen and he'd be unprepared. It was the way things went at Darden. Unlike many others he knew in D Ward, Rob didn't fool himself into pretending they weren't in a prison, even though it looked a bit like a hospital at times, and other times like an old junior high school.

He glanced at the others through the sprays of water.

Rob noticed how he stacked up against them. How much more masculine he was. How much more real. His chest and stomach had thin dark hairs, and his private parts (for he could not use the bad words for that area even when he tried) were not as ugly as other men's. His mother had always told him how beautiful he was because of his genes. Good genes were everything. Good genes and getting clean. His muscles, despite being in Darden, were still long and sinewy. He still had his youth inside him, and he knew that he would never ever grow old. He had been created that way.

Rob could tick off their names: Noodles, the guy who had cut heads off his girlfriends (and apparently had, Rob noticed, one testicle); Jake "the Whistler," a serial rapist and scalp collector (undersized penis); Arnie, the guy who had tried to assassinate the president's wife but never made it further than a debutante ball in San Diego; and then Scoleri.

Michael Scoleri.

Scoleri was sometimes brought in. Sometimes the ward mixed them together. It was a Program 28 directive. Early morning only.

Rob Fallon didn't like it one bit.

It also meant more psych techs were around.

Not that Rob minded being watched in the showers. He looked damn good, and he liked the attention.

But Scoleri.

Scoleri still looked like a kid, even naked in the showers. Couldn't have been more than twenty-six. A scared kid in a den of wolves.

On his stomach, those words.

SUFFER THE CHILDREN TO COME UNTO ME.

On the inside of his thighs, names.

He was a damn sideshow freak as far as Rob Fallon was concerned.

Like a fart: silent but deadly.

Rob grinned at Scoleri, holding his hands out. "Toss the soap."

Scoleri glanced at him. Scoleri picked up a bar of the yellow soap and handed it to Rob. Whether it was women or men, Rob knew that everyone loved him. He was beautiful, and smart, and irresistible. People told him their secrets.

That tended to coincide with the times that he'd cut their throats.

But not inside.

Inside he was a good boy because he was being watched.

He glanced at the orderly and the psych tech, standing in the entryway to the showers.

"You still don't talk much, huh?" Fallon said. He arched his back as he scrubbed the soap beneath his underarms. "Well, I got some news down the wire today. I hear Campbell's coming back."

Scoleri barely glanced at him.

"I like Campbell. Always have. Last summer, one of the women here went after him. And his family. But Campbell got through it okay. I knew he would." Fallon turned around, showing that he didn't care if Scoleri watched him or not. He flexed his muscles. Rob liked to turn men on. To turn women on. It was a trait of some of the smarter sociopaths and thrill-kill junkies.

When he turned people on, he got things. He found out their whys. Their most intimate secrets.

78

He was smarter than nearly everybody else, and once he figured out the whys of people, he could get what he wanted from them.

He knew that Scoleri had a why, hidden somewhere inside him.

He rinsed off his back. The hot water was delicious on him. It washed away all the grit and nastiness of the night. Cleanliness was good. Dirty things annoyed him a great deal. Most of the patients were dirty. Practically crawling with vermin. Some of them didn't even know how to clean themselves well. Rob liked the ones who did. Like Scoleri. He got scrubbed good.

"I guess you didn't know Campbell. He's one of the good ones." Rob nodded in the direction of the bulky psych tech standing guard by the entrance to the showers. "Not like him. He's what my mother would call a three-dollar bill."

Scoleri shrugged. "I don't know too many people here." He had a voice like a sparrow. Just a chirp. The water from the showerhead poured over his thin hair, matting it to the sides of his face. A halo of water. "I hear some things sometimes," he said barely above the noise of the showers.

"Oh yeah? So what's on the radio this morning?" Rob meant it as an idle comment. Scoleri's nickname was Radio since he seemed to be both on another wavelength from the other sociopaths and psychopaths of Darden State and because he claimed he got messages. Special messages. The COs on the hall talked about it. Scoleri would sometimes tell them things about themselves that he couldn't possibly know.

"He's out hunting, is all," Scoleri said in that little-boy voice that belied his six-foot frame and slightly receding hairline. "He wants more children."

"Who?" Rob Fallon asked.

Scoleri glanced at the guards at the shower exit and at the other inmates. For just a second, Rob Fallon felt fear, something he didn't always feel. It was refreshing to get a taste of it. It was a sexual fear. He suddenly had the feeling that Scoleri was going to touch him.

Scoleri stepped closer to Rob Fallon, pressing his lips almost to his ear.

Fallon thought he felt Scoleri's tongue on his earlobe as Scoleri whispered his answer.

Scoleri reached up, holding Rob's head close to him, so he could keep his mouth almost right inside his ear while he whispered all the secrets he knew.

When it was over, Rob Fallon drew back in disgust, furious that Scoleri had gotten so close to him. Invaded the space near his flesh. He was the one who did that to others. They didn't do it to him. He hated Scoleri. He hated him with a passion and wanted to hurt him. Nobody got that close unless Fallon himself was taking control. He didn't want men like that. He didn't want the touch of any man, not like that. He felt himself go all dark inside like when he'd been a kid and his mother had caught him doing dirty things to himself with pins and tape.

Rob made a fist and threw a hard punch into the side of Scoleri's mouth.

When the impact came, the crunch of knuckle to face was like a shotgun blast.

Scoleri slipped, falling against the tile floor.

Blood spurted from between his lips.

Rob watched the blood flow into the soapy water that ran pink down the drain in the floor.

Two of the other men stepped back, but Jake the Whistler leapt forward to grab Rob by the throat. The psych techs in the doorway were already running across the slippery tiles when Rob Fallon began to black out from Jake's expert strangulation techniques.

"Don't alarm!" one of the psych techs shouted to the other. "We can control this."

The other psych tech put his alarm pen back in his breast pocket. Then when Noodles, out of nowhere leapt upon him, he managed to reach in, press the panic button on the alarm pen, just before he fell to the slippery tile floor.

The strobe lights began going on and off, and the interward alarm sounded.

A brief period of shutdown would follow. The doors to the ward would close and lock automatically, and no one would be able to get out. COs would show up momentarily, and with luck, the psych techs wouldn't be too banged up.

Now and then a ward-wide riot might erupt if controls and restraints weren't in place fast enough.

Or if staff members, including the psychiatric technicians and the nurses and the ward doctors and the corrections officers didn't act in a timely and efficient manner.

5

Michael Scoleri stood over Fallon and the psych tech who wrestled around on the tiles. Water streamed off his pale skin.

A curious smile grew on his face as he watched the struggle at his feet.

The lights flashed on and off around him.

When a psych tech grabbed him from behind, Scoleri got violent.

He went for the eyes.

His fingernails went in the orbital ridge and he felt that warm moisture around the eye itself.

6

Michael Scoleri, in his room, minutes later, bound, the restraints impossibly tight around his hands, nodded his head as if listening to someone who was not there.

Chapter Twelve

Rob Fallon had been shut off into his room, still shivering from the shower, and with the taste of blood in his mouth from where he'd been thrown against the wall by a psych tech who was afraid of him.

He wrapped himself in his sheet, and when the staff nurse came around to give him some meds to help calm him a bit, he told her that he had an important message to deliver.

"Who to?" the nurse asked.

Two husky psych techs stood near the doorway, ready in case Fallon caused any trouble.

"My doctor," he said. "It's important. It's real important. I gotta tell her!"

But his psychiatrist wasn't in yet.

It was too early.

Chapter Thirteen

1

San Pascal County was something of a joke in the Inland Empire of Southern California, for it had been a diamond-shaped wasteland until the 1980s, when developers had seen a gold mine in creating a series of commuter communities beneath its mountains. Most of it was high mountains and canyons off a corner of Riverside and San Bernardino Counties. Its mountains connected with the San Bernardino Mountains and National Forest, briefly, and sustained ski resorts at elevations exceeding 11,000 feet. Far below, almost a plummet, lay the flat lands of the inhabited portion of San Pascal County. Now a bedroom community, it once had been a flood area. Some say that if it rained hard enough, it would be nothing but mudslides, like it had been in the 1930s when torrential rains swept through the then-uninhabited area, taking out a chunk of a hillside with it.

Early morning, too early to get up, but the little boy always got up early. And this was an extra-special morning. A morning that would be remembered forever, he knew, because it was going to be Lucas Day. Officially. His mother had declared it, and he reminded her of it every single day until the day on his calendar came up:

MONDAY.

Beneath this in red felt tip marker, his mother had written:

NATIONAL LUCAS DAY. NO SCHOOL. DAY OFF! CHRISTMAS VACATION STARTS!

Lucas, who was just eight years old, scruffed his hair with his hands and yawned. He smelled the morning, the threat of rain outside his window, slightly propped open with one of his hundreds of toy soldiers. The smell, also, of the woman next door, beneath the condominium, who always put her laundry out in the mornings. Fresh clean laundry smell mixed with that just-before-it-rains odor. He pictured Mrs. Randel running out as the rain came down, gathering up all her clothes from the line. It made him happy to think it.

When he got out of bed, he went over to the pile of toys in the corner of his room. He picked through them, tossing the little trucks to the side, stepping on some marbles and almost falling down. He picked through the toy lizards and bugs he collected. Finally, he found the large Mickey Mouse clock. He looked at the hands of the clock carefully. Then he picked up one of the big rubber spiders his dad had bought him when they'd spent the summer in Los Angeles with his dad's new wife. He stuffed the spider, named Charlotte, in the pocket of the shorts he intended to wear that day. Then he picked up a green toy soldier and stuffed it in the other pocket. He padded from his room, to the bathroom to brush his teeth and "go," then over to his mommy's room. She was still asleep. He got up on the covers and stared at her awhile.

Soon she opened her eyes, almost startled to see him.

"It's today already," he said. He thought she was so pretty. A lot prettier than his daddy's new wife.

"Ten more minutes," she said, turning over into the comforter, covering her head with the pillow.

"No more minutes," he said, reaching over and tugging the pillow from her arms. When he had it, he gave her a scolding look. "Go get ready."

"You first," she said groggily. Her eyes looked like they were glued shut. Still, she managed a grin. "All excited about today, are you, kiddo?"

"You know who you look like right now?" he said. He didn't wait for her answer. "Like a movie star."

"I feel like a very sleepy mommy," she said.

Then her beeper went off on the bedside table. She reached for it, her hand fumbling across all the books and papers she always kept there. When she picked it up, she lifted it to her face, squinting. "It's too early for me to see," she said. Holding the beeper to Lucas's face, she asked, "What's the number?"

He read her the number, then frowned. "I know what that is. That's work."

"Coffee," was all she said in reply.

"Can I take Stuart with us?"

"Coffee," she repeated.

He scrambled off the bed and ran out to the kitchen to turn on the coffee machine. He went to the cooler and poured out exactly enough water to get to the half-way point of the coffeepot. Then he carefully poured it into the machine. It was always up to Lucas to flick it on, so that it would start sputtering the coffee into the pot. As he watched it begin its steaming, he wondered if he'd be able to sneak a taste. Then he went and poured himself a bowl of Fruit Loops. He carried it with him, munching on the cereal as he went to feed his hamster. The hamster cage was in the small den, which was part play room and part his mother's home office.

"Hey, Stuart," he said, having named his hamster for the book his mother had read him, *Stuart Little*. He had had a guinea pig he named Charlotte, from *Charlotte's Web*. His mother insisted that the guinea pig shouldn't be named for a spider, any more than a hamster should be named for a mouse. But he liked both names and both books. When Charlotte the guinea pig had died the previous summer, Lucas had transferred the name more logically to his rubber spider.

"Stuart, come on, it's breakfast time." Lucas picked up some food pellets, dropping them in the little bowl at the bottom of the cage. For good measure, he set three Fruit Loops in the bowl, too, and watched his pet eat. He picked up *Charlotte's Web* off the lower part of the bookcase by the wall, and flipped through its pages. "See?" he showed the book to the hamster. "Charlotte is teaching Wilbur the pig things. She's spinning her web so people will see it. See?" He held up a picture from the middle of the book. Then he put the book down beside the cage. "Stuart, today is gonna be better than Christmas," Lucas whispered.

The hamster got onto the metal wheel in his cage and began running, spinning the wheel rapidly. Lucas went out into the hall, down toward his bathroom. It was wallpapered with Tweetie Birds and Sylvesters, and the shower curtains had Wile E. Coyotes and Roadrunners all over it.

After he jumped in and out of the shower, he climbed into his shorts and put on his favorite T-shirt and his sandals. In the mirror, he scraped a comb through his thick hair and brushed his teeth twice, once with Colgate and once with bubblegum-flavored toothpaste. In the mirror, while he was brushing, he thought he saw something move behind him, off near the door.

"Mom?" he said. He turned around. No one was there. Lucas shivered a little. He had been told at school all about the Bogeyman. He'd been having nightmares since then about how the Bogeyman waited for kids and grabbed them. He didn't like to think about it, and he wished he hadn't seen that shadow movement in the mirror. It was all pretend. No such thing as the Bogeyman.

He bravely looked all over the bathroom, behind the shower curtain, and inside the hamper. Empty.

"It's pretend," he said aloud, just in case the Bogeyman was listening.

He went to check on the coffee, leaving wet footmarks down the white wall-to-wall carpet as he walked to the kitchen. Carefully, he lifted the glass pot. He poured the steamy dark liquid into his mother's favorite mug. On the mug it said FOR THE BEST MOMMY IN THE WORLD. It had a big red heart right beside it. He'd given it to her for the previous Mother's Day. He'd saved his allowance of fifty cents a week for nine weeks running to buy it for her. His mommy loved her coffee.

He measured two teaspoons of sugar into it and stirred in a drop of whipped cream from the fridge. Then he walked down the hall to his mother's room. She was in the shower, so he set the coffee on the bathroom sink.

The phone rang. He went to pick it up. "Hello?" he said. "Hello?"

But no one said anything on the other end of the line.

His mother came out of the bathroom, wrapped up in a huge towel, her hair wet and sticking to the sides of her face in a kind of funny way. "Who was it?" she asked, sipping her coffee.

"They hung up," he said.

She held her small wristwatch up in her hand, and said, "Okay, well, slight change of plan, kiddo.

We still go to the beach, but I have a quick errand to do for work. Okay?"

Lucas said nothing. He felt the pout beginning to thrust itself out from under his skin, right about where his lower lip stuck out. He put his hands in his pocket and looked down at the floor. He was not going to throw a tantrum, but he really wanted to do it. He wanted to fall on the floor and kick and cry, but it would be too much like a baby. And since his birthday, he was no longer a baby. His hand clutched the big rubber spider in his pocket. It felt good to squeeze it.

"Oh, stop with the face," his mother said. "It's only going to be for a little bit. I promise."

"I know," he lied. "It's okay."

His mother sighed. "No, it's not okay, Lucas." She crouched down next to him, putting her arms around his back. "We are going. I mean it. But you know how Mommy's work sometimes . . ."

"Yeah, yeah," he said. He pressed his face against her neck. She smelled like lilacs. She always smelled like lilacs in the morning from the soap she used. It was purple soap. Just as he smelled like coconut from his favorite soap, she smelled like flowers from hers. He couldn't help himself. A tear or two came to his eyes. He felt himself melt into her a little bit. It felt good.

When he finally pulled back, he saw tears in her eyes, too. "You okay?"

She nodded and kissed him twice on the forehead. "It won't be long. I'll run in and then run out. I promise. Then I'll race back here, and we go. And

Nina's going to come over and be with you while I'm gone. But I promise to be back really fast." Then she brightened. "Knock knock."

"Who's there?" he asked, a half-smile creeping across his face.

"Boo."

"Boo what?" he asked, and then exploded in laughter, having spoiled her joke.

"Oh," his mother said, shaking a finger at him. "You've heard that one too many times. I need new material."

3

Twenty minutes later Lucas, wearing his Sponge-Bob SquarePants T-shirt that stretched almost to his knees, sat in the front yard with his rows of small green plastic soldiers. They were in battle position.

Lucas knocked at a toy soldier with a twig. "Take that!" He was pretty bored with playing soldiers when his PlayStation was inside the house, but he had promised his mother that he wouldn't play any games on weekdays. Even if this was a special weekday—his first day of Christmas vacation and his official birthday celebration day all rolled into one.

But playing with plastic soldiers was for babies. He had the toys since he was little, since his daddy had given them to him. That had been the only reason he still had them at all—because they were from his father.

Lucas reached into his side pocket, where he had

put Stuart Little, his hamster. The hamster was rolled up sleeping. Stuart had already eaten the six Fruit Loops Lucas had put in his pocket with him. Lucas always had to be careful to put Stuart only in his baggy shorts pockets, otherwise he tended to escape and run away. No matter how Lucas jostled him, Stuart was so used to going to sleep inside Lucas's pockets, nothing ever seemed to bother him.

His mother would be angry if she knew he'd brought the hamster for the trip, but Lucas did not trust Nina to feed Stuart while they were gone.

After patting Stuart's soft fur, he worked to bury a little toy soldier under a mound of dirt. Then he put a plastic pail upside down over it. "Here comes the tank down in the battle, tank tank tank," he said, picking up a rock that barely fit into his fist and pounded it along the grass, heading for its destination, the pail.

"It's gonna blow up now," he whispered, as he brought the rock up above the pail and was about to smash it down.

Lucas saw the man's shoes. It was as if the man had just suddenly appeared.

Lucas dropped the rock.

The shoes were black and shiny, but scuffed a little at the toes.

The pants were dark blue, almost black.

"Hi." The man's voice was almost squeaky, like a mouse.

92

Chapter Fourteen

Lucas looked up from the grass.

"Hey," Lucas said. "Want to hear a knock-knock joke?"

"Sure."

"Knock knock."

"Who's there?"

"Boo."

"Boo who?"

"Quit crying, you big baby."

"That's a good one. You're up early today."

"I got up with Mommy. We're going to the beach."

"Where's Mommy?"

"She had an errand. You want to talk to her?"

"I don't need to. Who's watching you then?"

"Nina. She's inside. She's reading. Want me to get her?"

"A babysitter?"

"I'm not a baby. I'm almost nine. She does breakfast, too. When Mommy's in a rush. Her name's Nina. Want me to get her?"

"Let's let her read, okay?"

"Okay." Lucas looked back down at his soldiers. "I'm bored with this stuff."

"Shouldn't you be in school?"

"Christmas vacation. It's my birthday." He didn't mind lying a little. It was, after all, the day that they were going to pretend it was his birthday and have fun.

"It is? Well, guess what? I have something for you. Back in my truck. It's pretty cool."

Lucas set his toy soldiers down, knocking a regiment over with his hand. He reached into his pocket, feeling Stuart's soft fur. Charlotte, his rubber spider, was in the other.

He was supposed to tell one of the grown-ups whenever he went anywhere, but it wasn't as if he really was going anyplace different.

Just a hop, skip, and a jump to the truck. He ran down the driveway to where the truck was parked.

"You got a new truck," Lucas said.

Droplets of rain on the top of his head. His only thought was that it was going to turn out to be a bad day for the beach if it started raining. It made him a little sad to think of his mommy probably canceling the beach by the time she got back from work.

Of him not getting a special birthday with her.

Just as he stepped up to peer into the interior of the truck, Lucas felt a jolt, like a big shock, on his left shoulder.

Chapter Fifteen

7:50 A.M.

It glanced around after it shut off the tazer and slipped it back into his jacket pocket.

It rolled the little boy's body farther into the seat of the truck.

It shut the door.

It glanced around the pretty neighborhood as rain began to fall.

It looked at the house, with its big picture window in front and its lawn, and the way the foothills rose up behind the suburban property.

It went around, slid into the seat, and started the truck up again.

It felt the Other One inside it.

It growled in its throat as it petted the boy's head, scruffing up his hair.

"Don't be afraid," it said.

Then it reached in the glove compartment and pulled out the duct tape and the box cutter.

A hypodermic needle and a small vial of pills nearly rolled out of the glove compartment, but he managed to catch them and push them back in.

For a second it closed its eyes and was suddenly in the other place.

The place where its father roared like a lion and the sky was raining with fire and brimstone down upon it.

Then, opening his eyes, he leaned over the boy, raising the box cutter and tearing out a length of duct tape.

The boy's eyes had been closed, but they opened suddenly.

It reached into its jacket for the tazer, but fumbled.

The boy opened his mouth, and it clapped its hand over the lips.

The boy bit the palm of its hand, and it dropped the box cutter.

The cutter rolled back into the crack of the seat.

The duct tape rolled to the floor.

It cussed as a 7-Eleven coffee cup spilled over onto the mat beneath the glove compartment.

Slapped the boy's face.

Boy's hands grabbed around its forearms, pushing.

Pressed its palm down.

Kept its hand on the boy's mouth even though the boy was biting down hard.

And it heard the sound of the Other One, shaking the bars of its cage. Trying to get out.

To devour the boy.

Right here.
In the truck on the pretty suburban street.
Rain came down.
Like blood.

It got the tazer out of its jacket, and pressed it on the boy's chest, at the same time withdrawing its hand from the boy's mouth.

The boy's body shook when the tazer touched it.

The boy was still.

Breathing.

Eyes open.

But still.

Alive.

It glanced out the windshield.

The houses all in a row, neat and clean with well-manicured lawns.

Somewhere nearby, a dog barked in a backyard.

It quickly duct taped the boy's mouth, and then wrapped the duct tape around the boy's wrists and ankles, using the box cutter to slice the tape neatly.

From behind the seat, it grabbed a blanket, the one its mother crocheted for it when it went out on cold days.

It tossed the blanket over the boy.

It turned the key in the ignition, started up the truck, and headed down the street, making a left when it reached the bottom of the hill.

It turned on the windshield wipers, and reached over to the dashboard, to turn up the radio.

It thought about its work day coming up.

It thought about how it needed to send a message to God.

Chapter Sixteen

8 A.M.

1

After a jog in the cooling, light rain, Trey Campbell went into his home through the sliding glass doors off the kitchen. In the kitchen, something seemed different. There was some kind of smell that did not seem to fit with the usual house smell. He went to the fridge and opened the door. Smelled fine in there. He checked to make sure the stove and oven were off.

"Just your usual paranoia," he said aloud, feeling foolish. He knew it was only an illogical fear based on incidents in the past. It might happen again, but the likelihood was, he told himself, that if someone wanted to come into his house to rob them or kill them, it would've happened. *Working around killers, breathing the same air with them, you get to thinking like this.*

They get inside your head.

When he passed by his daughter's room, he stopped for a moment. He'd spent the past several months being a full-time dad. Paid leave. So different than going to work every day and seeing his children just before they fell asleep at night. He knew things about their daily lives now. He noticed that Teresa had gotten rid of all her dolls—exiled to boxes in the basement. The room was messy. On her dresser were a Nancy Drew book, a small statue of a horse, and her basketball trophy from school. At times a little demon, at times a perfect kid, he was damn happy that he had this life with her, and with Mark. He was damn happy that life was not all about criminals and work routines and mind games.

Her brother's door was wide open, and Mark had all his Harry Potter and Lemony Snicket books tossed in a corner; on the wall a big poster of the Tyrannosaurus rex from *Jurassic Park*. Trey couldn't see Mark's face because of the blanket thrown over him, but he heard his son's steady snores.

"You've had months of being house-husband," Carly said, coming up behind him. "Ready to give it all up and go back to nine-to-five?"

"No," Trey said. He felt her arm go around his waist. "Yeah, I guess I am."

He reached for her, pulling her back, turning toward her. Her nightgown smelled sweet, and she smelled like morning to him, always. He reached inside her robe to feel her skin against his arms, and although it aroused him, he let that feeling come and go.

"Maybe I'll call in sick," he said.

"Or you can call in well," she said, grinning.

He wondered how he had ever come to deserve such a wife. She had put up with him all these years. She had even sat out his sabbatical and now his return to work as if it were just another part of him she cared for. He brushed the hair from the sides of her face. Kissed her lightly. Hugged her. "Sorry about the argument last night."

"Well," she sighed, pulling away again, "Yeah. Me too."

"Thanks," Trey said. "Look, for better or worse, that job is important to me." He knew that on some level she meant it, but it was a constant sore spot for them. As long as he even mentioned that place, it always would be. He wasn't smart enough to know if this was how marriage went. There was the good and the bad, and you lived with both, learned to get along, and just let some things slide. He wasn't sure if those things that you slide would come up later and bite you on the ass. But for now, it was okay. They had a good marriage. They had a few rocky points. It was life.

He gave her a kiss on her forehead.

"Now go take a shower," Carly said. "You stink." She turned and walked toward the kitchen.

"You are a vision, even before my first cup of coffee," he said.

As she padded into the kitchen, Carly replied, "And you look like a guy who's buttering up his wife so she'll forgive him for doing what he promised her he would never do again."

Damn it. It's what I want to do. It's what I need to do.

He knew there was some danger working where he did, but it was as if he felt more alive inside the doors of that place than he felt anywhere else in the world.

And yet, what kind of sane person would ever admit to that?

He watched her go and suddenly felt excited, if not entirely ecstatic about going back to work at the maximum-security hospital.

As Trey stepped into the shower, he thought he heard the phone ring.

2

"Jim Anderson left a message for you on the machine. And Conroy's office called twice already," Carly said. She passed him a towel and set an extra cup of coffee for him on the edge of the bathroom sink. "Just her assistant. Wouldn't let me know what it was. Must be top secret." She said this last part a bit sarcastically. "I'm telling you, Elise Conroy's got her sights on you."

"Well, she's going to have to wait until you dump me then," he said.

He toweled off, got dressed fairly quickly while glancing at the clock, and went to check the messages.

3

On the answering machine, Jim's gruff Texas accent. "Hey Bubba, looking forward to seeing you in the Crack-up Palace today. Listen, we got a live one on Program 28 I want you to meet first thing. Scoleri. Nearly took out Bobby Bronson's left eye this morning. A quarter inch from getting it. Dug right into his skin. Believes he's Lord of the World. Calls himself Abraxas. Has a whole mythology worked out about how he can hear the secrets. All that jazz. Brainard and Conroy are on him, and Conroy gave you a special pass to check him out. Can't wait for your assessment. I guess you're a big shot now. Conroy's been hunting you down, too. It must have something to do with this profiling case she's working on. Some kidnappings over the weekend. I didn't get the details, you know Conroy, and then that dude Eric is in spaceville half the time. Well, Bubba, I wanted to be the first to welcome you back to Thrill-Kill Row."

Chapter Seventeen

1

Trey arrived at work a few minutes early.

Nearly soaked despite his umbrella, he walked from his parking space into the main building. It was a large white-gray building. Were it not for the security fences, a person driving by might think this was some corporate headquarters, or perhaps a spa rather than a hospital for criminals. He nodded to the two men at the desk. Both wore blue uniforms, crew cuts; one of them seemed to recognize him even though Trey could not remember ever seeing him before.

He flashed his badge and walked down the main hall.

Ward A had low-security clearance. A central office area, off which three hallways, each with double-doors. Always flowers on the sign-in desk, as if this were a happy place. The smell of institution. They might as well have bottled it and sold it to be sprayed around every state institution in the world: rubbing alcohol, air freshener, pine cleaner, and something not so breathtaking, something between ammonia and urine in the blend of odors.

The fluorescents still flickered along the ceiling as they had since he'd last been there. The cork boards along the wall carried staff photos and notices about apartments for rent, dogs that needed homes, old cars for sale. An open window office to the right, behind which was an entire open room of administrative staff, as well as some of the legal staff.

At the sign-in desk, three nurses were in line ahead of him, and one, Joe Houston, turned and slapped him a high five. Trey was never sure of high fives. He generally just put his hand up slightly, more used to shaking hands than slapping them.

"I thought you were outta this joint," Joe said, laughing. "Who drug ya back?"

"I live here," Trey said. "Didn't they tell you?"

He took a deep breath before he turned left to go down to what was called Level Two, which contained Alphabet Wards A through G. He glanced toward the stairwell that went to the Rap Floor, as they called it. This was a bit easier as an area because the older patients who had been around for forty or more years were up there. They were less bother than Trey's floor—the older the patients got, the less dangerous they were to each other and to the staff. Additionally, the upstairs wards contained the least harmful young patients. The ones who had only committed one murder, or had not-even completed a murder but had merely maimed. They were more sedated up there, happier and with fewer attacks.

It would be like a promotion to move up to the Rap Floor, even if the salary and benefits didn't change.

But Trey was on the Alphabet Wards.

They were his territory.

2

He flashed his I.D. badge to the overweight security guard who nodded him past the second check-point.

Hearing the heavy slam of the protective metal doors was enough to bring bad memories back.

Joe Houston smacked his gum as he walked alongside him. "I was on D for two emergencies last month. Man, I do not envy you that place. I had to scrape up one guy off the linoleum."

Trey sighed. "Yeah, that's D."

"Man, I'd transfer out if I were you. Shit, you'd think they'd've gotten you off the floor after last summer."

Trey paused, adjusting his glasses slightly. "They did. They tried anyway."

"What happened?"

"I guess," Trey grinned, "nobody wanted my job."

3

An orderly he didn't recognize sat at the entryway to Ward B. The guy looked a little wild, and Trey saw the telltale signs of speed—the bloodshot eyes, the peach skin, the slight jitter.

It was a problem with employees at Darden. Sometimes they turned to drugs to help get them through their shifts. Occasionally, a few of them ended up as inmates a few years down the road. Sometimes you couldn't tell an inmate from a psych tech or an orderly. If it weren't for the white jackets versus the khakis of the inmates, it would be hard to tell which were the crazy ones.

The worst were not the Speedies, as the psych techs called staff who did meth on the weekends.

The worst were those staffers who were about one bad day away from becoming exactly like the patients they handled.

"Campbell."

The orderly checked the badge. Then put an X on a chart. "William C. Campbell the Third. Trey. You're the guy from the Hatcher thing, right?" the orderly asked.

"Christ." Trey shook his head. "Yeah, I am."

"That's cool." The orderly nodded. "I just read all about it in *The Times*. You beat the shit out of her?"

"Christ," Trey said again. "No. I was lucky to get away from her with my heart and lungs intact. That's all."

"Hope you don't mind if I feel you up," the guy said, a grin on his face.

"Get your kicks any way you can here," Trey said, lifting his arms as the guard passed a handheld metal sensor over his body. Then he reached between Trey's legs, feeling for any hidden weapons.

It was a precaution that Trey appreciated. Not for the cheap thrill. Because they'd had problems with staff smuggling things in.

Staff who got too close to the patients.

Guards could be the worst, particularly if they were working Darden because they'd failed the psych exams for regular duty. If they'd worked the prisons out on the desert, as some had, they thought this was a cake position, but they always ended up complaining that they'd prefer the general maximum-security prison population to Darden State.

At least with sane prisoners, you had logic and reason and motive.

He waited for the guard on the other side to unlock the steel door.

4

On B Ward, he passed the group rooms and the recreation center. One elderly man, tall and thin, propelled himself forward in his wheelchair.

As Trey passed by him, the old man said, "Goddamn motherfuckers. I'm gonna skin me the lot of you."

A nurse, holding a clipboard to her chest, flashed a smile at Trey. Lauren Childes—she'd been at Darden since before Trey's time. "Good to see you back, Trey," she said.

Her eye-patch was new. Her left eye was covered.

One of the patients had gotten her probably.

Trey didn't want to ask.

He didn't want to know.

5

Two COs at the double doors. Corrections Officers had been brought in to beef up security even further.

The two cops frisked him as he stepped across the grate at the entrance to C. Their ID tags said CURZON and BELLOWS. Curzon, the younger of the two, held up a metal detector and waved it over his body.

"Glad to see Darden's met twentieth-century technology," Trey said.

The officers said nothing.

Trey knew their silence was from nervousness. He held up his ID badge. They scanned its bar code. Double checks and triple checks were the rule.

No cop liked being in C or D Ward.

"When they have you guys come in?" Trey asked.

"Nine weeks back. Extra protection," Bellows said. "Ever since Program 28 went into effect."

"What do you do when something happens?"

Curzon shot the other a look and half smiled. "We bolt for the doors and get the hell out of here. Let the crazies kill the crazies, that's my take."

Bellows shook his head. "You're on D, right?"

"Right," Trey said. "New assignment: Program 28."

"Oh man." He laughed. "Oh man. We lost a guy there last month."

"Dead?" Trey asked.

"No. Early retirement. Some lucky SOB banged his knees up something good. Somehow got a pair of pliers from some asshole working on the pipes and just busted his kneecaps. Went out on disability. They've transferred half the SVPs from up in Napa down here, and they're . . ."

"Different," Curzon finished. They chuckled. "Two nights back some guy on D tried to pull some chick's head off. It was bad. Real bad."

Bellows chuckled. "She grew two inches."

"Damn." Curzon laughed. "Why can't we send 'em to Patton State? Or send their asses back to Atascadero. We don't need the pile up here."

"Let me keep my cojones, that's all I'm sayin'," Bellows said.

6

The first corridor had bars on its entry door, but after that, the hallways all looked like a cross between hospital floors and elementary school corridors, with fire doors at the end of each of them. The artwork and creative writing samples of many of the patients were pinned on long cork boards just above eye level along the walls. He passed the group rooms and the lounges. All the guards seemed to recognize him, even those he'd never seen before. He assumed this was because of the notoriety he'd received since the previous summer. Artwork adorned the walls. Outside each door, the clipboard hung with the various doctors' and nurses' names for the patients who occupied the rooms, as well as their daily schedules from morning showers to recreational therapy to who got cigarettes and who didn't.

For Trey it was like walking down a long and lonely tunnel to the place that almost cost him and his family their lives.

D Ward.

And an offshoot of D, the newly christened Program 28.

It looked, at first, like any other hall of the entire complex.

But it wasn't.

7

When he arrived at Ward D, he marveled at the beefed-up security. Cameras moved lazily back and forth along the ceiling. Reinforced doors of steel were everywhere it seemed—more than had been there when he'd last been at work.

"Somebody must be running for office somewhere," he told Mary Fulcher, who was doing soap and toilet paper counts near the guard station.

"Huh?" she asked. "Oh, Trey. Hey, old man. I didn't recognize you with those glasses." She threw her arms around him for a quick hug. When she pulled back, he noticed that she had aged ten years over the past few months. Her forehead was creased with worry lines—far too young to have them—and she had that over-stressed look to her eyes.

110

"Good to be back, Mary. I meant all the security improvements. The cameras. The guards and stuff."

"Oh, yeah. It was Hatcher that did that. Olsen got a call from the governor himself and it was all donated by some security firm in Riverside. 'To make sure no one ever escapes from D Ward again.' Good P.R. for the neighborhood, huh?"

"Yep. Good P.R.," Trey replied.

"Think it'll work?"

He smiled.

"Me neither," she said.

8

On Ward D, the night shift nurse and psych techs were off on their duties, so he made a pot of coffee in the lounge and drank half a cup. The lounge was a mess—crushed Dixie Cups on one of the round tables, the microwave was filthy, and someone had spilled Cremora around the sink.

Same old same old.

There would be three shift nurses making early rounds of meds on two different corridors. Six psych techs, most of them doing shower duty. Rise and shine wasn't for another ten minutes. Miraculously, another fifteen psych techs would arrive by 9:30 A.M. Then, three or four would be late for their shifts. Other staff would come in, and the night staff would leave. The patients would wake up at different times, depending on how heavily they had been medicated. The showers would go in shifts, as would the cafeteria groups.

Trey finished his coffee, which tasted bitter but strong enough to energize him. He tossed the cup toward the trash can by the lounge door, but missed it. He wondered if this were an omen for the rest of his day.

Because he'd been shift supervisor, he had one of three small offices at the opposite end of the corridor. He passed several patients' rooms, glancing at the charts as he went, noticing that Dr. Conroy now had six new patients and Brainard had two. As usual, Brainard overdosed his with too much Doltrynol, but it was the man's method: drug 'em and bury 'em. And before they die from lack of life, pretend that you actually care about their welfare.

Jim Anderson had been promoted to Shift Charge, and as Trey passed his office, he saw the desk covered in paperwork, and the small lamp on. Tinny music from the small boom box on Anderson's desk—was it from *The Mikado*? Trey wasn't sure. Anderson was a big Gilbert & Sullivan fan, which seemed so incongruous with Anderson's demeanor and way of talking. But somewhere along the line, he'd gotten hooked on light opera, and played it whenever he could. Trey smiled as he heard the words, "I've got a little list of people we could do without who never would be missed," from the tape that was playing.

They hadn't spoken since last summer.

It was as if what had happened had been too much to talk about.

Anderson was still on the ward somewhere. He'd

112

be there till noon. He was the one guy Trey was looking forward to seeing.

Then, two doors down, Trey's office.

The door was still locked. Had anyone been in it during those four months? When he unlocked the door and went in, he saw the tracks of others. The papers out of place, the computer terminal turned slightly to the right, the file folders stacked on the cabinet.

He went about his morning duties.

9

Trey signed for the alarm pens, to make sure they were accounted for. Next, he went down to the station and checked the razors, to make sure the correct number was there. After that he checked the sharps: scissors, razor knife, a special knife to cut restraints in case of fire, pliers, screwdrivers, a hammer, finger- and toenail clippers. The others had probably checked them, too, but as supervisor it was his ultimate responsibility.

And since what had happened the previous summer, Trey Campbell did not want to leave anything to chance.

After he checked out the sharps, he walked up and down the corridor of D Ward. Several fire extinguishers lined the walls, and he checked each one of these. Then he moved on to check the defibrillators and oxygen bottles. As he passed it, he glanced at a crash cart—used for hospital emergencies. It was full of bandages, neck, back, and other braces, flashlights, special hospital material for people in sudden and acute respiratory or cardiac failure. The nurse on duty was in one of the patient rooms—he saw her through the porthole. She was in there with two psychiatric technicians, tending to one of six patients in the room. It was Rita Paulsen. She smiled when she caught a glimpse of him through the round window. He nodded to her, but was unable to smile. He both looked forward to his daily routine and wished he had not come back.

Trey flipped through the roll charts to see if there were any other female staff members on D that morning. When women were on, he had to check with them every fifteen minutes. It wasn't that they were incompetent. But the patients often made their more gruesome attacks on the females. It was a dangerous job.

He checked the Site Incident Report at the nurse's station, but nothing out of the ordinary had occurred during the night. Walking the green halls, with the thick smell of rubbing alcohol and Clorox and then that all pervasive odor of mildew, it was as if he had not had time off at all. It was as if his life had begun and would one day end within these walls.

Within D Ward.

Any one of these patients was potentially dangerous in ways the community that surrounded Darden State could not possibly imagine.

Trey knew better than anyone that all it took was one.

He wondered if anyone was making the back hall rounds and the long hall rounds. Every fifteen minutes someone was supposed to check the ward and the patients' dorms. In a dangerous unit like D, no one wanted to miss those.

He did his own check of the ward, looking from room to room. Most of the patients were sleeping. Some had already risen and were with the orderlies down at the showers. All would be awake in a few minutes. Then the laundry detail and shower supervisors would miraculously appear from this silent ward, and the day would truly get under way as the med cart squeaked on its wheels down the bustling corridor.

10

After he'd gotten his phone messages and checked the computerized state forms, he went down to Conroy's on-site office, down through the corridors, on the opposite end of the building from the violent criminals' ward.

She wasn't there.

Her office, like all the psychiatrists' offices, was large and spacious—unlike the hole-in-the-wall he had as supervisor on D. She had a window to the inner courtyard, and a side room for her secretary. It smelled of lilacs and cigarettes inside the office. Elise always broke the rules and smoked in her office. So far, no one had complained too bitterly about it.

He went in and looked over her messy desk. Half

a dozen manila files, stacked one atop the other. A half-drunk cup of coffee—she was an early riser sometimes. A workaholic most times.

A framed picture of Elise and her kid. Trey had only worked with her sporadically and was often surprised that she had a life outside her work at all. She had offices at three different facilities, including the Riverside County evaluation site in Riverside. He had never known her not to work. Even after her husband walked out on her, she had been on the job the following day.

And she was a chain smoker.

Five cigarette butts in the ashtray. The staff was supposed to go outside to the yard or up through the locked area at the roof. Elise never left her desk if she wanted a smoke.

A notepad in the middle of her desk. A crazy doodle across it. As if she'd sat there less than an hour ago, drinking coffee, talking to someone on the phone, puffing on her cigarette . . . forcing a Bic pen down hard making circles on the pad.

He found the file he needed fairly quickly.

MICHAEL SCOLERI.

From behind him, in the doorway, someone said, "Trey?"

He turned around. It was Conroy's assistant, Eric Lombard. He was short, blond, and too much of a surfer dude for Darden State. He belonged in L.A. at the beach. He seemed sorely out of his element in Conroy's office.

"Hey, Eric. Where's the boss?"

"Some bad shit's going on. Here's her cell," he said, then passed him a number.

"Any idea of what's up?"

"She's not even telling me," he said. "She's doing some profiling with the San Pascal and Riverside sheriff's office, working on some new forensics case. She got called in over the weekend. That's all I know. She was here for about ten minutes and then took off like a bat out of hell. She won't tell me anything. But she wants to talk to you ASAP."

Then, "You can use the office if you want." Eric left, shutting the door.

Trey reached for the phone and dialed the cell phone number.

Elise picked up.

"Hello? Elise?" he said.

"Trey? Thank God."

"What's going on? You working on some case?"

"I'm in traffic. I . . . can't talk like this. I'll be there soon. I've got . . ." Silence on the line.

"Elise?"

"I'm driving over to San Pascal. I'll be back. Maybe an hour. Maybe more."

Another silent few seconds.

"Tell me what's going on," he said, expecting nothing more than a hectic schedule from her, as was her usual.

"Do something for me. Did Eric get you a file?"

"Yep."

"Okay. Okay. Read it. Just as an intro. And go see Scoleri. See if you can get him talking. About anything. Anything at all. Watch him. See if he's talking to anybody else. Staff. Anybody."

11

Trey grabbed the top file of the pile of papers on Conroy's desk.

"Okay. Scoleri. Tell me who you are."

He opened the file.

Chapter Eighteen

INTERVIEW SUBJECT: MICHAEL SCOLERI
INTAKE O/D : E. CONROY
PROPERTY OF THE DARDEN STATE HOSPITAL,
DARDEN, CA
CONFIDENTIAL

NOTES: Found guilty of the murders of six women, two men. Rape, mutilation. Post-mortem sexual activity. Fascinated with the dead. Necrophilia. Goes for souvenirs. Collection included eyes, noses, breasts, and genitalia. Activity: labile.

SCOLERI: Hi. You know my name, but I don't know yours.
CONROY: I'm Dr. Conroy. I'm a psychiatrist for the state of California. Do you understand that, Mr. Scoleri?
SCOLERI: Yes. It says E. Conroy on your tag. . . .
CONROY: Elise. Dr. Elise Conroy.
SCOLERI: Okay, Doc. But call me by my real name.

CONROY: Might I call you Michael?

SCOLERI: No. I'm not Michael. I'm Abraxas. I am the true God.

CONROY: Let's talk about what you did.

SCOLERI: The pretty girls. Okay. I didn't kill them. What I did was date them, and that was about it. We partied. We had some fun. It was all pretty innocent. Yeah, they came on to me, and yeah, I just should've not spent time with them. But I didn't kill them. It got a little rough. But I only did what they told me to. What they asked. They asked for all kinds of things. They begged for some of them.

CONROY: And you killed them.

SCOLERI: Only when they begged. I didn't do it. They used me as a tool. That's why they called me the Handyman.

CONROY: Who?

SCOLERI: The newspapers. They called me the Handyman. Like the song. Do you know the song? I'm a handyman for a lot of things. It wasn't the hammers and nails that got me that name. It wasn't the pliers and the wrenches and the ropes. It was because I knew what to give their hearts. They spoke to me in prayers. They pleaded for me. And I gave them what they asked for. There was one named Jenny and she prayed the most. She prayed so much that I had to answer her prayers. See, she'd been beaten when she was a little girl. She couldn't get away from it in life. That's how life is. You don't get away from your problems. You don't either, do you?

CONROY: Who had beaten her?

SCOLERI: Her parents. I think mainly her father. But her mother, too. Her father was a sadist, but I think her mother was like, you know, one of those little yappy dogs. You know? The kind that just runs after and bites at you. So she sort of encouraged the father to be mean. She was probably the kind of mother who liked it when children suffer. And pretty Jenny suffered all the time she grew up. And her daddy did those things to her that daddies are only supposed to want to do with mommies. So when she was in my presence, and crying, a big girl of twenty-four, bawling her eyes out, I showed her how to reach atonement. That means at-one-ment. That's where atonement comes from. She had to atone for her sins, and her father's sin. I told her what it would cost. What was demanded. And she begged. And then, she offered. It was just three of her fingers. She offered them because they were the part of her that still did bad things. That was her atonement. When it was done, she prayed that she would die. I was just the tool. The hand of Abraxas was upon her, and she thanked me when she left. She thanked me profusely. I stayed with her that night. All night long. I prayed with her. I knew how her life had gone to that point. Children really live in Hell. But I could offer her Heaven. And atonement.

CONROY: And how did you know that? About her childhood?

SCOLERI: I'm afraid if I told you, you wouldn't understand.

CONROY: And you believed her parents had beaten her and abused her as a child.

SCOLERI: Her body radiated it. She was small and weak from it. She had a little darkness in her head from where they'd hit her. She talked to me silently from the darkness. Do you know that's what we all have? All of us who are here? We were born with this small broken piece of glass—a darkness. In our brains. And then, some of us were tortured. By nice people who thought they were doing good. I know what they did to her. They saw into her darkness, and they hurt her so that her darkness would grow.

CONROY: Darkness?

SCOLERI: Yep. A small voice of darkness. Don't you ever hear them? You talk to enough of them. They grow up and do bad things later. Or they spend their lives being hurt. It's because of that voice in the dark. It grew in them. It didn't grow in someone like you. You're attractive, well-educated, smart. Not like the kind of people I'm talking about. They're lost, and they've been lost since that darkness grew inside them. I hear their voices as one voice. I do. All the time. They talk to me. The lost ones. The ones who get hurt. And the monsters talk to me, too. The ones who hurt. I know them. They send me their prayers.

CONROY: Do you think that what you did to her was worse than what her parents had done to her?

SCOLERI: Of course not. What I did to her was the best thing for her. I wasn't going to let her go through the life they'd mapped out for her. How would she have turned out? She would've been just another messed-up woman. She would've kept the species going, only her species. The messed-up kind. The kind who raises children all wrong. The kind of woman who doesn't achieve any balance in her life. The kind with darkness growing. Look around, Doctor. The streets are full of them. You may know some. They blot out the light. They're . . . well, they're not like you. And none of you are like me.

CONROY: Do you believe that you are a different species?

SCOLERI: It must be hard to understand any of this, Dr. Conroy. You don't live in the world of direct experience. You're watching a movie screen and you think that's life. But you're not out there, in contact. Very few are anymore.

CONROY: Do you feel bad for what you did to her?

SCOLERI: How? She begged for death. But I messed it up.

CONROY: In what way?

SCOLERI: I did it too fast. The knife slipped. She was supposed to suffer for six minutes. It was too quick. She was gone before I could tell her.

CONROY: What did you need to tell her?

SCOLERI: About the gift.

CONROY: What is the gift?

SCOLERI: Suffering. She was so lucky to have it. But she should've had six minutes.

CONROY: Why is six minutes so important?

SCOLERI: Six minutes is enough time for me to take out what I need so that she could've seen it before she died. She could've watched it fly. All it ever takes is the power of six. She could've seen it.

CONROY: Seen what?

SCOLERI: The beauty of the world can only be experienced through terrible pain. Joy is in suffering. Even the saints knew that. All suffering is where God lives. I showed them God. And they found me there. I showed them my beauty. My true face. The doorway between life and death is always open. And it swings both ways, Dr. Conroy. They still talk to me. They tell me things. I can't keep the dead from speaking. What does it matter what I did to them? If I took their sight? They passed through suffering. They still exist. It's ridiculous to lock me up like this. I am Abraxas. I am all that there is. I hold life and death in my hands. Death is the true freedom in life. I hold their souls in my kingdom.

1/00: Scoleri transferred to Atascadero following conviction.

09/03: Scoleri transferred to Darden State/life threatened at Atascadero/sixth patient for experimental Program 28.

Chapter Nineteen

1

"Hey Bubba," Jim Anderson said.

Trey glanced up from the page. He dropped it back into the manila folder, shutting it. Anderson stood in the doorway, taking up most of it. "Jimmy."

"My trivia dude is back in play."

"Absolutely."

"What's the name of the woman who wrote the poem that goes on the Statue of Liberty?"

"Easy. Emma Lazarus."

"Who was the first man in space?"

"Double easy. A Russian named Gagarin. 1961. We launched Alan Shepard up a few weeks after. You know I know the space race answers backward and forward."

"I need to check on that one. You may be wrong. Okay, one more. What was the name of Jayne Mansfield's dog?"

"You got me. No idea. She was in a Buick Electra

225 when she died, though. So was the dog. Does that get me trivia points?"

"No way, Bubba. No way."

Jim, a behemoth of a guy, larger than when Trey had last seen him several months before, growing wider the older he got. His blond buzz cut was still intact, giving him the giant teddy bear crossed with a Marine look. He had the telltale peanut butter and jelly smudges of a slipshod breakfast all over his white coat.

Jim cracked a grin, his gold tooth shiny at the front of his mouth. "Back for the love of the job. Man, it's good to see you."

Pointing to Jim's dirty jacket, Trey laughed. "Don't you think you ought to come to work in clean clothes?"

Jim glanced at the stains. He wiped at the peanut butter, then licked it off his fingers. "Ever since this new laundry service started up, I just throw it to them. Pretty soon, we'll have shoe shines here, too. And massages. It'd be like paradise here, if it weren't for the patients."

Trey rose, offering his hand, but Jim slapped at it, playfully.

"Hear you're going to work Program 28," Jim said. "Jesus, that's the shit end of the stick. I go in to help out, and I feel like I'm just waiting to get my head torn off. They're all labile in there. They move slow, they get you all relaxed. Then when they see an opportunity, well, you know the routine."

"It's what I missed about this place."

Jim offered a smile. "Well, you worked with Hatcher pretty closely, didn't you?"

"Too closely. Jesus, Jimmy, they act like 28's a promotion."

"Sure, the docs think so. That's because they're all going to run off and write their books about the monstrosity of the human mind or some bullshit. Conroy herself was writing up some book and got a deal with some big New York publisher just to talk about her unusual way of dealing with the patients. You and me, we just have to watch out for the crazies. One thing I'll give Program 28: They're in restraints so much, there's not a lot to be afraid of. But hell yes, they creep the crap outta me."

"Agnes Hatcher was in restraints," Trey said.

"True. And she managed to get out of them. But 28 is Olsen's baby, and Conroy runs psych with it. So you know we're all safe," Jim said, winking. "It's a super-duper freak show there. You think you've seen the worst? 28 is the scum in the toilet. Hey, you got a copy of *Sociopathic Times*?" Jim pointed to the file in Trey's hand.

Trey held it up. "Conroy wants me to consult. Not just work with him, but work with her. Christ, I had six messages from her when I walked in."

"Something bad's going on with her today. No idea what. She came in after seven, but left real fast." Jim snorted. "I wish Conroy had never come down to D Ward. She's good, but it's 'cause she's pretty. Sexist as that sounds. It stirs some of these guys up. Christ, Rob Fallon was all jumping up and down this morning talking about her. Jillian thought he was gonna kill her. You gotta watch Fallon."

"He cool down?"

Jim nodded. "Yep. He clams up and is all smiles like the damn cat with the canary. We thought we were gonna have to tie him down, but you know Fallon. He's basically a good boy."

Trey half grinned at the intended irony of this comment. "Fallon greeted me in the lounge."

"Yeah, he's tasting his freedom. He's got some girl on the outside with big bucks who's trying to get early release for him." Jim Anderson paused, not having to add that everyone in Darden knew what Rob would do if released: kill the girlfriend at some point. "She may just do it. She's some heiress to some fortune. Lives in Beverly Hills or something and drives in here for long visits with him."

"A lot's happened since I left," Trey laughed. "At least for Rob. Man, someone should counsel that girlfriend of his. Does she understand the definition of 'sociopath'?"

"We tried, Bubba, we tried," Jim said. "So now that you're back, what's the first order of business, boss?"

"Tell me about Scoleri. The stuff I can't find out from a psych file."

Jim shruggd. For a big guy who had taken down some seriously dangerous killers in his time, having to wrestle them to the floor when they got hold of broken flourescent light tubes to use as weapons, or when someone did a body slam at his kneecaps, Jim always seemed to have an air of innocence about him. "Okay, what I know: He talks about how he used to work in carnivals. You know, the kind that go town to town. I've seen him do some stuff. Real carny tricks like he does this contortionist thing where it's like he can suck his own dick. Pardon my French. No, really. I mean, he can get in these weird positions, like his legs all the way over his head. He also told me and Bobby that he used to stick needles all the way through his body. Long needles. A real sideshow freak as a kid, apparently. He had his first girl when he was sixteen. When he talked about it, I thought he meant sex, but what he meant was something different. I mean, he had her. He cut off her big toe as his first souvenir. When he was a little kid, he grew up in group homes all over the place—mainly between here and Chino. He said they were all Jesus freaks and he claims he was battered into his whole God thing. He is Abraxas the Great or something. He reads comic books whenever he can. The basics: Superman, Spiderman, Batman. That and children's books. He's basically hooked on reading anything a ten-year-old might read. But he's sharp. He had one year at a work farm in Arizona because he'd committed some crime as a little kid that might've involved hurting another boy. I'm not sure. You gotta ask Conroy about that if you want. All I know's what he told me with his big fat mouth."

"He kill more than once?"

"I think so." Jim nodded. "Every time he talks about one of the people he killed, he acts like they're still alive. Still talking to him." Jim paused. Reached into his pocket and drew out a pack of

Wrigleys. Offered a stick to Trey, then unwrapped one for himself, popped it into his mouth, and began chewing. "You know something? On the outside, he was like Hatcher. He collected souvenirs. You know, the usual: jewelry, fingers, eyes. He liked having mementos. He looks like a kid sometimes. He's late twenties, but looks like he's eighteen. But this one started early. He's labile, so you have to watch yourself around him. But he hasn't caused much in the way of problems. Till this morning."

"The thing with Fallon?"

"Yep. In the showers. Scoleri was there. Whatever happened, Scoleri ended up jumping on Dave Fenstler and Bobby Bronson. Nearly got Bobby's eyes."

"Why was he on Fallon?"

"Rob says that Scoleri wants to do him, but Rob thinks everyone wants that. Scoleri claims he had a message for Conroy, and that's as far as I know. He's definitely agitated. Maybe it's the weather. You know how it goes sometimes. The barometric pressure goes all screwy and they start getting sinus headaches and then one of them gets all screwed up. Last night, Scoleri started carving on himself."

"With what?"

Jim held up his fingers, displaying fingernails. "We cut his nails down this morning. He wrote on his tummy 'Suffer the children to come unto me.' He spouts scriptural stuff a lot. He is the great god Abraxas." Jim laughed. "You'll like him. He reads minds and talks to dead people, too."

Trey got out of his chair and went to the door. "I guess it's time to go to God."

"Sure," Jim said. "Room 6 on Program 28. Hey, you'll love it down there. It's like an isolation tank. Times six. Hey, got another one. What's the oldest written story?"

"*The Epic of Gilgamesh*," Trey said. "Man, you'd think that my brain could remember complex mathematical equations, instead of this stuff. You lead the way."

The two men began walking down the green corridor, toward Program 28.

2

Two COs stood at the entrance to Program 28.

Big, muscular guys who looked like they were hyped up on testosterone. That was good. They needed some scary guys to keep the really scary ones in line.

"This is Ash Freeman, and this is the infamous Pete Atkins," Anderson said by way of introduction.

Trey shook their hands, and the one named Atkins couldn't seem to make eye contact to save his life. Trey never liked that in people who worked on his ward. Even a CO. It might spell trouble down the line. It was a psychological check point, and when a man couldn't look him in the eye, particularly during an intro, it might mean that man was hiding something or, at best, not all there.

It wasn't like Trey had never had problems with COs before. He had learned the primary rule of working with the forensics patients. There were three kinds of people who liked working with them:

the ones who had a talent for the work, the ones who had the background for it and needed the job and could handle it. Then, there were those who worked there who either actively hated the patients or liked to have positions of power of people they considered lesser.

Trey tried to engage Atkins in conversation briefly, but the CO exuded a bland disregard for him.

Years before Trey had had to separate a CO from a patient when the CO had nearly beaten the patient's brains out of him. It was a guy just like this one: young, smart, strong, and something was up. He'd not been all there. Half the battle at Darden State was just making sure that the staff was saner than the patients.

It was the problem with life outside these walls, too.

But inside, it could be deadly in a way that wasn't pleasant to contemplate.

Familiar patterns, back one day, he thought. *Put it aside. Deal with it later.*

For now, Scoleri.

3

Program 28 was entered via the standard reinforced double doors, but when Trey glanced through their porthole windows, he saw a different kind of hallway than the norm. This one looked as if it were for medical quarantine. It was completely metallic and gray instead of the usual light green of Ward

D. It gave him an eerie feeling. It wasn't made for warmth or human habitation. Whoever designed and then built this special hallway knew the effect it would have on the patients.

They would feel especially trapped and separated.

It was like a twenty-first-century science fiction dog pound, with minor adjustments for human beings. Shiny and metallic and very cold.

It was a nightmare.

Trey felt as if this were more dehumanizing than necessary, but when he thought about the kinds of crimes these particular forensics patients had committed, he knew that Darden State was at a loss. None of the other state hospitals wanted the six patients in Darden's Program 28. It was an experiment that the Executive Director was willing to try, mainly at the behest of Dr. Elise Conroy and a consortium of medical personnel from among the psychiatric community. They worked closely with the law enforcement agencies when the possible psychopath was out in the real world, to try to understand the inner workings of the kind of human being who had stepped into the territory of human monster.

And Trey, coming back, now would have Program 28 as his supervisory group. He would be spending the next several months working daily with each patient.

He both dreaded it and couldn't wait to find out more.

4

When he got through the doorway, with Anderson following him, they had to turn and lock the doors behind them. "Added security," Anderson said. "The sweet thing of it is, if we have a lockdown, we're fucked. See that?" He pointed to the ceiling, toward what looked like a series of small round lights, recessed into the ceiling itself. "Those are the strobes. But every third one is a camera. Every fourth one is for gas."

"Gas?"

"I told you it was unorthodox. If they have a breach here, those doors—" Anderson pointed back down to the doors they'd just locked—"can't be opened until the folks up there—" he pointed up to the small recessed orbs—"see that whoever is in here—and that means you and me, too—is down on the floor, either in sleepytime or overdose land."

"Jesus, it's like smoking bees."

Anderson arched an eyebrow. "Say what?"

"When you want to get the honey from a hive, you can use a bellows and get smoke on the bees. It makes them dormant. Like freezing them."

"I wish we'd just freeze these guys sometimes," Anderson said. "My love for humanity sort of goes south in here."

"Can't be true about gassing people. That sounds like Nazis."

"I don't know. It's what I heard," Anderson said, chuckling. "Maybe it's another Darden rumor, like

134

the little pill that simulates death to try to get the worst patients to stop killing. I like those myths. Frankly, I'd rather pass out without knowing whether some loon had chewed my nuts off."

They were several feet from the first room. The rooms were all on one side of the hall. "Patients don't look at each other here. They can hear each other sometimes, but it's basically isolation. Some outside stuff comes in. But it's very regulated, and three doctors have to sign off on it."

"That can be good or bad," Trey said. "They don't hear each other, they don't get in an excited state. But they spend too much time not interacting, they start to go *kaboom*."

Anderson grinned. "God, I'm glad you're back. Nobody knows about *kaboom* like you do. Here you go, first room."

Chapter Twenty

1

Each of the six rooms had the illusion of being open to the hall, but with a thick transparent wall. Behind this, more bars. The door into each was barred also. Each room held a large cot, a wash basin, a toilet in the corner, and a table with two chairs. Trey was about to ask about the chairs—they could be used as weapons—but noticed the floor where the chairs were bolted down. The walls were bare. The ceiling of each room seemed fairly high, and at the top, there was a rectangular window that no doubt also had thick Plexiglas in it, as well as bars. The window was close enough to the ceiling that it would've been extremely difficult for even the most agile athlete to leap to them.

"They never hurt themselves?" Trey asked. "The Plexiglas? I'd think that might be worse than a little padding."

"It's not quite Plexiglas. It's a reinforced glass

and plastic, bonded together. It's a bitch to keep clean. Especially when they scratch them up or put all kinds of crap all over them. But on the patients' side, it has some give to it. These guys never hurt themselves that way. They think they're little messiahs. They believe too much in themselves. Scoleri tried to kill himself, but using his fingernails. I don't know how he gets those suckers so sharp. We keep them as clipped down as possible, but he grows 'em fast."

"Is he on a suicide watch?"

"Scoleri? Naw. He just had a moment. He said he wanted to prove that he was God. Or something. You know the routine."

2

The man in the first room was naked, and his body was covered with what could only be feces. He had been wiping his own shit across the walls, writing out long sentences that were unreadable.

"He's the artist," Anderson said. "Calls himself Ivory. Fingerpaints like this all the time. He is probably the only one I feel bad for here, just because he's alive. If I were like that, I'd want someone to put a bullet in my head."

"What was he on the outside?"

"Murdered his wife, his five kids, the dog, the works. Then started taking out the paperboy and the old man next door to him. He said he'd gotten word that it was time."

"Time?"

"Time to kill. Apparently the secret of all human life is something that was revealed to him by voices. Sort of like Joan of Arc. And the secret must've involved a pretty sadistic death, too. I think it's on record that he didn't just shoot 'em. He played with them before they died. Look at him. He thinks he's doing the goddamn Sistine Chapel. Twice a day at least they have to hose this room down."

Trey was used to this, as was Jim Anderson. They had spent their adult lives working among society's most violent.

Yet, Trey felt an inward shiver. *A goose walking over my grave.*

They passed the next room and the next. Each held a patient whose crimes seemed worse than the one before. It was like walking into the mouth of nightmares.

"Jesus, it's still a zoo in here."

"And we're the zookeepers," Anderson said. He pointed to the fifth room, fifth patient, who lay on his cot facing the side wall. "That's Mandolar. He's in for beheadings. He's pretty depressed right now. Last night at one of his sessions, Brainard got him talking about his childhood and it turns out Willy's family had weekend incest parties involving Dad, Mom, Grandma, the whole bit. He's been a little under the weather all day. And now . . ." They approached the last room on Program 28. "Your new boyfriend."

3

"Anything I should know before I go into the tiger's cage?" Trey asked.

"Want more Scoleri trivia? Absolutely," Jim Anderson said, keeping his voice low. "Michael Scoleri is the worst. His crimes on the outside were beyond any of those. He cuts them up, gets off on it. Some men, too. Likes to collect souvenirs, you know that routine. Gets off on the memory of the kill. Went high profile when he killed that porn star, Fiona Raleigh. Her sugar daddy was pretty powerful in the governor's office, so when Scoleri finally got picked up, they really went to town. Nobody was happy he ended up here. They wanted the death penalty. They got us. As I mentioned, he likes to carve into his skin. Claims he feels no pain whatsoever. Gets off on the pain of others. On fear. He told Bobby once that fear is a magical drug you could inhale and get power from. He completely believes he's God and pisses off too many people to mention with his curses on them and his pronouncements of the end of the world. He'll be in here until the day he dies, I suspect."

4

Before entering the room, or "pod" as Trey would soon come to know these Program 28 rooms, he wanted to get a sense of the man within it.

Scoleri sat at the table, reading a book.

He looked too young to have committed the murders that had landed him here.

He looked too young to have raped, mutilated, and killed other human beings.

He looked like an innocent.

Once inside the pod, Trey felt differently.

The familiar sense he had around sociopaths returned: a feeling of human cold. Of being in the same room as a lion. Only with less compassion. It was almost an aura around them. Scoleri's was strong—the feeling of not being all there. Not quite being human. The sense, perhaps instinct, that some enormous gulf existed between the two of them.

A feeling of emptiness, of something being terribly wrong.

A preternatural sense.

"Campbell, William, 36, Caucasian, brown, brown, not quite as tall as you look," the youngish blond man said, not bothering to glance up from his book. Trey didn't know books were allowed here. He was never sure, in these experimental programs, where the rules twisted. The young man's voice was sonorous, and had an oddly hypnotic quality to it. He didn't seem like the killer Trey had just read about. "Poor family from Yucaipa, or maybe Barstow, or San Pascal, or Yucca Valley— that kind of place that feels like nowhere when you're growing up in it. Brought yourself up pretty much on your own. Maybe some group homes. Jesus Camp and Bible School and memorizing the book of Revelations like it was the Boy Scout Handbook. Lots of dreams of getting far away from your parents. Not your parents, though. Your foster parents. You were one of those unfortunate kids, at least you think that. I can smell it—that insecurity, that feeling that it might all be taken away. Sometimes you wonder who your parents were, your real parents. But you leave that door closed. Because you know one thing about them. You know your mother was put in a place kind of like the place you're in now. Only hers was for nice people who went crazy. Not like this place, where only bad people go crazy." His legs were crossed, and the book was spread open between his knees.

When the young man did glance up, sighing, he didn't look the way Trey expected. It was as if a man of twenty-three had dropped six years. He looked like a kid, not an adult. His face was peach, his jaw elfin, his youth startling. His eyes, pale blue, were the only distraction. They seemed to quiver, as if keeping his steely gaze on Trey's face were impossible. As if all the young man's nerves were in his eyes. Scoleri glanced down to the book again. "They call you Trey."

Trey Campbell shook his head. "Amazing. You're sharp, Michael."

"Thank you." Scoleri wore the tan fatigues and olive drab T-shirt of the ward. Scoleri grinned, the sweet shit-eating grin of a farm boy. He didn't look up at Trey's face again, but stared at Trey's midsection.

"Like I told you," Michael said. "I created the world, so I know every secret in it. I was there that

141

day, watching your foster father take the strap to your brother. And then, after he stopped moving, your father left him with you in your room for nearly a week and locked you in. Always in the dark. You had to be with your dead brother for seven days. And then, he touched you. Even after he was dead."

Trey took it all in: Scoleri. Reading material, intuition, rapid eye movement, creative delusions, family construct, two brothers, one dead?

"Something about your eyes," Michael said, in a hushed tone. "You see a lot, don't you?"

"What are you reading?"

"*Beautiful Joe*," Scoleri said, rubbing his hands over the book. Trey knew it. He'd read it as a kid. A dog book. The kind of book that got kids crying. His daughter had read that book when she was in third grade and wept for a week.

"You like that story?"

Scoleri nodded. "It's wonderful. They chop off a dog's ears and tail. Another dog gets shot at."

Trey nodded slightly. He was not going to try to set Scoleri off. Sociopaths could be like lions if you tapped the wrong emotional key. It depended on who was watching. Since Trey had never before interacted with Michael Scoleri, he didn't want to chance anything. "Dr. Brainard tells me you've been doing okay. You've been talking up a storm today I gather."

"No complaints. I really had nothing to say before. So, Trey," Michael grinned. Eyes still down, unwilling to look him in the eye again. "I heard you had a run-in with one of my better creations."

142

"Really?" Trey returned the grin, unsure of where this would go.

"Miss Hatcher from D Ward. Catalina Island."

Trey glanced at Jim Anderson, who stood at the doorway. Anderson, big as a house, filled up the doorway. Jim suppressed a laugh.

"Word gets around," Trey said.

"Well, rest assured that it was not my intention to have her hurt you or your lovely family. Sometimes even these creations get out of hand." Michael set the book aside, bringing his knees up to his chest. The scars from his attempted suicide were clearly visible—striations along his wrists, still healing. "I was sure you wouldn't return to my domain so soon."

Trey shrugged. "Well, you know how it is."

"Have to earn a living, yes," Michael said. "You're already taking classes toward your Master's."

Trey lost his good humor. Again, he glanced at Jim, who raised his eyebrows.

Trey squatted down beside Scoleri. He knew to keep his balance and push his face slightly forward. Sometimes they went for your eyes. It was the easiest way to debilitate you. He had spent years making sure both his eyes stayed in his head. He wanted Michael to feel comfortable talking with him. "So, you know all this because you're God, right?"

Michael threw back his head, laughing. He had a girlish laugh, high and sweet. He closed his eyes, opening them wide.

The pupils moved so rapidly back and forth they were a blur. It was almost too horrible to look at.

The eyes moved independently of each other, seeming to spin and spin until all Trey saw was a viscous darkness.

How the hell does he do that? Trey thought.

Then Michael Scoleri whispered, "I'm Abraxas. I'm God. But there's a very bad Devil out in the world right now. He's making his little angels fly to me to give me messages. But I don't answer the Devil's prayers. Let me tell you, Trey, you're going to want to have God step in soon to stop the Beast before the world ends. Which might be in just a few hours, at least as far as Dr. Conroy is concerned. Do you know something?"

"What's that?"

"I hate the rain."

"It won't be that bad. It's pretty light."

"I like snow. But not rain. Have you ever made snow angels?"

"Sure. When I was a kid."

"I wonder if kids still make them," Scoleri said. He glanced up to the barred window that touched the ceiling.

"Would you mind showing me what you wrote on yourself last night?" Trey asked.

Scoleri closed his eyes. Opened them. They were normal again. Not moving rapidly in their sockets. "No. I'm tired," he said. "I don't want to talk anymore."

5

Outside the room, locking the door behind him, Jim Anderson turned to Trey.

"So, I didn't know that about you and your family," Jim said, patting Trey on the back. "You had a brother who died?"

Trey said, "None of it was true. He wasn't talking about me."

6

Trey continued, "The physical stuff about my height and weight were pretty accurate. My family was pretty middle class, and my dad was a nut job, but other than that, it was an okay childhood. Not quite what he was saying. Most of the stuff he could learn from nurses or heck, even you. But the other stuff—I wasn't raised in a foster family, I never was beaten, and I never had a brother get killed. But he has."

"What?"

"He was telling me his life story. That's how he does it. He makes himself 'you' and he tells his whole history," Trey said. His throat was dry. "I wouldn't mind that Wrigley's now."

"Spearmint pleasure coming right up," Anderson said, bringing out the pack of gum.

"Sometimes I just want to round up all these families and put them out of their misery. Or save them. But I don't know if they can be saved. I just don't know."

"Everybody can be saved."

"You think that?"

"I don't know. Maybe it's nuts," Jim said, "but I still have faith that things can work out. Even after everything I've seen here. No matter what." Then, he brightened. "Man, he had me going. I was beginning to feel sorry for you."

"Well, he's good at it," Trey said, unwrapping the stick of gum and popping it into his mouth. "So, he's mine now."

"Him and three others."

"What's with the book? I thought this was major psych isolation."

"Part of the program. They get some media, newspapers, books, a little radio, TV now and then. We even have Movie Fridays and Sunday Night Old Time Radio shows."

"Meds?"

"Heavy."

"Sedation?"

Jim shrugged. "Pretty constant. It's Brainard. He's the zombie doc. Conroy's more anti-med and pro one-on-one sessions. I think she wants to cut back on his meds so he can be more . . . lucid. Maybe."

"He seemed pretty lucid. Sometimes I wish we had fewer meds and more techs." As he walked ahead of Jim, glancing at the charts outside the shut doors, noticing Dr. Brainard's marks in red felt tip across all the graphs, he added, "And fewer zombie docs. What the hell does Brainard get out of all this?"

"I heard he's writing a book."

"Jesus, you and I should write a book. We'd have the real shit," Trey said.

"Yeah, mainly about how insane the psychologists are."

"Brainard is . . . a piece of work." Trey tapped his

fist against the wall lightly. "Somebody ought to load him up with his own meds. Why is it some of the craziest people we know are psychiatrists?"

Jim laughed, catching up to him. "We've got Paulsen on the desk till four on D, and then Somers takes over."

As they walked toward Trey's office, Trey asked, "What was that thing about making little angels?"

"One of his fantasies," Jim said. "He keeps telling me how the Devil started sending him little angels two nights ago to tell him about the end of the world."

7

A half hour later in his office, Trey picked up the phone. "Campbell, D Ward."

"It's me," Elise Conroy said.

Chapter Twenty-one

Trey went back down to the end of Ward D, past the security doors, to her office.

"Elise?" Trey said when he stepped through the doorway.

She sat behind her desk. Her hair disheveled. Her eyes were bloodshot. She looked like hell, a sharp contrast to her norm of looking beautiful and pulled together.

"All right. I'm really all right."

"I don't understand. . . ." Trey said. "What's going on? Elise?"

"I couldn't say it on the phone. I couldn't. Trey. Just a few hours ago, just . . ." Nervously, she reached into a pack of cigarettes, then stopped herself and set the pack down. Before she spoke again, her eyes filled with tears, and she pressed the palms of her hands against her face as if she could blot them out. Her voice sounded like a little girl's, not the sharp tone of Ward D's primary psychiatrist. "My baby. Got taken. My Lucas."

The Day

Chapter Twenty-two

1

Trey went around Elise Conroy's desk and wrapped his arms around her.

She leaned against him, her face pressed into his neck, and whatever she'd held tight within herself, she let go of it.

He held her for as long as she would let him, and felt as if she needed whatever warmth he could offer.

2

Then Trey said, "Do you want to talk? Do you need me to drive you home?"

She dried her tears, reaching for tissue after tissue. Her face, normally so lovely, had crumpled in on itself, a mass of lines and a kind of sorrow he'd only rarely witnessed. A private sorrow most people never showed the world.

"No. What's the use of going home? What's the use? Trey, I was working with the police to help catch him. And he has my baby. My Lucas. He's so helpless, Trey. He's so little. I can't let anything happen to him. I just can't."

The rain outside battered at the office window.

God, Trey closed his eyes. *God, please let this turn out good. Please let him be found. Safe. Alive.*

Chapter Twenty-two

Chapter
Twenty-three

1

The San Pascal County Coroner's Office employed two pathologists, four part-time supervisors at the morgue, as well as several part-time and full-time employees, from clean-up to bagging to cutting.

San Pascal County Morgue is in the basement of the old Baseline building off Vineyard and Pepper Streets. Originally a small teaching hospital from the 1930s until the 1970s, it had become primarily a research and development facility for the county and for the tri-county alliance interests, and the main housing for the coroner's office. It was the subject of controversy, the Baseline building, because it was old, had ventilation problems, and was due for a major renovation. But the county had not yet allocated funds for its improvements.

It was part of a complex of buildings, including

the sheriff's department and other local law enforcement agencies, at the edge of the Annex, an industrial park beyond the suburban sprawl off the freeway. Once the entire area had been vineyards and orange groves.

Jane Laymon had grown up wishing she could go into the morgue with the county coroner, hoping to do forensics research (thus, her bachelor's degree in both criminal justice and forensics). But after spending two years primarily on child deaths in the county, she was weary of the trip to the morgue and the unnatural camaraderie of those who worked there.

Seeing dead children, whether from natural or unnatural causes, always made her hate the world a little more each time.

2

Once inside the facility, you took the stairs rather than the service elevator, unless you were bringing in a body. An increased case load in the area, plus spillover from the Riverside County morgues, had made Baseline (as the place was known by those working in it) overcrowded. The elevators were for the dead. The stairs, the living. Even the refrigeration units, where the corpses were stored during examination and autopsy, was inadequate, and the corridor at the bottom of the stairs was often used as cold storage. Central air-conditioning as well as swamp coolers chill the halls below the building. Decomposition was the norm for those bodies that the coroner and his deputies couldn't get to immediately. The remains were covered or sealed in body bags on gurneys. The detectives and trainees joked about the place as Valhalla, the hall of the fallen.

Jane Laymon thought it was the entrance to a slightly chilled version of Hell.

Whenever she went into Valhalla, Jane took a palm-sized face mask, slipping it over her nose and mouth. Additionally, she breathed primarily through her mouth when she pushed through the thick door from the stairs into the corridor. She generally slipped on a pair of latex gloves, as an extra precaution, annoyed by the talcum powder that ended up on her hands and wrists.

The stench was definitely something she had not gotten used to, despite visiting the morgue often.

There were four large rooms, all the size of school cafeterias, subdivided into smaller spaces by drywall, freestanding dividers, or the refrigerators in the basement morgue. Two of the four rooms were used for embalming and other services of the county related to the dead. The county embalmed some of the bodies, subcontracting out to local mortuaries for the work, depending on its need for revenue. The two remaining rooms were the refrigeration units and the small rooms within them, known simply as the cutting rooms. The coroner's and the two deputy coroners' offices were off these rooms. The offices were glassed-in. There was inadequate floor drainage, so that Jane had more than once needed to wipe her shoes before leaving

the cutting room. There were emergency decon-
tamination showers—three units, two in the
women's room at the end of the hall and one in the
men's. Jane showered only once here—the first
time she'd had to view an autopsy performed on
the body of a six-year-old boy.

She had felt, during that autopsy and what it revealed, a revulsion for the human race, and looking
at him had reminded her of her little brother when
they'd been kids, and she'd had to turn the hot water up on the shower, nearly scalding her skin, to
just wash away the memory.

3

Jane Laymon walked in as if she owned the place,
and, turning to the Chief Deputy Coroner, a middle-
aged man who seemed more of a shopkeeper to
her than a medical expert, said, "I need to see all
three of them."

She had gotten used to the mutilation done to
the corpses. She barely took a breath when she saw
all three laid out. Something in her turned off, like
a switch she could manually toggle so that she
didn't think about the method of the killer.

Three bodies lay on three metal tables. They
were so small they made the tables seem large. The
usual equipment—saws, bonecutters, scissors—lay
on the table in their individual holders.

The children seemed haunting. She had already
seen two of them. It was not easy to look at the face
of a dead child.

Particularly not after what the killer had done to two of them—their faces, their arms.

The bites.

Jane had some small comfort in knowing that the killer did not mutilate them until after he had taken their lives.

But it didn't matter.

You violated them, even if you think you didn't. You could not leave them alone. You have to come after them, even in death.

You hurt them only after they're dead. Why? What does that do for you?

Chapter Twenty-four

1

At the morgue, Jane Laymon looked over the victims on the metal tables. It was a double check she did, in case her first impressions had been off. She'd spent an hour going over the details of evidence, mainly standing in the background while Sykes, Tryon, and Fasteau asked the questions of the pathologist. She was a keen listener and used a rather unorthodox approach that she felt might help add a fresh perspective her colleagues might've missed.

2

She felt as if she were alone with each victim as she looked over the body. She tried to clear her mind. Empty her thoughts, hoping she'd approach the dead now as a blank slate.

Tryon had taught her this technique. It slowed down the process, he'd said. It opened your mind to possibilities other than the ones first presented.

Sometimes it was worse for her.

Sometimes she felt as if she were going inside the mind of the killer when she looked at his handiwork.

3

The light was bright in the room. It was chilly—the refrigeration units were behind her. She worked to keep her mind clear. Hoping. Waiting. Wanting something to come to her. She felt a strange desperation there. She wanted to make her mark with this case. It would have the profile. It would be important.

But she was fairly sure that despite Tryon's backing of her in the investigation, it would go to a team comprised mainly of veterans. If they didn't come up with something solid within a day, after two days of nothing, the FBI would be on it and its manhunt would be so profoundly superior that the local cops would look bad.

The pathologist, the coroner, and Tryon and Fasteau were at the third corpse, talking quietly over the body. Tryon had a hand-held voice recorder and repeated what the pathologist said into it.

4

The first child, a boy, had no name yet. The missing child hadn't been reported, and they had not yet found an identifier for him. He was simply Victim 1.

The second victim, a boy named Steven Latimer, had been reported missing too late. The body had turned up in the orange groves at the same time that his mother and father had discovered that he'd never made it to his Cub Scout overnight camp out. He had never even made it to the rented van that would take him there.

And finally, the third victim.

They had a name for her: Gina Parsons.

From San Pascal, like the Latimer boy.

Found in the Santa Ana River near the town of Bannock.

Hanging from a group of trees in the middle of the river.

The coat hanger around her neck with the wings, like a noose.

5

Preliminary matters were discussed, but none of them seemed interesting to her until the coroner mentioned the soap.

"Camay," Tryon said.

"Little bits of pink soap. Under her fingernails," he said, indicating the dead girl. "Because the river hadn't washed it away completely, it may be that she was only in the water for an hour. At the most."

We just missed you, Jane thought. *You sack of shit. But someone could've seen you. It would've been daylight. You washed her hands. You wanted*

her clean. But not for us. For you. You wanted her
pure. You killed her, and you wanted her scrubbed
clean. "What else?"

"The bites."

She looked more closely at the victim's arm. "But
after death." She said this as much to confirm as to
alleviate the tickle of dread she'd felt since viewing
the body.

"Correct. It would appear that all mutilation oc-
curs after the child is dead. He kills them. A little
morphine to help them to sleep. Then he drowns
them. That's the first two. It's probably the same
with this one."

"Morphine?" Jane hadn't heard this before.

"We found traces in Victim 1's bloodstream. And
2."

"Jesus. He has access to a hospital?"

"Nurse, doctor, orderly. Maybe," Tryon said.
Tryon had been hanging back, letting her look at
the bodies. "We're running checks all over the
place. He's going to trip up somewhere here."

"Or she," Jane said.

But instinctively she knew this was wrong. The
killer was male. The murders had all the signs of a
man killing. Only the morphine seemed feminine.
Putting them to sleep. *A gentle death.* The thought
of it disturbed her more. If the murderer had just
been a vicious killer, it was one thing. But he gave
them morphine to sleep. He didn't want them con-
scious for the pain of death. He wanted them to go
to sleep like . . . "Maybe he works for the pound.
Maybe . . ."

"Sure." Tryon nodded his approval.

She noticed an imperceptible smirk on Fasteau's face.

She shot him an acid glance. "He's putting them down like kittens. He doesn't want them to know what's going to happen. Or hurt."

This is a test, Jane thought. *He wants to see how far I can go with this.* "If he only kills after they're asleep . . . well, he doesn't enjoy their pain," she said, thinking aloud. "Our guy doesn't torture. But something happens after that."

Fasteau shot her a glance. "Sure. He mutilates them." Then, more to Tryon than to her, "We'll get him from the bite marks. This guy has priors. I know it."

"No," Jane said. "He's stopping himself. He's re-sisting. Something is forcing him to attack them. Maybe. I don't know. Maybe he . . . well, it's prob-ably whatever's inside him. Forensics get a good look at this?"

Fasteau nodded. "The odontologist took the im-pression. The bruises blurred it. This guy chews 'em up and spits 'em out."

Gallows humor, particularly around the child murder cases, pissed her off. She ignored him, as she often did. As hard as it was, she kept her focus on the dead child who lay before her. "No semen, right?"

"None. Everything intact below the waist."

"He doesn't want them sexually. That's one for the books. I was sure this was a sexual predator." Then it occurred to her. *You care for them. You want*

162

them clean. You use Camay. They don't arouse you. You don't kidnap them because you have to. You kidnap them because . . . But the thoughts led her nowhere. She hated where her mind wandered at times like this. She needed to focus on evidence and what it told. Not go off on her own mental gymnastics. It was one of her problems in life: In breaking down a problem, she sometimes found that she overcomplicated things. As Tryon had told her more times than not: *Let the evidence tell its story.* "Maybe the bite marks will lead to someone with a prior. But I doubt it." She brought the twisting lamp down near the face of the little girl found that morning.

It looked as if a scavenger had mauled the face.

A whiff of necrotic tissue entered her mouth—even though she was used to the twin smells of death and steryl alcohol in the room, now and then it made her feel seasick.

She turned her back on the metal table, the small body, and the men.

Hold it together.

She managed to get out, "We'll check dental records in San Pascal County," before she felt as if she was going to be sick.

Count to three.

One, two, three. Let it pass. They're dead. She's dead. Their pain is gone. They went to sleep, like a patient on an operating table. They didn't know. They didn't feel it.

She could tell herself all this and believe it, but the one thing that she knew was a lie:

They were not afraid.

Of couse they were. You keep them for nearly a day. You take them and then you keep them somewhere. Where? Do they know you? Are you a friend of the family? What is your connection to them? And why do you want them for such a short period of time? What's erupting in you after ten or fifteen hours with them? You don't rape them. You don't torture them. What do you get from them that you need? What is it you want? What is compelling you for three days in a row to expose yourself to suspicion and discovery and arrest and even death, to go to their front yards or to their neighborhoods and get them to go with you.

Why now? Why these days?

Is it Christmas? Did you do this before? If you did, we'd know. You're still young. Not too young. But you're not thirty yet. I can tell. You're frustrated. You look at these kids. They have something you want. You can only get it by taking them. And then, you have to kill them. Without hurting them in any way that we can tell.

And, once they're dead, you have to attack them. Once they're beyond life.

You make them angels.

Do you think you're protecting them? Is there something that you're stopping by killing them?

She took a deep breath, feeling it come over her again. The sense she had in those few murder cases she'd worked on. The sense that she understood the killer in some small way. "He's new to this. Something happened to him and he snapped. Some pressure built up, and our guy is going on pure instinct. He's trying to control it. He's trying to hold back. You use a knife if you want to obliterate someone's face. You don't use your teeth. You don't bite them all over after they're dead unless you get sadistic, sexual pleasure from it. But not our guy. He doesn't want to hurt them. He doesn't want them in pain. My guess is, either there are two killers, or . . ."

Fasteau ignored her. He went to one of the other tables.

The coroner kept his gaze on her. "Jane?"

"Or," she continued, "one guy with two distinct personalities in his head. Both of them killers. One is just insane. The other is a sadistic monster." She glanced up from the body.

Thoughts came to her, but she didn't say them aloud.

You're a frustrated artist. Maybe. No. These are definitely angels. These are messages. Are you God? Do you believe in God? Are you doing this because Christmas is coming? Is that it? These are Christmas angels? Angels. Blood angels. Red angels. Bird wings. Flight. Found in or near rivers or streams. Cold streams. Water. Liquid. God. Angel. Devil. Fallen angel. You're religious. You have these conflicting thoughts. You want us to see them as angels. You want us to know that you are making angels. You're showing us—or someone—angels. Angels are a message. To us? To find you? You could bury these children somewhere. But you're putting them out for us each day. It's your game. Are you afraid? Do you not want to do this? Do you want us to find

165

you? You want us to find you because part of you wants to stop this. You believe in God. Or you mock God. But you have this in you, this terrible thing.

You can't control it, and it's coming too fast.

Something is taking you over.

Then the one that made her feel cold.

Possessing you.

Something else is living inside you. You have a conflict. You kill these children. You cut off the wings of the birds. Water fowl. Big wings. Angel wings. But you don't want to. You want to stop. But there's something inside you that keeps going. Maybe at night. Maybe at dawn, you put the bodies out for us. But at night, something else comes through. Something you can't control.

It annoyed her when her mind started spinning on its own like this. She knew the people who perpetrated this kind of crime were evil. She had no other word for them. They were not misunderstood. They were not passive victims of a larger world. There was genuine evil among humankind. She had seen it firsthand.

But something in her brain always tried to understand the killer.

To catch the perpetrator, you had to get inside his head.

She stood over the metal table and glanced at the others around it.

For just a second, she imagined the moment when the killer strung the two torn bird wings together with the wire coat hanger.

"Those are duck wings? Geese?" she asked.

The pathologist glanced at the evidence in the plastic bag that lay beside the victim's body. "Sure. A duck."

"So we're looking at parks. Bodies of water. Someone living nearby. Someone who sees these birds a lot and can get them easily."

"You're good," the coroner said out of the blue, looking up from his work at the second metal table. "Water's in the lungs of Number 1 and 2. He drowned them. Strangely, there was a little burn in the throat."

"Burn?" Tryon asked.

"Not much. Like soup. Like they'd been given soup, but it was the water. I think hot water was used. No real scalding on the face, but the water was hot that they drowned in."

"He puts them to sleep, then drowns them," Tryon said, mostly to himself.

Jane appreciated Tryon, even when she didn't always like the assignments he passed to her. The entire team was somber. It was the difference between finding adult victims and child victims. In cases of adult murder, there was seriousness, but also the nervous laughter and chit-chat—a way of removing oneself from the gruesomeness of the metal table. But in the case of a child death, generally there was an aura of enormous tragedy. It was the human part of all of them, and Jane felt that those gathered around these corpses paid them respect, even in the examination of the minutiae of their deaths.

"He doesn't want them to suffer," she said, nearly a whisper.

"Jane?" Sykes asked, looking up from a small plastic evidence bag.

"He likes them," she said, speaking up. "He doesn't sexually touch them. He doesn't cut them. Doesn't shoot them. Doesn't seem to have tortured them in any way. He puts them to sleep. Then washes them in hot water. Maybe the drowning is accidental, but I doubt it. He washes them to get them clean. Maybe. He's religious. I can feel it. He has a religious mania. That's why he makes them look like angels. He's sending them to heaven. Pure. Washed. He's showing us that he's doing that. Or showing someone. Maybe God. I think he's going to crack and show himself to us soon. Tell me about the families. Do we know them yet?"

Chapter Twenty-five

1

After putting the little bird in its cage, it felt the rumbling of the Other One coming out of itself. It ran up the path to the hill. The path was all muddy, and its shoes got suctioned, but it kept running until it got to the house above the Mad Place.

It nearly broke down the door because the Other One was getting loose, and the only way to control the Other One was energy release. It heard all the angels singing, but it covered its ears.

It first checked in on its mother, who was sleeping. The visiting nurse had come and gone, but had left a new set of pills on the dresser and replenished the morphine in the drip.

It then went into its bedroom, and there was Monica, laying facedown on the bed, wrapped up in the quilt, but her skin pale and naked beneath it.

It took off its clothes, dropping its shirt and trousers as it stepped forward into the room, shutting the door behind it.

It couldn't control what the Other One wanted.

The Other One was lusting.

The lust was evil.

But it could turn the valve. Let the lust out. Let the sin out.

Let the perversion out.

Monica was a whore.

Monica was a sinner.

Whore of Babylon.

It went and lay down on the bed, and pressed its thing between her thighs. She groaned, waking up from deep sleep. She had been asleep for less than six hours, and she didn't like this.

But it didn't care.

The Other One was out.

The Devil.

2

"What the hell are you doing, Duane? Not now."

"Now."

"No. Get off me."

"Now."

"I said—"

"Bitch."

"You—don't you touch me."

"Whore."

"You son of a bitch."

"Shut up. She'll hear you."

"Like I care—"

Three slaps.

"Now."

"You asshole. Don't you hit me ever again. I am carrying your baby. Your baby. Don't you ever hit me. Again."

"Now."

3

The Devil pressed itself into her. She fought it, but the Devil wouldn't let her go, and the friction she created when she lashed against it only made the Devil stronger, as it bucked and moaned and growled against her ear, as it took her there.

A white-hot feeling of moisture and anger all in that one spot, where it had her between her thighs.

WHORE!

SHE WILL GIVE BIRTH TO THE BEAST! SHE WILL BRING ABOUT THE END OF THE WORLD WITH THE BIRTH OF THE ANTICHRIST!

It felt the hammers in its head and the sound of its father's voice shouting from the stone angel in the Mad Place. Shouting about THE DEVIL LIVES IN YOUR HEART AND YOU MUST SCOURGE THE BEAST FROM YOU! YOU MUST RAVAGE THE FLESH AND SAVAGE THE CREATURE THAT COMMANDS YOU TO EVIL!

It wanted her. Wanted her stinky body. Her putrid flesh. It wanted her sex. Her every fold. Her innards. Her privates. Her devil passage.

Wanted to bite and tear her. To put his face into her womb and find where the baby was growing. It wanted to rip it out of her and hold it in its teeth while her blood ran down its face.

It pressed its devil member into her.

Ah, it thought. *Ah.*

And then something within it exploded.

Like a bomb in its head.

And the release came.

Too soon.

But the release made the cage door close again.

It fell against her, and she swore at it. She shoved back, and it rolled off her. Her curses float into the air, unheard. She took up the quilt, drew it to one side, wrapped herself in it, covering her face with pillows.

Inside her, its son.

The Beast.

It lay there, staring at the ceiling.

Bringing the end of the world into flesh.

Just like its daddy said it would.

Then it closed its eyes and journeyed into the wet tissues of Hell.

Chapter Twenty-six

1

Dr. Elise Conroy's office. Daylight shattered by rain, beyond the window.

Trey Campbell, across from her.

Silence.

Silence broken.

"I've consulted with these investigative teams before," she said. "On each case where I was called in to help profile the killer, they never caught the guys until after too many bodies had piled up. I've had seven years here, and during that time two previous consults. In one case they never caught the killer at all. They're not going to catch him in time. Not to save my son. He kills after sundown. Before morning. So far. That's the best they've figured out." Her voice, cold and distant, as if she were trying to move away from the problem in her mind.

Trey knew one thing about the psychiatrists at Darden State that was a key to their personalities.

It probably was why they had studied psychiatry in the first place: They knew, within themselves, how the human mind had too many doors inside it. That some locked. Some opened. Some never opened. Some were wedged open and should be closed.

As he watched her, he wondered what door she was closing inside herself. If she was trying to keep the one closed that had hope in it. Or if she was trying desperately to open that door herself. By herself. Within herself.

But he was fairly sure she had closed a door. She looked as if she'd locked it and thrown away the key.

Her face, smooth, set.

She was a woman who had made up her mind, had locked a door, had opened another.

It worried him.

It even scared him a little.

2

She drew a cigarette out from the pack on her desk. She shot him a look that he translated as: *Don't tell me it's illegal to smoke on premises. I break this rule all the time. Screw the rules.*

Trey reached across Dr. Elise Conroy's desk to steady her hand as she finally lit her cigarette.

Elise Conroy took a drag off her cigarette. "They've already had police on this. The FBI is stepping in. I know they won't find him. At least not in time. They threw me off—told me to go home and get some rest. Goddamn it. My damn babysitter didn't even know it happened." She brought her hand over her eyes to hide the tears. She let out a string of curses as she pressed the palms of her hands against her eyes.

"Could he just be missing?"

At first she didn't respond. Then she looked up at him as if seeing him for the first time. "You know Scoleri."

Trey nodded.

"Fallon came to me this morning. He said it was urgent. He said that Scoleri had told him that something terrible would happen to me today. I asked him what. All he would tell me was that Scoleri had told him something terrible and that it had to do with Lucas. That Scoleri even knew my son's name was something. He may have seen his picture, but he wouldn't know his name. Maybe he overheard it. I don't know. I don't care. I went to see Scoleri because I thought someone here must have mentioned it to him. Dr. Brainard, perhaps. Someone who had heard when I heard. Scoleri told me, point-blank, something that I can't get out of my head."

"He knows the killer?"

"No. He told me that I should've just taken Lucas to the beach this morning."

"Why?"

"Trey," she said, her voice hard, as if she had come to the most difficult decision of her life, "because that is what I was supposed to do. I was supposed to take Lucas to the beach today. I came here to pick up some papers. Between the time I left

home and the thirty minutes I was here, Lucas . . ."
She paused. "I wanted to take a few days off at the
start of Lucas's Christmas break. We hadn't spent
enough time together. This damn job. Other things.
I could consult on the Red Angel case just a few
hours a day, then be home for the rest. And Scoleri
knew. He told me that he gets messages from the
man who took my son. And then he told me that
the beach would have been awful today, anyway,
what with the rain."

"Okay," Trey said, his mind crackling with ideas
that came at him too quickly. "Scoleri has some
contact. We don't know who. Let's find out."

3

Elise ordered sandwiches from the canteen to be
delivered to her office. She spread out the files that
she had on Scoleri. "I give you full access."

He glanced up at her. "You sure you want me to
see this?"

"The rules of this place are not going to save my
son," she said.

Chapter Twenty-seven

1

In Tryon's office, in Riverside, Detective Jane Laymon picked up a styrofoam cup and poured coffee into it from the small Mr. Coffee machine on the corner table. Then, turning to Tryon, who sat at his desk, she said, "So when does CASMIRC get to work on this?"

CASMIRC was the Child Abduction and Serial Murder Investigative Resources Center that the FBI used in cases like this one.

"They already have. I heard from Tommy over at the Bureau yesterday. They've been running priors, trying to see if this is in line with some kidnappings from three years ago down in San Diego."

"But it's not," she said. "You need to get better coffee."

He ignored the comment. "You're not going lead on this one, Jane. I'm sorry to say."

"I suspected as much. Who is it?"

"Jenkins. And then Sykes, over in your area."

"Well," she said, tilting her head slightly to the side. "They're the best."

"They're mainly going to be working with Tommy and Bill Murphy on most of the forensics."

"So what's my connection?"

"You'll work on your side of the line."

"Sure. But why call me in at all?"

"I think you're good. You've got the goods. You have intuition on your side. A knack for this. That's talent. And I need talent on a case like this. We're fucked here. We have a nut killing a kid daily, leaving them out in the open, and we don't have a thing yet." He paused, did a back and forth of his head like he was weighing options. "Plus, you know the terrain. Every kid was taken from your backyard, not ours."

"But they get dumped in your sandbox. And San Bernardino's. And mine."

"Yeah," Tryon said. "It just screws with us when that happens."

"We'll get him."

"You should come to work for me."

"I thought I was. At least in this limited capacity." She urgently wanted to change the subject. "Look, we have a report of one kid missing already. So far. My guess is that our guy is going one after another. Grabbing the kids and offing them pretty fast."

"A sexual predator."

"Not quite. Nothing evidentiary to suggest sexual contact. This is a psychotic who just snapped."

"Just?"

"I think so. Fasteau thinks otherwise. He thinks there'll be priors. I don't think so. Or if there are, it'll be juvy stuff. Maybe. Takes ten years or more to work up to this psychosis. Competely disordered mind. Has a focus, but has cracked. Something was always wrong, but it just got worse." She glanced over at him. Tryon watched her with fascination. "Hey, I was a double major: criminal justice and forensics psychology."

"I hope we don't lose you to the Bureau someday."

"I like being a cop," she said. "My dad was a cop. My mom worked dispatch in San Bernardino for twenty-six years. I like this life."

"So what else? What do you figure?"

"Haven't gone over everything. I got the nudge from Morrison at the morgue and couldn't hang out long enough to ask the questions I really wanted answered. But I'm not sure they could even answer them yet. Our guy is not cunning. He's got dumb luck. He's got some way of accessing the houses near the country club in San Pascal—that's where the girl's family lived. Right behind the links. Maybe he's a golfer. But I doubt it. He's blue collar. He aspires, maybe. Maybe not."

"White? Black?"

"White. Maybe twenty-seven. Twenty-eight. I'm guessing, but I don't think CASMIRC's going to come up with priors. I think it's his first week on the job of murder. He's learning as he goes. The first victim had two broken fingers. No marks on his

179

body at all. Suffocated. Second, he had two broken fingers. He bit his cheek and his lip. By the third, the bites were all over the victim's body. Whatever is inside this guy is coming out now. Maybe he had episodes as a kid. But I'm guessing he's spent ten years trying to keep this down. Trying to live right. But he can't help himself. It's a compulsion."

"Why right now?"

"Something in his life is messing up, big time. He's under some pressure, but I don't know what type. Maybe he's just lost his job. Or is about to. Or his wife left him. Or let's see, maybe he's had some emotional trauma re-enacted. The death of his own kid? I'm guessing. But something set him off, and he's going off fast."

"Tell me about the one today."

"Happened a couple hours ago. Scrub Jay Drive, nice hill-top community. Pool in the backyard. Volvo in the driveway. Professional mom, off to work for a couple of hours, planned on taking the kid off for his birthday. She had a sitter at the house, but the sitter was out back by the pool reading, and the kid was in the front yard."

"No witnesses?"

"None that we've found. Nobody was looking out their front window during the minute or two it took to get the boy out of there."

"Checked neighbors?"

"Ongoing, but this is our guy. I know it. Something goes on where he's invisible in the neighborhoods."

"Delivery guy?"

"That's my guess. Or the gas guy. Or mailman. A gardener. Someone ordinarily in these neighborhoods. Someone nobody notices. Someone who goes into their lives every day. Maybe even into their houses. They let him in for all I know. Even the kid knew him. He must've just done whatever our guy said. No signs of struggle. Nothing but toy soldiers and a plastic pail in the front yard. The kid was playing, waiting for Mom. Just like the others did. He gets them in the early morning, or right after school, but he gets them within a hundred feet of their front door."

"The Invisible Man," Tryon said. "Christ."

"We're checking everybody who drives those streets on a daily basis," she said, and glanced at her watch. "I better hit the road. I want to go take a statement from the mother before all hell breaks loose." She looked out the window behind Tryon's bald head. "I wish this rain would let up. I wish I were up there." She pointed to the snow-capped San Bernardino mountain range. "Maybe Big Bear. I could be skiing. That's a nice thought for a day like this. We get the crappy rain; they get beautiful snow."

"You'd freeze your ass off. I like a little rain," Tryon said. "So what's the bug up your ass?"

She laughed. He was normally so dignified in his speech. "What do you think?"

"Johnny Fasteau."

"He's the flea on my dog."

"He's all I got for you."

181

"I could work with Sykes more. Or you."

"I want that to happen. I really do. But right now, this is too big a thing for me to break up the current team. And you know what? Part of me feels like he teaches you something."

"I already finished school."

"What's the worst thing about working with him?"

"He stares at my boobs. Too much."

"File a complaint. We have a department for that."

"You know I can't do that. You know if I do that, I'll be shunned by the rest of the old boys. A little silent treatment."

"You might be surprised. You believe in taking his guff? That's all it is, just guff. Look, Jane, he's not my favorite either. But you two will work out whatever you need to, and then you'll move ahead and you'll see that guys like Fasteau pretty much stay where they are."

"If I believed in that fairy tale, I'd already be married to Prince Charming."

When Tryon's phone rang, she kept her back to him to afford him some small measure of privacy.

Tryon turned to her, still on the phone. "They found another one. In Little Orange. Look, Jane, we've got to get the Bureau in here fast. This guy's crapping all over the place. I have a goddamn press conference to give with the sheriff in two hours. I don't know why we have to play with the damn media like this."

"You always look great on camera," she told him.

RED ANGEL

2

They didn't call it the Bullpen, as she thought they
would when she first began learning the inner workings of the homicide investigative unit. They called
it, more simply, the Map Room, because of a large
map on an erasable board that covered one entire
wall of the conference room. The table was littered
with coffee cups and memo pads that had been left
behind from the earlier meeting.

Jane went to the board, took up a marker.

San Pascal County. San Bernardino. Riverside.

Where the counties met, she circled in red
marker.

They had sticky notes up where each of the victims had been found and a blue check mark where
each of the children had been taken.

Knowing that she'd have to erase it when she was
done, Jane began connecting the lines—from Caldwell to Bannock to Little Orange to San Pascal.

This is your territory.

This is your hunting ground.

You're coming from somewhere here.

She circled a spot where the foothills met the
valley.

You're like a mountain lion, coming in.

Then she said it aloud: "The mountains."

She glanced up at the towns in the mountains,
from the majestic Lake Arrowhead to Big Bear, Blue
Jay, Moon Lake, Windsock, and Slipping Springs.

"You think?" a voice behind her said.

She turned around. Fasteau. "My doppelganger," she said.

He stood in the doorway, bottle of water in his hand. Slurped some of it down. "You planning on snowboarding?"

"Maybe," she said. It annoyed the hell out of her that she was saddled with Fasteau, but she had to make the best of it. *One day, you'll be free of him.* "Just an idea. The victims are from the foothills." She pointed to the places on the map where they'd been taken. "The country club area, the hill-top houses, and over here, a little lower, but still near the foothills. Then, look, this is where they end up."

"Sure," Fasteau said. "Sykes already got on that. They end up in the valley."

"Flatlands," she corrected him. "The rivers and streams that feed into where they were found, all follow a pattern from the foothills. See? These are the washes that flood this time of year and feed into the river." She tapped out areas on the map. "Where he dumps them is the farthest he's willing to go after he takes them. He must time it. He keeps the kids for a day or less. Kills them. Then, I'm guessing, he only wants to go an hour or two from home. His home is . . ." Here she took the marker and made a dotted line radius that went up to the mountain range, and down past the 10 freeway, into Rubidoux and Moreno Valley, getting into the tip of the desert out at Banning but not quite to Palm Springs."

"So?"

"He's linear."

Fasteau gestured with the bottle. "Sure."

She could tell he didn't quite get what she was saying. He had that cowboy look in his eyes again, like everything was all about riding horses and roping dogies and riding off into the sunset on the way to a strip joint.

"Well, look. If this is point Z." She tapped Bannock, where they'd found Gina Parsons that morning. "And this is point, let's say, F." She tapped the foothills. "Then point A, his origin, is somewhere here." She made five points along the map in four different regions of the three counties.

The valley. The flatlands. The mountains. The desert.

"He's not down here in the flatlands," she said. "And since he has to kill these ducks, he has to find them someplace. Now, he might raise them. But that sort of eliminates the desert, since it would be hard to raise or catch ducks out there. And that leaves the valley, the foothills, and the mountains. There are four man-made lakes in the valley, mostly at city and town parks, none that I know of in the foothills, except the reservoir, unless he's raising the ducks in his backyard pond. And then, up here." She tapped the mountains. "Big Bear Lake, Lake Arrowhead, Moon Lake, Green Valley Lake. It's the damn land of lakes. Ducks aplenty."

"Hey," Fasteau said. "Wouldn't they fly away now? The ducks?"

"Maybe he has a way of keeping them."

"Maybe," he said.

185

She could tell by his tone that he was not interested.

"Those are interesting concepts," he added.

She could hear the condescension in his tone. What was most annoying about it is that she wasn't even sure if he understood what the word "concepts" meant.

"This guy has a route. A daily route. He grabs a kid, stashes the kid, murders the kid, and has his route set up. The kids are ones he knows. Somehow he knows them. Each victim's an only child. He knew that. A large family would've scared him. He couldn't deal with more than one child. I'm guessing each of these kids were loners of sorts. Didn't play with a lot of kids in the neighborhood. As only children, they might've been good at talking to adults. I think he knew them in some way, even if the parents didn't know them. Each of the victims lived within fifteen miles of each other. Want to take a drive?"

"Up the mountain? It's probably snowing up there. We'd need an SUV. It's snowing up there today."

"No," she said. "Just here." She tapped the map at the designation for the foothills of San Pascal County.

186

Chapter Twenty-eight

When Lucas awoke, he was surrounded by gray darkness that was only interrupted by twinkling white lights. He looked up to the ceiling. Not a ceiling at all, but rugged hanging rock. Christmas lights were strung along them. It freaked him out.

Bad dream.

At first he thought he had been dreaming and was back in bed.

The fact that he'd peed in his pants made him remember where he was. He shivered from cold. His hands were duct taped together, but he was able to reach down into his pocket. In one, Stuart, his hamster. Lucas was more worried about his pet than about himself for the moment, but as he smoothed the animal's fur, he felt the stirrings of a very sleepy hamster. Cushioned with a bit of napkin wrapped around it, Stuart had managed to survive the trip that Lucas wasn't quite sure he would. At one point, in the darkness, he'd been afraid Stuart had been smushed to death. But the hamster was fine.

In the other pocket, two quarters and his favorite giant rubber spider, Charlotte. Lucas squeezed it, feeling its familiar contours. He said the Lord's Prayer three times, at first fast, but by the third time so slowly, trying to imagine God hearing him.

Then, as his eyes adjusted, he saw shadows all around him.

He was in some kind of cellar, but maybe it was a cave. It was a strange place. Rock walls like a cave, and they had really scary drawings all over them, but they were only drawings. He knew not to be that afraid of them. The big statues nearby made him think of church, and that made him feel a little better. He liked church and always felt safe in church. But it reminded him a little of the kind of place that monsters lived. Ogres. Nightmares.

He kept hearing noises, like water trickling and like something moving, but not all the areas of the place had the Christmas lights hanging over them.

The flickering lights bothered him.

The room seemed like a giant box. Dark shapes in parts where he couldn't quite see. Piles of something. He couldn't tell. His head hurt so much, he thought it would split open. Where was his Mommy? Where was Daddy? Why weren't they there to protect him? His confusion increased with each second. Maybe this was some game. Some strange game. Maybe he had done something really bad. Something he shouldn't have. He thought back to the morning, and the weekend. All he could remember doing that might be considered bad was stealing the picture from his father's drawer when he visited him over the weekend. The photograph that had his mother, father, and him as a baby in it. All of them smiling. He had stuck the picture in his pocket. When he'd gotten home from the weekend with his dad and his dad's new wife, he'd hidden the picture behind some books on the bookshelf. Maybe that's why he was being punished.

Maybe Duane was the punisher.

Why would Duane do this? Duane was his buddy.

He was Duane's helper whenever Duane came by, just like he helped the gardener, Mike, in back when he came over to check on the roses. Just like he helped Mrs. Portrero with carrying books to her from the public library. He didn't know Duane that well, he figured, but Duane had always been nice. Nice and friendly, and one time gave him a dollar for helping him.

But maybe it wasn't Duane. Maybe it just was something wearing a Duane mask. Duane was always nice to him. Duane laughed at his jokes. His mommy even let Duane in whenever she was home. So did Nina. Why would Duane do this?

Duane even called him his "little helper" when he'd stand and watch Duane work.

But that thought again: Maybe it wasn't Duane. Maybe it was just someone who looked like Duane.

Like nightmares where things came for you looking like your mommy or daddy, but they turned into something different.

Or maybe he was the Bogeyman. Lucas had heard terrible stories from other kids in his first grade class about the Bogeyman. One of his classmates, Sandy Shapiro, told about how the Bogeyman lived in the dark of closets and under the bed. She told him how at night he came out and grabbed little kids and put them into the dark.

Just like this place, he thought.

Then he remembered one of his own nightmares, when the Bogeyman came up behind him and grabbed him, and then slithered under the bed with him. In the dark under the bed, Lucas had screamed for his mommy, but she had never come.

He should've known.

He should've know that this was the day the Bogeyman would come out of the shadows and grab him.

He wanted to wake up from this nightmare. He didn't want to be here. It hurt to think all this. And his shoulder hurt.

He closed his eyes as hard as he could and wished himself back in his bed, asleep. Wished himself to wake up. At the count of ten.

Ten nine eight seven six five four three two one.

Lucas opened his eyes.

Water dripped in one corner of the room.

He heard a shooshing sound, like the sound the shower made when he took his bath.

When he had to pee, he struggled, but he was bound up too tight. He peed in his pants and felt ashamed. It hurt down around his thighs where he'd already peed.

His head felt like it was full of stones smashing against each other.

He felt Stuart crawl from his pocket up his arm, and along the floor beside him. He wanted to tell Stuart not to run away, that he wouldn't ever be able to find him again. He watched his hamster skitter along the floor.

Come back, Stuart. Please.

He wished his mom would come and get him soon.

Then he heard a muffled noise—a human noise—from somewhere in the dark near him.

He saw a dark shape of movement, as if an inky blackness had just begun pouring from the shadows.

Chapter Twenty-nine

1

It spent a little time with its mother, inside, sitting with her, talking to Nancy, the visiting nurse who was filling in, who checked the morphine levels and triple checked the pills. "You sure this is all the Roxicet?"

It nodded.

"There should be more."

She leaned over its mother's bed.

Its mother seemed to it like a jellyfish for a second. Tubes running in and out of her. Her skin crackly and pale. Her hair thin and white.

It felt nothing for her, but it didn't like to think of her like this.

"She seems to be in more pain that usual," Nancy said. "But she seems to be dosing herself well." She leaned closer to its mother. "You need to be careful, Mrs. Cobble. This is just for when you feel pain." She pointed to the intravenous tube and the button on its edge where the patient could self-dose.

"Maybe she needs more," it said. Hoping. It could use more.

"She seems fine as she is," Nancy said in a low voice, as if she didn't want its mother to hear her.

Nancy wore all white, like a nurse should. She was good to its mother, and although it didn't like her that much, it appreciated when she came around. The other nurse, Betty, was better, it thought, but Betty was on vacation until after the holidays. It only saw the nurse once a week. It felt a bit nervous about the nurse being there now, but the little bird below was silent and since the Other One had control of all this, it was fairly sure that Nancy would not wonder too much about the morphine level being down, about the missing Roxicet or the Valium that were gone. Its mother had last seen a doctor six days earlier, at the office over in Big Bear, when it drove her there. That was when its mother had talked about dying. About not being around.

That's when the home care had begun, and the morphine had seemed to it to be a godsend.

Morphine helped people not feel pain.

It didn't like pain at all.

"Did you get a flu shot this year?" Nancy asked, interrupting its thoughts. She had her little dark bag full of all the wonders: needles and pills and plastic bags filled with liquid sleep. She reached into it and withdrew a syringe. "I could give you the shot right now. Mr. Cobble?"

"Flu shot?"

"It's one of the services our visiting nurses association offers to family members of our patients. There's a nasty strain of flu going around. This'll help prevent it. It won't hurt much—I'll use a butterfly needle." She leaned back over the bed, her face so close to its mother's that she must've gotten a good whiff of its mother's awful breath. "How about you, Genie? I'm going to give you a very little shot. A teensy one. It'll keep you from getting sick this winter."

The nurse drew out a small syringe from its plastic casing.

Its mother nodded, closing her eyes. "I feel like a damn dartboard. I've had more needles in me than a pine forest."

The nurse laughed, but it did not. It knew that its mother was serious. She'd had blood tests and shots of things, and intravenous tubes for weeks. Ever since she got worse. Ever since she called the hospice and the visiting nurse place.

Ever since she told him that she was going to die before Christmas. *"I know my body is going. I don't want to die,"* she had said to him. *"But God is calling me."*

Didn't even like thinking of it. Didn't even want to imagine what its life would be like without her. Lost Ruthie when she was a little girl. She didn't go to Heaven, not according to Daddy. She went to Hell. But his mother was going to Heaven. She was pure and holy. She was above all the filth of the world. Ruthie had been part of it. Daddy had told it about Ruthie and her sins and how she came into the world bloody with sin and how she was the

194

Whore who must never see the light of day lest she unleash her disease and vermin upon all mankind.

Ruthie was in Hell.

But the idea of its mother leaving it was something that made the hammers go off in its head. Pounding and thrashing inside it. Making the cage rattle. Making the Other One stronger.

Its mother was going to die.

Its dog Jojo was going to die.

It wanted everything to just stop. To just keep everyone alive.

Its dog.

Its mother.

She was the only thing who had protected it.

She had saved it, in the last minute.

Saved. Not saved like the baptisms Daddy gave it all the time.

But saved from the place in the earth where its daddy had tried to bury it alive.

2

It didn't like to dream, but when it had been awake for so many hours—nearly four days, it reckoned—it began to dream with its eyes wide open, even sitting behind the wheel of its truck. It wondered about the child, the little dove, but it had to keep moving on its route or else nothing would go right.

It remembered how it and Ruthie would be down in the Mad Place with its daddy and how Daddy would read scripture, and rock back and forth on his knees, raising his hand up to the dark above his head and crying out against the vileness of human-kind. How Ruthie would begin speaking in tongues, and then it would follow her lead, although it felt fake. The Holy Spirit never came into its head, not like the Other One did. But Ruthie was holy and she got chosen young to be a blessed one of God. "Thou art a vessel!" its daddy would cry, his hands on Ruthie's scalp like he could feel the Jesus energy coming up from her. "You are chosen by the Lord! You are righteous and pure and your purity will be a light unto the world!"

It was not sure if that was exactly what its daddy had said, but in memory, that's what it seemed like. Its memories and dreams got all mixed up, and it had blocked out so much of what had happened in the Mad Place that it wasn't sure if it all had happened exactly like it remembered.

Ruthie's face had been truly pure. It remembered that much. It remembered how he had loved her more than he could've if she had been his flesh and blood. She came to them and stayed before the other children. The others were all bad, but Ruthie was sent by God. Its daddy had loved her, too, like she was his own daughter, and it even had gotten a little jealous when it saw the two of them together, singing hymns in the Mad Place or saying prayers so loud that their voices echoed.

His mother had been there, too, but its memories of her were weaker. It remembered her perfume, which was like juniper berries, and the way she never said much in front of its daddy. Sometimes its daddy hit its mother, and it got really mad, but then it was usually punished in the Mad Place and it knew that was right and godly. It never heard from God directly, but that was because it was born in sin. That was a problem it could never get away from.

It was born in the filth, that's what its daddy had said, and when its daddy had told it about how its mother had been a sinner and how she had given her soul to Satan until its daddy had SAVED HER. SAVED HER AND BROUGHT HER INTO THE HEALING LIGHT OF THE LORD!

"She was a whore, as all women are whores until they are saved by the hands of men who are of the Spirit! As your sister is a whore! Ruthie is cursed by God with her twisted spine and legs. She was born into sin, and she will remain in sin until a man brings her to light and redemption. And you, you children, the Lord saith, "Suffer the children to come unto me." And you must go to Him. You must feel the Spirit in you. You must let only God speak through you, for what is your flesh is the Devil. If thy right eye offend thee, cut it out. If thy right hand offend thee, chop it off. If thy twisted legs offend thee, saw them and toss them into the fires of Hell! Do not mistake your flesh for life. Your flesh is death. Burn your flesh. Scourge it. Your weakness must become your strength!"

And then its daddy would bring out the cigarettes and press them into its back. "You are nothing. Your flesh is nothing. You are born of evil. You are an 'it.' Say it. Say it. You are an 'it.' "

Andrew Harper

And it would say it, over and over again. "It! It! It! It! I am an it! I am! An! It!"

And Ruthie would say over and over again, "Whore! Whore! Whore! I am! A! Whore!"

And then, in the dark, she would hold it and tell it that one day Mommy would stop all this.

And Daddy would get better.

But it never believed that.

It knew that the Other One lived inside it, just like Daddy had been telling it since the day it was born.

3

Its workday didn't begin until nearly one. It worked for six hours. It was a part-timer, and could only take so much daylight and interaction. It was lucky to have the job since its daddy died.

It arrived at the gate. The guard, Pete, waved it in. It passed the dome and the main office and drove its truck right up to the back. Then, it parked. Others were there, and it said a few words to them. They joked a bit about the crappy day. About the possibility of a storm brewing.

One of the guys said, "Man, that's the one pisser about Southern California. It won't just sprinkle. It's gonna end up pouring for two weeks straight if it starts."

Another said, "Naw, I bet this'll just be sprinkles. I predict sunny skies by Christmas. I bet it's snowin' up where Duane lives."

"How's your girl, Duane?" a guy in a red jacket asked.

It looked up. It was good at mimicking them without them knowing. "She's great."

"You old dog," he said.

It smiled. Uncomfortable. It didn't talk to many of them if it could help it. It wished that Monica never had come around work that one day, wearing her skimpiest outfit, nearly flashing her tits for the guys. They all had talked about her afterward. About how they wanted to get her panties wet. About how they wanted to stick themselves into her, all at once. It didn't like men when they talked like that. They couldn't help it, just like Daddy couldn't help it with Ruthie because whores did that to men. Spirit was strong, but flesh was weak. The Devil made flesh to tempt man. These men were easily tempted.

But Monica had worked at it.

It didn't like Monica being so cheap. She was like a whore when she did that, and it had rescued her and taken care of her just so she'd never become a whore.

"How's your mom?" the one named Jeff asked. He was different from the others. He was saved and went to church and talked about his Bible Study group. It liked Jeff.

But it had no reply for him.

"She's got my prayers," Jeff said, then passed on to his truck.

"Aw, dang, here comes Randy. Now we're screwed. Well, have a good one, Duane. You too, Chad."

"Ditto," it said, then went to get its designated truck for the day's work.

4

It didn't even notice its routine anymore. It had been doing this for nearly six years, and it was used to the stopping and starting, the traffic on the 101, the side streets, the hills with their winding streets and the houses with their winding driveways.

It was dreaming instead. It saw its daddy, gaunt and with a harsh expression on his face, one hand raised to Heaven, the other wrapped around a big fat worn Bible.

When it dreamed with its eyes open, it was always back in the big stone room with the pool of water and the angel.

And Ruthie was there, too.

Ruthie, with her face so like a spoon, shiny and curved, and her hair all smoothed back because it would comb it with its fingers for her.

It had felt that Ruthie was its only happiness.

Ruthie with her little crippled legs and leg braces that didn't help her.

Ruthie with her smile that was like sunshine even in the shadows.

And in the dream, their daddy began shouting that they were possessed by demons.

"And the demons need to come out!" his daddy shouted, slapping the Bible down hard on Ruthie's head. "OUT! OUT! OUT!"

200

Then Daddy went to get the barbed wire, and the first time Daddy did that was the first time it heard the Other One rattling the bars of the cage in its head.

Chapter Thirty

1

Eating a turkey and swiss on rye while poring over transcripts of tapes, Trey was beginning to get a picture of what had made Scoleri. Taken from his original mother soon after birth because she had been keeping the baby up at night with the same speed that she took herself, he bounced through Southern California, group homes, some of which Trey knew of that were down in Chino, some in the outlying areas of San Bernardino. He followed the cadence of Scoleri's speech, his pontificating in this other personality he called "Abraxas" of how he created the Earth, how the dinosaurs were his dragons, how he and the Devil knew each other too intimately, among other delusions and constructs. There was a history of hurting other children, particularly girls, and three admittances to hospitals before the age of thirteen; each time someone had beaten him up. Once, they'd used razors on him.

Despite this, Trey developed little sympathy for Scoleri. Trey was not a bleeding heart, and he knew that there were other kids who were tortured the same or worse, whose psychological makeup allowed them to grow up into healthy, productive, contributing members of society. They got help. They worked at it. But in Scoleri's case, and in the case of other sadistic sexual predators Trey had seen and studied, he had the X Factor. That was the one mysterious thing—perhaps organic from birth, perhaps it had been the speed he'd been given as a baby, or perhaps, as Trey sometimes thought, human predators were a throwback in evolution. Every single human being exhibited a predatory nature of some sort, whether it came out in a competitive spirit that rejoiced while others failed, in manipulating others to do one's will, or any number of mindless activities that involved one-upsmanship. It was not just getting ahead for some people. It was about destroying the competition.

But those people were nothing compared to the predators Trey had come to know. These human beings were akin to lions on the hunt, seeing a herd of antelope, picking out the weaker, the sicker, the less able to survive members, and targeting them.

The only word that came to mind as he read Scoleri's file was "evil." Not cosmic evil. Not spiritual evil. But ordinary human evil that was willing to break the social contract, to go outside normal behavior, that experienced great pleasure at the suffering and pain of others. It was that element of enjoying suffering that most disturbed Trey in nearly every single case file he had ever read.

Scoleri's was no different.

Then, as he quickly scanned the last file, he said, "What about 1984?"

Elise looked up from her cup of coffee.

"He talks specifically about nearly every year of his childhood, except 1984. He would've been about eight years old then. We know he left the group home in Mentone that year. All it says is 'Transferred.' Then, over here—" Trey lifted a sheaf of transcript papers—"he talks about his God year, but he doesn't answer your questions about it."

"I don't have all the answers," she said. "He only tells me what he tells me."

"Well, maybe it means nothing. But I feel like I know the guy backwards and forwards from all this." He set the papers down, closing two of the file folders. "I still think he's talking to somebody. To get this information. It's an inside job. He reaches the kidnapper somehow. Maybe one of these group homes or foster families that he kept bouncing around from. Maybe it's one of those people he's still in contact with."

Flipping through page after page, Trey came up with a list of people with whom Scoleri was in regular contact. None of them were anything other than trusted employees at Darden State. No outside family, no lawyer, no cop even. Nobody but the ward staff.

"Someone here?" Elise asked.

"I wish I could say that. Maybe. Let me go talk to him about it."

"Look, Trey, I wouldn't ordinarily say this in any other circumstance. But I've been working with Scoleri for four months. Since his transfer from Napa. He believes he's psychic. He believes that he talks to others with his mind, and they talk to him. I am not leaving this up to the police. Not my little boy. They don't understand the criminally insane. You and I do."

"How much time do you think we have?" he asked.

Through a haze of smoke, she said, "Eight hours. Maybe less. Between now and tomorrow morning. That's the longest he's gone. He doesn't want ransom. He doesn't want anything that he doesn't already have once he has one of the children. He kills the victims within several hours of taking them. The longest one was twenty-four hours. Maybe. I'm not sure." She took a deep breath, steeling herself. "He's dead. My baby's dead already."

Her hands trembled, and she stared at them as if she didn't know what to do with them anymore.

2

Another silence, brief.

Elise took a few deep breaths. Trying to control it. The thing inside her. The thing that wanted to explode. "It's been hell this morning. I want to believe he's fine, but I'm sure he's dead. The rational part of me knows he's dead. But the emotional part can't accept it."

"He's alive," Trey said. "You've got to believe that."

"It's the only thing I can believe. Right now. Look, I think Scoleri is a link to the Red Angel. He believed the Red Angel is the agent of the Devil. And he knows things."

Trey shrugged.

"Didn't Hatcher feel a connection to you?"

Trey laughed nervously. "You could say so. She thought we were past life buddies."

"Were you?"

Trey was astonished. "You're a doctor. You don't believe in reincarnation, do you?"

"Do you?"

Trey was silent. "Okay I concede the point. I'm not sure."

"And I'm not sure with Michael Scoleri, either. I'm not sure, but if he's even ten percent right, call it perceptive, call it intuitive, I don't give a damn. I am not going to trust the same detective and his cohorts who had two days to try and save the Red Angel's last victim and screwed up because they wouldn't listen to a man they consider criminally insane sitting at Darden State. Did you see what he wrote on himself? With his fingernails?"

Trey nodded. "I heard. 'Suffer the children.' "

"Not just that," Elise said. "He had names. There are seven of them, and the sixth one is Lucas. The fifth one is Mary. Trey, they haven't even found a fifth child yet. What if they do? What if her name's Mary? What if Lucas is the sixth, and then the seventh is named Billy? How would that happen, that a psychopathic personality in Darden State knew who the kidnapper would take next?"

Trey took a breath. Then, "Elise. You do not believe that he is telepathically linked to this killer. Tell me that."

"No. I don't. But there's something. I can't figure it out."

"When was the last time you had a session with Scoleri?"

"Friday. Normal day. We spent three hours together. He seemed especially troubled."

"In the pod?"

"There. And here. Bronson and Marcovich were here, too."

"Restraints?"

"Not completely."

"Hands free?"

"Hands only. Leg cuffs."

"Not full shackles?"

She shook her head.

"Who else came in your office on Friday?"

"No one that I can think of."

"Any deliveries?"

"People come in and out of here all the time. But I'm here when they do that. I would've noticed someone. Or Eric would've."

"Did he have access to any writing material?"

"No. We cleared sharps before he came in."

"Did he do anything while he was here?"

"He stood most of the time. He said he was tired of sitting."

"Did he go to the window?"

"Maybe. I don't remember. Yes. He looked out on the grounds. He looked at—" she pointed to the pictures on the wall, calming images of waterfalls and countrysides.

"I have to ask you a question that you probably already heard from the cops, Elise. But, here goes: Why do you think Lucas was targeted?"

"Targeted? Trey. This is a random kidnapping. The cops said the main link was the upper-middle class neighborhood and San Pascal itself."

"Okay. I guess I'm just doing scattershot here. But I just don't believe in telepathy. Or that he has some psychic link to the man who kidnapped your son. Those three hours you spent with him may be crucial."

She heaved a sigh of frustration. "I wish I could give you more. It was just a completely normal day with him and with others. I didn't connect him with this at all. I only got pulled in on the Red Angel that night."

"You see any others who might have a link to the outside?"

"Program 28 only," she said. "With the other patients, I went to the pods."

"Why give Scoleri these little trips out of his pod?"

"He's not an animal, Trey. He may be a sociopath. A psychopath. But he was responding to some extent. I thought we were near a breakthrough." Her voice trailed off as she lost confidence in her own words.

"Okay," Trey said. "This is all we have to go on. Let's see what I can get out of Scoleri."

Abraxas

Chapter Thirty-one

Twenty minutes later, Trey sat across from Scoleri.

Scoleri was spread out on his cot, arms crossed behind his head. Eyes closed. Grinned, as if he knew too much.

"You know what's great about this place?"

"What's that?" Trey asked.

"You kill someone in here and all they do is transfer you. Either to another ward or to another institution. If I were to, say, kill you—not that I intend to—I'd get some extra meds and maybe a more comfy bed."

"Is that what you want to do?"

"No. I don't like hurting people. I only do it when they attack me. But I was just saying it as a 'for instance.' " Then, turning his head slightly, he said, "I knew you'd be back once you talked to Elise. I knew you'd be here. You want to know about the Red Angel now. But you don't believe in me, Trey. You must believe in me. I am the way."

"Sit up," Trey said in as authoritative a voice as possible.

Scoleri blinked. Then he grinned. "You gonna be my daddy?" he asked in a little boy voice.

"I mean it. Sit up. I want to ask you some questions."

Scoleri made a strange move with his body. Trey remembered what Jim Anderson had told him: *contortionist*. It was as if Scoleri were a snake, and his body movied fluidly into a sitting position. "Yes sir, herr doctor. Oh, but you're not a doctor, are you? You're just a cut above janitor. Psych tech. A nice title for somebody who wipes my ass. You meet Creep down the hall? He's paints his shit all over like Picasso. Somebody should wipe his ass better."

"Sit up," Trey said.

After a minute, Scoleri decided to sit up. It probably helped that Trey had the two COs from the end of the hall come in and pick Scoleri up, put him in the chair at the table, and then bind his hands behind him. "Very nice, Trey. Very nice. You got me where you want me. I used to do this to some pretty ladies I knew. They enjoyed it. Me, I'm more of a hands-free kind of boy."

Trey took the chair across the table from him.

"You're not at all afraid of me?" Scoleri asked. "Not the teensiest?"

"No."

"You should be. I'm God. I like hurting people."

"Tell me about the Red Angel."

"What do you want to know?"

"Who is he?"

Scoleri shook his head. "You don't get no pussy without some flowers and chardonnay."

"You don't know anything about him, do you?"

"Well, I know something about him. He's a very bad man."

"What else?"

"He has little Lucas Conroy in his secret hidey-hole. He calls it the Mad Place, and it's not because he's insane. It's because he's nuttier than a shit-house rat, and he thinks that it's where you're allowed to get very angry when you want, and nobody's around to hear you scream about it."

"Who's telling you all this?"

"Ah," Scoleri said, narrowing his eyes a bit. "You don't believe in me. That's right. Let's start with that. If you become my disciple, I'll let you in on my sacred secrets. There are six sacred secrets. In each of the six, there are another sixty. And within those six hundred. That's six hundred sixty-six, or 666. The mark of the Beast. And I am not the Beast. I am Abraxas. Believe in me, or I will never tell you anything more."

"All right."

"Oh goody. A follower. First, only call me Abraxas. This Scoleri garbage has to go. Michael Scoleri was the flesh I had when I was a boy, but that got burned away when my Godhood came out. I was about eleven, when—"

"I don't care. I'll believe in you. All right?"

Scoleri paused. "Believe in who?"

"Abraxas."

"That's more like it. God likes to be called by his

real name. The Red Angel was once one of my disciples. He was one of my most beloved. But he got a little too much Devil in him, and now he's trying to bring about the end of the world. He's completely crazy. He thinks that by . . ." But Scoleri stopped himself. "You know what, Mr. Trey Campbell? I want you to show me you believe in me."

"How?"

"Do something for me."

"Okay."

"A magic trick."

"You're God. I think you should do the magic tricks."

"I know, but I'm trapped in this." Scoleri pinched the skin on his face. "I can't quite cut my way out of it. What I'm thinking of is a vanishing act."

"You want me to leave?"

"Both of us. I want you to take me to Elise Conroy's office. We can all three talk there."

"I'm afraid that won't happen."

"Well, it was a test of faith. And you failed."

"How about you tell me a little bit more? Maybe with some more information, I can get around the house rules."

Scoleri closed his eyes. When he opened them again, he said, "I just heard from him. The Beast. Do you know one thing that the police don't know about him? He's been kept at bay. The part of him that's not Beast has been kind up to now. He put the little angels to sleep before he sent them off with their messages. But this one is going to be different. This one is number six, and number six is a magical number. It is the Beast's number. This one, sweet little Lucas Conroy, isn't going to go to sleep. The Beast is taking over fast now. The man who he was is burning away. He is losing the last of his soul. The others he's only tasted. After they've gone off with their messages to me and then on to Heaven. This one he is going to devour alive. He bites them. The Beast. The Red Angel. He bites them, but he doesn't eat them. He's going to eat this one. He's held back. He's fighting his nature. But he won't win this time. This little angel is going to get eaten alive and may not make it to Heaven."

Chapter Thirty-two

3 P.M.

Trey held his breath in the last second while Scoleri spoke.

Then he exhaled.

"Where is he?"

"I had it on the tip of my tongue," Scoleri said.

"Where is he?"

Scoleri leaned forward, and Trey smelled his breath, which was foul.

Scoleri's face was less than an inch away from Trey's.

Briefly, and so quickly it was nearly imperceptible, Scoleri's tongue flicked out from between his lips and touched Trey's upper lip.

It was like being touched by a snake.

Trey recoiled, drawing back fast.

Scoleri grinned.

From the doorway, one of the corrections officers stepped toward the table where the two men sat. Trey recognized him. The guy named Atkins. The one who might have something not quite right within him. Trey didn't want a confrontation. He wanted information now. He didn't need a fight.

Particularly not with a CO ready to smash someone's head in.

Trey took a deep breath. *Fight the fear. Put it down. He's trying to put you off guard. He won't attack you. He's under control here.*

Trey motioned to the COs to stay where they were.

"Tell me," Trey said, staring at Scoleri. *I will stare you down if I have to.*

"You can't stare me down," Scoleri said, as if reading his thoughts.

Trey felt a shock go through him.

He tried not to let it shake him.

Damn. I know you can't read minds. Up yours, Scoleri. Abraxas. It's a trick. It's a trick based on the obviousness of the situation. It's a trick you learned in your carny days. You are smart. You have some enormous I.Q., and you have some nastiness inside you. You are a snake. A rattler. Waiting to strike. Somehow, some way, you are going to tell me how you know about the Red Angel and where he is.

"There's only one way in Heaven or Hell that I will tell you where he is," Scoleri said.

Chapter Thirty-three

Trey had that feeling again: of cold. Of being stunned.

The way a rat must feel just before a python opens its mouth.

Scoleri's face seemed to change. He seemed younger, as if he fed off the fear he was sensing in Trey Campbell.

His eyes began moving rapidly, blurring so they seemed to fluctuate between all white and darkness.

Then Scoleri moved suddenly forward, grabbing Trey by the ears before Trey could lean back fast enough—

Trey heard the COs at the door shout, and other noise—

Scoleri pulled Trey's face close to his in a motion so fast Trey felt as if the wind had been knocked out of him—

Scoleri's lips went to Trey's ear and in that second or two before the officers pulled Scoleri back,

lifting him up out of the chair and practically slamming him into his bed, quickly tying the restraints—
   In that second or two—
   Scoleri whispered, "Get me out."

Chapter Thirty-four

1

"That's insane," Elise Conroy said.

"Insane" was not a word she used lightly.

She stood in the corridor, outside Michael Scoleri's pod on Program 28.

Trey glanced back into the room. Scoleri watched both of them from his cot. In full restraints, he could barely move a muscle.

"We could go to the police with this. Maybe there's a way . . ." Elise began.

"Like you said, it's insane," Trey said. He drew her back from the pod, down the hall a bit farther. The COs watched them from a distance. "I don't want anyone else hearing this, Elise. But we could help the police catch him. They have no idea where he is, or something would've happened by now. Scoleri knows something. I don't know how. I don't know why. But he knows something. If we can get him to feel comfortable, he'll tell us. Look, we call the police in. Or the Feds, if they're involved. Maybe they could interrogate him and get it out of him."

"Not if he goes catatonic."

"He's done that before?"

She nodded. "Sure. He did it for two weeks after he first got here. Nobody could get a word out of him, and we had to feed him intravenously. I don't know how he hypnotized himself into that state, but he managed to do it. When he came out of it, he ripped the tubes out of his arm and started screaming that he was being buried alive. But during those two weeks, not a word or a movement. I'm not even sure if he blinked. His respiration was so low, that . . . well, it was like a mild coma, if that were possible."

"He's a magician. A carny," Trey said. "In his late teens, he worked the carnival circuit. He probably learned tricks from others. He probably had a natural talent for it."

"Let me talk to my friend in Caldwell's police department. Maybe there's another way," Elise said. "Do you believe him when he says he's in communication telepathically?"

"I don't think so. I'm not a great believer in that kind of stuff. But he knows things he shouldn't know. And it doesn't seem, in a pod in Program 28, that he'd be able to get much information from the outside world. Unless a CO or a psych tech is delivering it. Now realistically, it could be someone here. It could be someone who is as screwed up as any patient here and is passing messages on to Scoleri. But unless it's you or Fallon, it doesn't seem like anyone has been passing messages to this guy. I've checked the logs. How does he know? I have one guess: He knows the Red Angel from when he was free. Or maybe even from Napa. He was told the Red Angel's plans years ago. Or else he knows, based on the Red Angel's psychosis exactly what this pattern of killing means. Maybe Lucas and the other kids who were kidnapped have something in common. Maybe. It would probably take a few days of sitting down with the cops to figure this out. By that point, Lucas's dead. I'm sorry to put it that way, but it's the only way I see it."

Elise thought for a moment, lit a cigarette. "You're right. We're going to get him out. I'll arrange a day transfer to Patton for observation."

"Right. Nothing more than that. If we can just get him outside for an hour, maybe he'll do what he says. Maybe he'll give us more. Then we can pass that information on to the police. Look, I don't believe in telepathy. I don't believe he's God either. But I do believe Scoleri knows something and wants to tell you. I think he likes you, and I think he respects you."

"It's impossible for him to respect anyone."

"I don't know. He respects me. I don't know why. But he could've easily hurt me bad in there. He was showing that I could trust him. Even when he had an opportunity to do so, he didn't want to attack me. Scare me, yes. And besides," Trey said, "he'll be shackled and cuffed. We'll get a transport car so that there's a screen between the front and back-seat. We'll have two COs sitting next to him. He just wants to get out for a while. He wants a drive. We'll give him a drive, and maybe he'll help us. If not, we'll get the Feds in to talk to him. Look, Elise. We'll do this. It will work out. We will get Lucas back. Alive."

She touched him lightly on the shoulder. "Thank you. All right. I'll go make some calls and get this arranged. It'll probably take a couple of hours. I have to call the EC, and then Olsen will have to be in on it. Get some lunch."

"I can't believe you're holding up."

"It's a nightmare," she said. "But I'm going to get through it."

"So will Lucas. They'll get this guy."

"I guess I have to believe that. I have to," she said, as if trying to convince herself.

2

Trey found Jim Anderson in the employee canteen, sipping a Diet Pepsi and flipping through *Popular Science*. Anderson glanced up. "My man. Want half a bad ham sandwich?"

"No, thanks." Trey briefed Anderson on the situation. "Look, Scoleri is somehow getting messages from outside. Any idea how?"

"None," Anderson said. "He has minimal contact with staff."

"I didn't like that one CO. What about him?"

"Atkins? I know what you mean. He's the kind of guy who flies hard and fast. But unless his background check was screwy, he's not the type who would slip messages to Scoleri. He despises the patients in 28."

"How about the cleaning staff? Or the midnight crew?"

"Again, minimal contact. And there are usually two to four people around whenever there's an interaction with Scoleri. Even when he's with one of the docs, he's got at least two people right behind him. They'd have to pass that message pretty quietly if they were going to do it." Taking a bite from his sandwich, Jim Anderson nodded as if answering a question in his head. "He's had a bad few days, though. Scoleri. Fallon punched his lights out this morning. Cut Scoleri's lip."

"Fallon's not passing messages," Trey said. "I wish I could think it was him, but he's the last one who would do that. He'd be more likely to hump Scoleri."

"What about the cafeteria?"

"He never goes in there. The most freedom he gets is in the morning for showers and then at nine. Snack time."

"What happens at snack time?"

"We bring them in here. One at a time." Anderson pointed to the vending machines. "They get Twinkies or Ho Hos or a soda. Four men supervising. Ten minutes each. It's their big treat."

"Who put that policy in effect?"

"Conroy and Brainard. It's for observation, I guess. They're pretty much shackled, though. It's just one way to give them a little something to look forward to before beddy-bye time. Only three on 28 are capable of doing it, though. The others are pretty much in another world."

Trey looked at the first vending machine. Fritos, Cheetos, the basics of snack foods. Then to the soda machine: Coke, root beer, Dr Pepper, Pepsi. Then the Snapple machine. Then the bottled water machine. Then the sandwich and fruit machine. He came up blank.

"When do the vending guys come in?"

"Depends. But never when Program 28 is here."

"Okay. I guess I'm just hoping."

"Hoping for what?"

"That Scoleri's just like the rest of us. At least in terms of how he gets messages."

"Aw, Bubba, you *know* he's not like the rest of us. Well, at least not me."

3

Trey checked out the showers next. It was eerie being there when they were silent and empty. Outside, a tiled room full of benches where the patients would disrobe. There were green metal lockers for them to store their clothes. Then the towel room— empty except for a laundry basket.

He stepped into the shower area. It seemed huge with only him standing in it.

How could a message be passed without one of the psych techs or orderlies noticing?

Trey stood at the center of the showers, where the drain came out. He went so far as to get down and check the drain.

And then he knew one other way a patient in Program 28 might get a message.

One other time of day when he might speak with someone other than psych techs and COs.

4

Back in Elise's office, Trey sat down across from her desk. She was on the phone, but quickly hung up.

"You," Trey said. "You met with him on Friday."

"I meet with him every day."

"But in your office on Friday. What did you tell him last Friday?"

"Trey. There was nothing that would have given him any information."

Trey reached for the picture of her son on her desk. He held it up to her. "He knows your son. Scoleri knows your son. He named him because he knows him."

"He wouldn't know his name," she said.

"That wouldn't be hard to find out. You've been treating Scoleri for months. Not just here, but at Patton, too. You've spoken to him. You mentioned your son. Maybe in front of him. Maybe when you didn't think he was there—when he just was leaving your office. But he knew Lucas's name from you."

"What would that matter? Someone got a message to him."

"And it's not telepathy," Trey said.

226

And then he knew. He didn't know how, or who, or even where.

"No," Trey said, feeling as if his mind was processing information too fast. "He didn't get a message. He delivered one."

Chapter Thirty-five

1

The second victim's house.

The living room. It was simple, classic, elegant.

Reminded Jane Laymon of a spread from a magazine like *House Beautiful*. This was the country-club area of San Pascal. It was nicer than where Jane grew up.

She sat across from the mother and father.

They'd been polite and haunted at the same time.

Fasteau was out in the car. He hadn't wanted to talk to them. He thought she was wasting her time.

Something about these two people across from her on the beige sofa reminded her of her own parents. These were wealthier people, but they were still just people.

And their son had been killed four days earlier.

"We've spoken to officers twice now," the father said. "I'm not sure what else we can add."

"There might be some detail we've missed. That's all." Then she added, "Thank you for letting me see his room."

The mother sipped a cup of tea and looked as if she hadn't slept in the nights since they'd gotten the news and had to identify their young son's body.

"That day," the mother volunteered. "That day . . ." She hesitated. The father gave her hand a squeeze, but she pulled her hand out from under his and rested it on her lap as if it was a thing and not her hand.

"Was there any delivery scheduled?"

The father shrugged. "I was at work. Nothing I knew of."

"Maybe something you ordered?"

The mother closed her eyes. Leaned back, sinking farther into the plush sofa. Opened her eyes. "Nothing. I mean, the mail came. The newspaper. No packages."

"How about workers? Do you have a gardener?"

"He's a fine man. They've already spoken to him," the mother said.

Then the father said, "I'm not sure, Officer, if we really can illuminate this further."

"He's got another one, doesn't he?" the mother asked. "You don't know anything. You can't know anything. That's why you're here. He's taken another child. I saw the news last night. He's taking one every day." She leaned forward and pulled a paper tissue from the box on the coffee table. She dabbed at the edges of her eyes. "I imagine the FBI are involved."

"Yes. But I wonder if there's something that you might be forgetting. About that day. That morning."

"I was upstairs, doing some work on the computer," the mother said. "He was just outside for a few minutes. He goes out—" she stops herself. "He was the friendliest little boy. The nicest little boy. I still can't believe it. I can't."

The father put his arm around the mother's shoulder. "I think we need to stop for now. We need to ask you to go."

"No," the mother said. "Maybe there's something. Maybe there is."

The father rose. "Can I get you anything? Tea? A Coke?"

Jane's throat was a little dry. "Maybe some water?"

"Sure."

The mother began openly sobbing. The father looked at her, then sat down and embraced her. The mother pressed her face into the father's neck as her shoulders heaved.

"I'll get it." Jane stood and walked across the room, down the short hallway to the kitchen, which she had seen when she first came in. She opened the cupboard, grabbed a glass. Then she turned to the sink. Noticed the water cooler by the kitchen door. Went to it and pushed the blue button, put the glass beneath the spigot, and poured the cool water.

She noticed the three big bottles of water by the cooler.

Back in the living room, she asked, "When does water get delivered here?"

"Water?"

"For the cooler."

"Oh," the father said. "I don't know."

When the mother calmed, she said, "Maybe once a month. No, twice a month."

2

Jane didn't necessarily think a lot about this until she was back in the car with Fasteau, who told her that he had gotten a call from Tryon, who was not happy that Jane had taken it upon herself to re-interview the families.

"That's okay," Jane said. "Let's check on something else. You get water delivered at home?"

Fasteau let out a laugh. "Sure. Who the hell drinks the water out of the tap?"

"I do," Jane said.

"It ain't always good for you. There's a lot of stuff floating around in the water out here."

"What kind of water do you get?"

"Usually Arrowhead. Since I was a kid."

"Ever heard of Moon Lake Spring Water?"

"Sure. It's that little outfit that's been trying to go national. I see their trucks all over the place."

"They get it. Delivered. I asked her if there was one particular delivery guy, and you know what she said? She had no idea. She said she never even noticed the guy who delivered it. It's like he had no face. She just lets him in her house, he goes in with the bottles, spends some time in the kitchen, and then leaves. She said she wouldn't even recognize him or if it was even the same guy each time. All she knows is she thinks of the water delivery guy as Green Shirt, because that's the uniform color. I wonder if the other families get Moon Lake Spring Water, too."

Rain began coming down hard.

"What the fuck," Fasteau said.

Chapter Thirty-six

1

Conroy's office. Gray light from the overhead, from the overcast sky outside. The rain slashing.

"Elise, who does he know on the Outside?" Trey asked. "Who came to see him at Patton? Or up north? Someone visited him. Someone on the Outside knows him. And wants contact. Who is it? Because that someone is either the Red Angel or the person who knows the Red Angel well."

Elise leaned back in her chair, lighting yet another cigarette. She took a few puffs.

"Who was at the trial? Who came to watch? Who knew him when? That's who this is. This is someone who has known Scoleri before."

"It could be anyone," she said. "Trey, this would take days to go through. We don't have days."

"Shit," Trey said. He wanted to pound the desk and kick something. "I know that he has a way of getting messages out."

233

"Or in."

"I wish we had more time."

Elise glanced at her wristwatch, a pained expression on her face. She took another drag on the cigarette. "It'll be dark in a couple of hours. Trey. Look, I'm going to go talk to Olsen. I think I can get this arranged. We'll get an escort, get him in the back of one of the transport vans, and just take him out. Get him over to Patton, see if he'll talk."

"Okay. But I have this feeling. I just think . . . I think if I stay on top of him . . ."

Suddenly, Elise slammed her fist down on her desk. "Damn it!"

He leaned forward and touched the tips of her fingers with his. "This is a terrible thing, Elise. But we have got to put it in the hands of law enforcement. We can talk to Scoleri to see if there's any information he can give us at this point. But nothing else."

"Here's the thing. I want to give him something small like this. Something inconsequential. If it gets him to talk, that's all I care about."

"You're not talking about roughing him up," Trey said. "I wish you were. I wish you were talking about using sodium pentathol. Or sedating him further and then getting him to free associate before he blacks out. But you're not."

"I wish I thought that would work. I know him well enough, Trey. I know what his demons are. Whether he's getting messages through staff or whether he thinks it's all coming through the ether like a radio, I don't care. He knows things. I want to find my son. The man who took Lucas kills them after sundown. I need him talking. He won't talk this way. He may talk outside this place. He may just need to feel in control for five minutes. To me, that's worth whatever it takes to get information to the police. To save my son. How the hell are you going to feel if sometime before dawn, they find Lucas in the Santa Ana River and that patient knows exactly where this killer is? Jesus," she said, "it's my baby. It's my Lucas. You can't even understand. I would lay down my own life to make sure he gets back alive."

"Give me one more chance," Trey said.

Elise pointed out her window. The rain. "Look at that. That's how I feel on the inside."

"Just one more chance."

"Sometime between sundown and midnight, it happens. I'm guessing that it's an internal clock the killer's on. Lucas is somewhere out in that world and I am sitting here. He'll be dead. I don't care about procedure. I don't care about the law. I have a gun. I can . . ."

Trey drew back in the chair. "You what?"

"When I went home. I got it. I keep it locked up. I brought it with me. It's in my car now. A Sig Sauer."

Trey tried to quickly piece this together. This was irrational for Elise. *I need to get her home. She needs to get away from this. She's too entrenched. She's not thinking right.*

"What are you talking about? Elise? A gun? Come on. This is real life. Don't go off like this." He reached over and picked up the phone and held it in front of her. "Call your friends at the police department. Tell them that there's a patient you've been treating who might have a connection to the kidnapper. They'll know what to do. They'll handle this."

She took the phone from him, but set it back down in its cradle. "I spent an hour with them this morning. Trey, they're not even sure that Lucas was kidnapped yet. They keep saying it's a possibility. They don't want to hear from me again. At least not at this phase. Not till they know for sure. By then, it'll be too late."

"Do you know for sure this is what happened to Lucas?"

"I don't even want to go around on this again. I was called in on Friday night by detectives in San Pascal. A body had been found two miles from here, over by some orange groves. It was the first one. Then, when I was working up a profile based on some evidence they'd shown me, they found another one, same killer, in Little Orange. Bannock. Every day, another one. I am telling you, Scoleri is communicating with this killer. Somehow, some way."

Trey glanced around trying to take in everything, hoping that something would catch his eye. Desk. File cabinets. Telephone. Wastebasket. Water cooler. Bookshelves. Books. Magazines. Computer. "The trash can. You threw something out. Notes? A phone message?"

Elise sighed. "Enough. I don't even care anymore. Here's what I do know. Here's what I care about. Lucas. Scoleri knows the Red Angel took him. Do you know what this killer does? He kills them. Drugs them, then drowns them. Then he takes a coat hanger and twists it around their neck. He cuts off bird wings and sticks them on the wire ends of the hangers so that they look like angels. That's why they call him the Red Angel—blood on the wings. He's making little angels out of them. When I spoke to the detectives today, they tried to keep me calm, but there's another detail. He's biting them. The last one found, this morning, her face was chewed up, her arms and torso bitten all over. I know what this is. He's been resisting doing it. But he's building up to it. The first one, nearly untouched. The most recent one, torn up like a dog got to her face. I've seen this before. So have you. With all the cases that come through. He's testing. He's trying out. He's getting more and more violent as he goes. Trey, his life is falling apart and he's taking it out on these children in monstrous ways. Jesus, I know this pattern of behavior. I've watched it before. I can't just sit and wait for these cops to find my son alive. It won't happen. He'll be dead. He'll have been tortured, too. He'll have the worst kind of death. Not my baby, Trey. Not my beautiful little boy. Not my angel."

2

"Call Olsen, then," Trey said gently, after she'd composed herself again. "Get the transfer set up. Get at least two COs in the back of the van with him. I'll go in the front, and we'll make sure the driver is armed. I don't trust him. You can sit in the back with him, so long as there are shackles and cuffs. A neck brace if you really want to make sure he won't try anything. Don't ever forget he's labile."

"You've known him one day," she said. "I've known him longer. I know what to expect from him. I know what he's like."

Chapter Thirty-seven

1

Hanging from the wall on a hook, large bird wings, blood dripping from them.

On the ground, a large dead duck.

Lucas was still crying because of what he'd just seen, but he fought to dry his tears. He felt stunned, but something in his brain was beginning to switch on. Something that was overcoming his fears.

It was a small gasp of a survival mechanism.

Duane had untied him, pulling off the tape. It had hurt, but it felt better than having it all over him so that he couldn't really move. He had to rescue Stuart, his hamster, too. He had to somehow get out. Somebody would come for him. He was sure. His mom or dad would be there. Lucas knew it. He also prayed to God to send someone to help him. He knew that if he prayed hard enough, it would all work out. He just knew something would happen that would rescue him, just like on TV or in some of the books he read. Everything always worked out. He was sure of it.

But he shivered nonetheless and felt as if every moment made him more and more scared.

"You're in the Mad Place," Duane said to the boy. He seemed friendly again. It weirded Lucas out to see him like this. It frighened him too much. His head hurt from trying to understand it.

"Do you remember me?"

Lucas nodded. "You're Duane. The water man."

"No," the man said. "It was Duane. But it is the Beast now. It is the Devil. Do you understand? You are the angel I need to send to God. God needs to know. The war is about to begin. Are you aware, little bird? Between Heaven and Hell, on Earth, it will begin. I am the Omega. I am the Last. You are my messenger."

Duane's look changed slightly. Lucas was worried that this was a bad thing to ask. Duane's face scrunched·up, not like he was mad, but like he was confused. He looked over at the bird wings hanging there. He stomped over to the small bed, and touched the tip of one of the wings. There was blood on it. He wiped it on his fingers, and then wiped his fingers across his mouth.

Fear clutched at Lucas's heart, and he stepped backward, tripping on something on the stone floor.

Then he saw what he'd tripped over.

It looked like a rubber doll's head, larger than it

should've been. Large and distorted, with fine wisps of hair off its scalp.

Attached to a body.

It made a noise that sounded like a crow cawing.

2

"You boys have been bad again! It's time to find your salvation before the demons get you! You want the demons to find you? The Devil is inside you. The Devil won't leave. The Devil is coming out!" Duane shouted, only Lucas was no longer certain it was Duane because his face had turned all red, and the sweat shone across his forehead, and his eyes were large and wide. Suddenly, Duane clutched himself around the middle. His throat seemed to get larger—Lucas had never seen anything as horrifying in his life—it was as if his throat were twisting around on itself and growing. Then a deep voice boomed from within Duane's throat shouting obscenities.

The voice grew soft.

Light.

Then the worst thing happened as far as Lucas was concerned.

Duane fixed his awful gaze upon him and whispered, "Do you know that demons live inside my flesh?"

Duane began ripping at his own face with his bare hands, his fingernails slicing away at the skin beneath his eyes.

241

In its mind, it felt the presence of greatness, of the Beast rising in its blood, taking over the hands that tore, the teeth that bit, the very soul of the it known as Duane Cobble.

The past and the present mixed together in its memory: Its foster brother; God, who had taught it about its inner nature the same way that its daddy had; about the Other One; The Beast; the Great Darkness known as 666, within its cage of flesh and bone. Its destiny marked by its little angels, sent to God to warn the Almighty of the coming fires of the world and the emergence of Hell.

Memories of Daddy holding it down in the hot water of the spring in the Mad Place, praising Jesus while he tried to cast out its demons, praising Heaven while slamming and dunking its head beneath the too hot water. "You are an It! You are less than a worm! You are not worthy of the evil sinful serpent from which you came! Your serpent is strong, but I will cast out the Devil from you! Do you hear me? Do you?" Its daddy cried out.

And then it was beaten so badly that it could only crawl, beaten with Ruthie lying there, her eyes blank and staring.

Locked in the Mad Place for weeks at a time, it lay and ate the scraps thrown down to it and drank the cold water along the ground, hearing its daddy reading the gospel to it from on high, hearing its daddy ranting in the dark about the demons its wicked mother had given birth to—given form—

"From her cursed place, you crawled, you whore, and then the it followed, a child of darkness, a child who was not human, but was full of sin! The mark of the Devil upon you! Dear Sweet Lord, save these two sinners, save them from the foul creatures that inhabit their bodies! Save their eternal souls! Keep them from the fires of perdition!"

Its two foster brothers with it, screaming as they watched its father break Ruthie's legs, but it knew that its daddy was right. Ruthie was the Whore of Babylon. She was the beginning of sin, and if Daddy did not subdue her—tread upon her as the serpent underfoot—then the last days would come.

Inside the Mad Place, bound for a thousand years, the world was safe from the Devil.

But when its foster brother left and Ruthie went to Hell, it was alone with its daddy.

And then, one day, Daddy died.

It was the man of the house.

It worked hard to hold the Beast in its cage so that it could take care of its mother, so that its girl, Monica, who had been a homeless whore down on its delivery route, could get cleaned up. But Monica's whoredom had tempted its flesh.

It had all fallen apart.

And now Jojo, its only friend for the past fifteen years, was dying.

And its mother was dying.

And it heard the voice of the Other One within it.

Louder.

Stronger.

Coming out.

It knew it was falling apart, and that the Devil was coming through more and more every day.

Christmas approaching.

God's birthday.

It had to send messages to Abraxas, the God of All.

Through the angels going to Heaven.

Through the signs and portents along its Moon Lake Pure Spring Water delivery route in the foothills and flatlands from San Pascal to San Bernardino, from Moreno Valley to Riverside.

It knew where God lived.

God spoke to it in omens.

It spoke to God with angels.

Chapter Thirty-eight

Jane called Tryon as Fasteau ran through the rain into a McDonald's with too long a line at the drive-thru window.

"I've spoken with three of the families. They all three get Moon Lake Pure Spring Water. I think it's the delivery guy. The Latimers told me that the Moon Lake guy talked to their son all the time. Funny thing is, none of them remember one specific guy. I think he grabbed the kids on his route. I think that's what he's been doing. These kids happen to be the ones who give him the opportunity."

"You following through?"

"Sure. We dropped by the distribution plant and got the names of three of the guys who work the area. They alternate routes. All part-timers."

"Good going, Laymon," he said. "Names?"

"James Pratt, San Pascal; Lou Barron, Mentone; and Duane Cobble, Moon Lake."

"What are the odds he lives in Moon Lake?"

"That's by the distribution center, but the guy at

the plant told me that Pratt lives on Sierra Ridge. That's within a stone's throw of Dr. Conroy's and within two miles of the Latimers'." She read the addresses and telephone numbers for each one.

"Okay," Tryon said. "We'll get officers to each residence. Might as well cover our asses."

"You heard from Conroy yet?"

"Yes and no." Tryon failed to explain further. A pause on the line. "You and Fasteau are where?"

"Not far from the Latimers'."

"Okay, you two get up to Moon Lake. Check out Cobble. This may be one of many goose chases, but we need to nail the Red Angel, pronto. If one of these three pans out, you done damn good."

He hung up.

" 'You done damn good,' he tells me." Jane closed her cell phone.

High praise from Tryon.

Chapter Thirty-nine

1

Trey Campbell spent forty-five minutes waiting for Dr. Brainard at his office, and then another twenty trying to convince him of something that Trey was sure he would sign off on. He and Elise needed both Olsen, the Executive Director of Darden State, and two psychiatrists to sign off on this kind of day transfer for a patient from Program 28.

When Campbell left Brainard's office, Jim Anderson, waiting in the hall, said, "So what's the verdict?"

Trey shook his head. "Maybe if Elise had luck with Olsen, we can do an end-run around Brainard."

But Elise's office was locked.

"Maybe she's talking to Olsen?"

"She'd phone it in," Trey said.

He reached into his pocket, brought out his cell phone and punched in the number of the Executive

Director's office. "Shelly? Trey. Hi. Listen, is Dr. Conroy over there?"

2

He felt a peculiar sense of panic as he walked swiftly down the corridor toward Program 28. ID badge flashed to the COs. Unlocked the double-doors.

Down the metallic corridor, past the first several pods.

Scoleri's was empty.

Anderson, following behind him, said, "What the hell?"

Trey cussed a blue streak.

"Chill, boy," Anderson said.

"Jimmy, she got him out. She couldn't wait. She did it. I don't know how, but she did it."

3

He didn't want to expose her. She might not be in any trouble. She might be fine. She might have gotten him to her car. That would be it. Trey was sure. She would be out in the staff parking lot. He told Jim Anderson he'd call him within ten minutes and explain what all this was about.

Out in the staff parking lot, Elise Conroy's space was empty.

He checked the log at the front desk of the main entrance.

Elise Conroy had left with "Guest."

248

Trey stood at the front entrance to Darden and weighed his options.

Lucas Conroy will be dead by sundown.

There is no option.

4

In his Mustang, out on the 10 freeway, he punched in Elise's cell phone number. Windshield wipers sliced against the heaving rain, increasing as the sun headed over into the western sky. Temperature 64 in the flatlands and dropping.

She picked up.

"Where are you?"

"I'm sorry, Trey."

"No need. You got him out. Right?"

"Olsen said no. I'm sorry."

"He's with you?"

"Yes."

"Cuffed?"

"Very."

"How did you do it?"

"It was easier than you'd think. For the guards, I faked an ID. They don't know Scoleri from Adam in on Wards B and C. They thought it was a Program 9 med transfer."

"But you kept him cuffed?"

"Yes."

"Shackled?"

"No. But he has leg cuffs on now."

"That's not enough."

She hung up the phone.

He turned off the freeway exit and up into the foothills of San Pascal.

In the rain, traffic slowed. No one in Southern California seemed to know how to drive in the rain. It was as if anything that smacked of weather scrambled brains as well.

Palm trees lined the fat sidewalks. Small bungalows blurred along as he drove up toward Baseline, then west on Date Palm Drive, zig-zag back up to Baseline.

He pressed redial. He hated being on the cell while driving. Hated people who did it.

She picked up on her phone on the first ring.

"Don't hang up on me."

"Don't condescend to me."

"Where are you?"

"We're driving."

"What is he telling you?"

"He knows the killer, Trey. We should've done more of a background check. They were in the home together for a year. His God year. The Red Angel's family took him in. They got close."

"He may be lying."

"Enough, Trey."

"Don't hang up. Let me meet up with you. You need someone with you."

She paused.

He turned up a side street, north. Stucco beige suburban tract homes littered the slight incline heading toward the hills. "Are you near your house?"

"No."

Shit. He had just turned up into Sun Ridge, just on the other side of San Pascal, and Elise's neighborhood.

He wanted to ask her more questions but knew it would be pointless. Scoleri was right there next to her. He had no doubt that Scoleri intended to use her to get away. *You could have a medical degree from the best school in the country, you could work with serial killers for more than eight years, diagnosing, treating, studying, observing. And still, when your kid gets taken, you're just somebody desperate enough to risk your own life with someone who happily would rape, mutilate, torture, then kill you.*

"Where are you headed?" he asked.

"Up the 16. Into the mountains."

She was taking the side road, the old highway, up toward Big Bear. He had hoped that if she took any roads, they'd be main ones. Big ones. Ones where highway patrol might possibly be.

He had an instinct to call the police in the mountains.

You're over-reacting. We can bring this one in. Whether Scoleri has information or not, we can control this. Get Scoleri back to Darden, talk to Olsen. Clean it up. Anybody would understand Elise's actions in the face of what she was going through. Given her record, this could be smoothed over. He knew there was a way to do it.

But he also feared something else. More than just what Scoleri might do.

He had a fear that in working so intimately with

251

Scoleri, Elise had begun to identify too closely with him. She was a professional. But then he'd known other professionals, people who should've known better, who got too close to that insane fire and burned themselves.

"Have you reached the first rest stop?" he asked, carefully maneuvering a twist in the road. "You know, the one near the falls?"

Pause.

"No."

"Pull over there. I'll meet you. It'll take me twenty minutes."

"You won't call the cops?"

He thought for just a second that he might lie to her. But decided that this could be controlled. He could help take Scoleri back to Darden State. There'd be a way to make it all work. He was sure.

"I won't. But Elise, do not let him get inside your head. Not on this. He knows your weak spot. He knows that you'll do anything to get your son. He may not know this killer. He may—"

She hung up the cell phone.

He pressed redial.

No answer.

She'd turned off her phone.

5

As he drove, crossing into higher elevations, it was no longer rain coming down, but snow. He went up the 18, all the way to a small clutch of houses just where the mountains really began beyond the

252

foothills. A dip in the slender highway indicated the turn-off to the old Route 9. He knew it well, from his make-out days as a teen, going up with girl-friends, going hiking with his buddies. It had mountain streams flowing down along the old road, and it had two rest areas off of it, usually used for picnicking or just parking.

It took him nearly half an hour of the windy road that was impossibly narrow to get to that first rest stop. The snow fluttered down, making the whole area seem magical and beautiful. It was piling up—he figured must be at about 3,000 feet above sea level.

Elise's Volvo was parked just inside the curve of it, near the picnic tables.

As he approached it, something seemed wrong. His mind began reeling, thinking of the possibilities, imagining from what he'd read of Scoleri as to what the man was capable of doing. *The mutilations, the torture, the souvenir-gathering, the murders.*

The dreadful images came up to him, things he'd seen in forensics casebooks, pictures he'd seen when there'd been a trial of one of the patients and he had gone to the courtroom with the psychiatrists and COs: dead woman, women like Elise Conroy, beautiful, torn, their faces staring at nothing.

His heart began pounding too hard, hammering in his chest.

Don't let anything have happened to her.
Don't let her be hurt.

Chapter Forty

1

Trey parked his car and went over to Elise's.

Thank God.

She glanced over at him, but she had an unreadable expression on her face.

Flakes of snow fluttering down, wet.

2

He leaned into her opened window.

Scoleri lay in the backseat, his head against the inside door handle. His arms were behind his back, cuffed. His legs, shackled.

Elise looked up at Trey.

"He knows where Lucas is," she said.

Her eyes, bloodshot. Her hair, a mess.

He noticed the revolver on the passenger seat beside her.

"All right," Trey said. "Let's take this slow."

3

"Let's talk about this," he said. "Outside." As an afterthought, he added, "Bring the gun."

4

He kept watch on the car in case Scoleri made any move to get out.

He and Elise stood on the edge of the pavement and curb, close enough to run back to the car at a moment's notice and subdue Scoleri.

Far enough away that Scoleri wouldn't hear them.

"We have to turn around right now. Take Scoleri back. We can smooth it over. Right now. Every minute we delay it will be that much harder to fix this."

"No," she said. Her voice was far too calm. "He knows where my son is. I'm going to go get him. And kill whoever did this."

"That's nuts, Elise. You're out of your league. You may be a smart person with degrees up the wazoo, but this is beyond what you, or I, can handle. You're going vigilante on somebody's ass? With your gun?"

"Yes."

"Elise, do I need to wrestle you to the ground and put restraints on you, too?"

"If it were your son, Trey. If it were Mark. If you knew the man who intended to kill him within a few hours. If you knew how the police worked. When your family was attacked on Catalina. Hatcher. Did the police save you? Did they? Would

255

they have gotten to your kids in time? Trey? Tell me truthfully. You tell me that I should take him back. My only hope. I've gone over and over this in my mind."

After a few seconds he said, "Ok. One hour. We give him one hour to help."

That was it.

5

He went around and got in the car. She passed him the revolver. He put it carefully into the glove compartment. Shut it.

Then he got out and opened the back door.

Looking up at him, Scoleri said, "I love rides in the country."

6

Trey sat in the backseat, with Scoleri sitting to his left. Scoleri kept his eyes out the window.

Elise watched them both in the rearview mirror.

"All right. You have your fresh air, Scoleri."

"Call me Abraxas."

"Abraxas, then."

"You want me to just deliver everything on a silver platter," Scoleri said.

"Why not?"

"Doesn't work that way. You live in this realm of consciousness that's milky and clouded. You think that what you can see in your little bubble is all that there is. But there's more to existence than that,"

256

Scoleri said. He looked out at the snow falling. "I love snow. I created snow because it makes everything seem more beautiful than it is. The world is an ugly, grimey place. Filthy. Wallowing in it, people. People who are not really people, just pulsating amoebas, crashing into one another. The earth is a woman, and the parasites infest her scalp and her pussy. The earth is a whore, and she fucks the Devil. It gives her these lice and vermin called mankind. But I created snow to dress her. To blanket her. To freeze the lice. Isn't it beautiful?"

"Look," Trey said. "Tell us about the Red Angel."

"He once was a real angel, you know. Once, when the world was innocent and new. He was pure, but the Devil got inside him. The Devil came through into him, like the Holy Spirit comes into others when I inspire them. The Devil came into him and tore at his innards. He was strong, but not strong enough. I helped him build a prison for the Devil, in his head. We spoke through the divine radio, and I struggled in the whorls of his brainshit to build a strong enough cage for the Devil. But the Devil gets out now and then. The Devil knows his weaknesses. And something's happening to him now. The Devil is stronger."

"How do you know him?"

Scoleri turned to face Trey. Smiling. "Aren't we going for a drive? I want to see the mountains."

"I would think Abraxas would make the mountains come to him."

"Ha ha ha," Scoleri said, slowly and deliberately. Trey's heart pounded. He felt heat in his face. *We*

257

are fucked if this doesn't go right. "It's snowing. The roads might be bad."

"I think we should go for a ride," Scoleri said. "Up, up, up."

Chapter Forty-one

1

Moon Lake.

Weather forecast for the San Bernardino Mountains: cloudy, chance of snow, 28 degrees dropping to 20 by nightfall.

That was the forecast. At the higher elevations, it was already 18 degrees by six P.M.

Snow covered the town of Big Bear and Moon Lake.

It was a peaceful snow. Winds, but no blasts. Made the whole world look like a snow globe. Santa's village. Christmasworld.

Moon Lake was surrounded by twenty miles of shorefront property, but had not become commercialized in the least. It was out of the way, a community that rose from a recess in the mountainside, going flat along the lake, surrounded by trees, mainly incense cedars, sugar pine, white pine, and other conifers. The sheriff's station was a beige trailer down in the town area of Moon Lake. Town was simply a bar, a coffeeshop, and a sundries store. Six houses nearby, all occupied by those who work in either the sheriff's station, bar, coffeeshop, or sundries store.

In the forest beyond the lake, there were 125 cabins along the outcroppings and rises that could be reached via unpaved roads. These were used primarily in the summer, although some came up in the winter for skiing up at the city of Big Bear, twelve miles northeast. Few arrived after December 1st without four-wheel drives, although some of the flatlanders risked the windy road up to Moon Lake just to make fun of the locals, who were a bit country compared to those who lived below the mountains, or to take in the quaintness of the small, tight-knit community. Most of the cabins were empty until ski season kicked into high gear in January, so even just before Christmas, the handful of winterized cabins were mostly empty.

The Moon Lake distribution plant was ten miles from the lake itself, but the town prided itself on being known for its spring water. "I go down and take a piss in that pure spring water every morning," is a favorite thing that locals told visitors over a few beers.

On one edge of the lake, the remnants of what looked like a small camp.

A semi-circle of small cabins. One larger one, more of a house than simply a summer cabin.

An old, rotten arch of a sign in front of the gravel drive up to the house said, COBBLE CHRISTIAN SUMMER

CAMP FOR SAVED CHILDREN. The lettering, gray and faint.

Wind blew it back and forth. The lights on the porch of the house wavered.

The snow came down in the darkening wood around it.

A girl yelled inside.

2

Monica Scrubb had been sixteen when she'd first met Duane Cobble, and she had run away from her third group home up in Palmdale just to be with him. That was back when he did the route up through the mountains, instead of down into the flatlands below. She had been desperate to get out of the last place and had met Duane at a truck stop. He'd been eating creamed chipped beef, and she'd had a cup of watered-down coffee and a bear claw, which nabbed her last dime. Duane had not been cute, nor had he been particularly charismatic, but she knew when a guy was hot for her, and she needed to get the hell out of Dodge and find a new place to live.

He'd been good to her, at least better than the guy running the group home, who'd pawed her up and down, and the damn lesbos, who had been on her like flies on shit every night when she went to bed. She was only just eighteen now, and had thought that she and Duane would be okay together for a while.

But then that witch, his mother, had been taking

him over, slowly but surely. Monica Scrubb hoped that the witch would die so she and Duane could start their little family without the nastiness.

The witch and the dog. Death's coming for both of 'em.

Monica slept five hours a day. Pissed her off to no end. Got up in the middle of the day to relieve Duane or the visiting nurse to go sit with the damn witch and hear her complain about life and about how Jesus had forgotten her.

Then, at nine, she had to change back into her Donut Queen outfit and head back down the mountain to Bannock where the Donut Queen's Castle awaited her, full to the brim with the stink of grease and day-old coffee.

It wasn't the life she'd signed on for, and pissed was her normal state of mind.

And Duane had been getting worse. Duane had been spending more time down in that cave than with her.

And he'd been getting rougher with the sex. He didn't care about her feelings anymore.

But she'd show him.

3

"We're havin' a baby!" she shouted, throwing a spoon at him all the way from the kitchen.

The spoon barely missed his scalp and went clattering onto the floor by the TV. The old dog perked up and raised his head to start howling.

"Shut up, Jojo!" she cried out. "Goddamn it,

Duane, you promised that when the baby comes we'd have our own place."

"We got the other cabins," Duane said, his voice small, like a little boy's.

"Rat traps," she said. "That's all they are. Leaky roof, black widow infested, snake hotels is what they are. I should just burn those cabins down. Jesus, Duane. I mean, Jesus."

"She's usin' the Lord's name in vain again!" the old woman shouted from her bedroom.

"Shut the hell up!" Monica shouted, half turning to stare at the door. Then, in a quieter voice, "You tell that bitch to lay off talkin' about my family like we was white trash, Duane, or so help me God I am gonna put her face in her own shit next time she starts in on me."

"Don't talk about her that way," Duane said. "She's a saint. She's a saint."

"She is a sick bitch," Monica spat. "And you are a sick fuck, and we are gonna have a baby, you goddamn Jesus Freak. You and me. Whether you like it or not."

That's when Duane rushed over to her and slammed his fist as hard as he could against her jaw.

Before she blacked out, Monica heard a slight cracking sound.

4

She woke up seconds later. He had already brought her to the couch, and he sat on the floor next to her.

"You okay?"

She hesitated before answering to draw out that worried look on his face. "I guess. You sorry for hittin' me?"

"Yes."

"Good. Get me a ciggie."

"Okay."

"Jesus, Duane, we got a baby coming in six months, and you ain't done none of the things you promised. You ain't done all the big world things you said you was gonna do when I met you. You had plans then, baby. Plans. I shoulda stayed in Palmdale and let Granger play poke-Monica for all it matters. We got a baby. Thanks," she said, snatching the cigarette from his hands. She leaned forward as he flipped up the lighter and got the little flame up. She took a nice deep drag. "I gave up meth for this baby, honey. You need to keep up your end of the bargain. I'm killin' myself, I mean killin' myself at that place, donut crap in my hair, customers grabbing my ass when I pour coffee." Her voice went from a young woman's to a little girl's, a baby voice. "I just want you to be my daddy and take care of me and our baby, Duaney."

"I will."

"I know you need private time. I know all men do. But you been spending all that time down in that cave."

"I talk to God there."

"Sure you do. I understand. It's important to you. That's why I never go down there. Men got private things to take care of." She didn't want to tell him that she was happy when he spent time in that old bomb shelter. It kept him from bothering her if she was home. "But I need you to start makin' plans for our baby."

5

It watched her but didn't want her to know. It had let the Other One take it over. Watching the whore with her talk about babies, when it knew that the only baby that she'd pop out would be the Antichrist. It knew that the only seed it had was the Other One's seed. That was why it was chosen. That was why its daddy had tried to teach it to hurt itself, to drive the Other One out of its body.

It had only begun to think of how it would stop the Antichrist from being born.

But other things were on its mind.

Jojo, the only good dog who ever had lived. He was dying.

And its mother. She was a saint. She was second only to the Virgin Mary. She was a Queen of Angels.

And she was going to Heaven too soon.

The whore and her Devil child would go to Hell.

It just had to figure out when it would send them to Hell.

Whenever it looked at Monica, the whore, it remembered its sister Ruthie and how beautiful Ruthie had been before she was sent to Hell.

Monica was like Ruthie.

Ruthie and it and its brother playing together as children.

Playing together and finding out their badness.
Their hellish natures.

Its daddy with the boiling water, showing it how it didn't have any pain because it had the Devil inside it.

6

Monica glanced at her watch. She shook her wrist slightly. "Damn, I just bought this two weeks ago, and it already's slowin' down. I gotta go in at seven tonight, baby. Don't drive me this time. I can just take your truck."

"I need the truck," it said.

"Well, my car ain't making it down in the snow."

"I need it."

She sat up on the couch, touching the edge of her jaw, and back to her lips. She was used to being hit. Even liked getting a slap sometimes, it knew. But it felt bad for hitting her so hard. "Okay. Take my truck. That's okay. You need to go into work."

Then its mother began calling out to it from the other room.

7

"Mama?"

"I don't wanna die," she said.

It shut the door behind it, and went to sit in the little metal chair by her bed. It moved the tubes that hung down around her so that it could see her better while it was talking to her.

"You won't die."

"I will, Duane. I will. I'll go to Heaven and see Daddy again."

"Don't talk like that."

"I guess I got to die. I guess that's the Lord's way."

It reached across the covers and took her hand in its own, feeling the rough warmth.

" 'Member when Daddy used to talk about the sweet hereafter? The angels?"

It smiled. "Sure."

"I thought you were dead once," she said. "I dreamed it. After Ruthie died. I was so sad, Duane. I slept for days. Do you remember? I slept and barely ate anything. Daddy kept telling me that it was the Lord's way. That the Lord was calling Ruthie and it was my pride that kept me from seeing that."

"Ruthie went to Hell," it said, and then wished it hadn't said anything about Ruthie.

"I don't know," its mother said. "Sometimes I think Daddy was wrong. Ruthie was headstrong. She was a fighter. And yes, the Devil was upon her at times. There's no denying that. Remember the revivals? Remember the camp?"

"I was born after the camp closed."

"Oh, yes. Yes. Now I recollect, that's true. We used to run the most wonderful Bible studies for the children. All children are little angels, Duane. Even Ruthie, as much as Daddy tried to get the demons out of her, even Ruthie was a little angel. Maybe I'll see her. Maybe if I go to Heaven, I can see her."

"Maybe," it said. But it knew that Ruthie was in Hell. In the darkness of Hell forever. Until the end of days. Ruthie was the Whore of Babylon the Great. Ruthie brought Devils out when she spoke. That was what his daddy had preached.

"If I die soon," its mother said, "if I die soon . . . there's something I need to tell you. I can't feel good about dying if I don't let you know."

"Mama?"

"I promised your daddy I wouldn't tell you. But I should tell you. You should know." Its mother cleared her throat.

It felt her hand clutch its tighter.

"Pain's comin' back."

"Want more?" it said, reaching to the small button on the side of the tube where the morphine came down.

"Little more," she said. "More."

It pressed the button slightly, then released.

Then again.

"You know I always loved you the best. We took in those other children. I never understood Ruthie or why she was so troubled. You weren't like that. Not as much. You kids got up to no good some-times, but I know children do that. But the other children we took in. Do you remember them?"

It nodded. "My brother."

"Yes, there were three little boys at different times. Andy and Brian and Mikey."

"I talk to Mikey sometimes."

"Do you? How is he?"

"He's perfect," it said.

"I loved that little wild boy. I loved all my children. All of you troubled, but just in need of prayer and saving. Remember what it was like back then? I woke up every morning happy. Your daddy did, too. He had his troubled times, but when we helped other Christian children, he was happy. He took you boys down to the shelter to pray every day. Every single day. And when you ran away . . ." She kept talking, but it didn't listen much. It pressed the little button on the morphine so she'd have an easier time of it. Her pain could be fierce. It didn't like her talking about those days, back when it was a kid, back when it was in the Mad Place too much.

It had not run away from home at all, but its daddy had put it down in the Mad Place for days on end. It had been a secret from its mother, and it knew it deserved to be there. But its mother had thought that it had simply run off to go camping in the woods the way, its daddy had explained to her, that bad boys sometimes do.

Its mother had never known what they'd all been up to in the Mad Place. Or why its father spent so much time there, trying to save them.

Trying to save Ruthie from her destiny, preordained in perdition.

Its mother never even knew how Ruthie had gone straight to Hell. Its mother had been that sensitive, that gentle, that she had no idea how Daddy had sealed Ruthie up in the place between Heaven and Hell, buried alive in the bowels of the earth.

"Duane?" its mother asked, her gnarled hand

pressing against his fingers. "Duane? You thinking about that whore?"

"She's gonna be my wife. Don't talk like that."

"She's a whore if there ever was one, and you know it, and your daddy'd know it if he were here. Don't you let her ruin your life, Duane. She's trash and she knows it and she never even got baptized, she's that bad. After I die, I want you to find a good woman. A woman like me," its mother said. "Someone who . . ." Her voice trailed off.

"Mama?" it asked.

Then it looked at the hand that was not holding its mama's hand.

The other hand had been pressing on the morphine too much.

If thy left hand offend thee, cut it off.

It let go of the intravenous tube and let go of its mother's hand. She was off dreaming, sleeping without pain, and that was all that mattered.

"You won't die tonight, Mama," it said softly. "I love you too much."

It always gave her a little more morphine at night, just in case one of the little birds in the Mad Place started screaming.

She didn't need to hear that kind of thing.

Chapter Forty-two

1

Fasteau took the curves of Route 18 too fast, and when they started hitting the accumulating gray slush as they reached higher elevations, Laymon put her hands on the dashboard as if this would somehow save her in an accident. The road up the mountain was windy and gave her a lurch in her stomach now and then, particularly the way Fasteau hugged the outer curves, giving Jane a murky view of the canyons and valley below.

"We're not rushing."

"What the fuck," Fasteau said.

"Just slow down," she said, nearly under her breath.

It would normally take thirty minutes to get to Blue Jay, one of the first major communities up in the mountain range, but because of the snow, they clocked it at fifty minutes, and then, with the sun just going down, visibility "sucks big time," Fasteau said.

"Ever the poet," Jane said.

"I gotta pee," he said.

"Okay. Pull over at the next lookout area. See? Look, it's coming up," she said.

2

They pulled over onto gravel, and then onto the paved area that curved out a bit from the mountain road, overlooking the entire valley. It was misty gray with rain below, but that was nothing compared with the snow coming down.

She got out of the car, stretching.

He went over to the edge of the guardrail to relieve himself. "Tell me if you see anyone coming!" he shouted back.

"Are you kidding? I'm selling tickets."

When he'd zipped up and headed back to the car, he pointed at the wooden sign that had the words SCENIC OVERLOOK on it. "I bet you couldn't hit that sign."

"Don't get my competitive spirit up, I just might do it."

"You couldn't do it if you wanted to."

"Fasteau, sometimes I feel like I'm partnered with a great big ape, only that's an insult to apes everywhere."

"I just think you're not up for the requal tomorrow."

She actually had to bite her tongue—press down

on it with her front teeth to keep from saying the nasty words she'd begun thinking.

Then she said, "Let's think more about Lucas Conroy and a little less about who has the bigger dick."

The sun was far over to the west somewhere, hidden from the gray-white view of cloud and storm.

The world began to darken as she got back into the car.

She didn't pray a lot, but she sent a little prayer out for Lucas, just because she didn't want to believe that God wouldn't somehow protect him. But God hadn't protected the other kids.

And that's when they got the call from the valley.

Another kid had been found.

Chapter Forty-three

Elise drove up the narrow road that went beside the main highway. The wind had picked up, and the snow came down at a slant. The sky darkened gradually.

Elise flicked on the car's interior light.

Scoleri kept up his chatter. "I used to come up here when I was a boy."

"So the Red Angel is here?"

Scoleri shut down. Closed his eyes. No words.

Trey glanced at Elise's eyes in the rearview mirror.

"What's going to get you to tell us what we need to know?"

Suddenly, Scoleri opened his eyes. "You want to be inside my head? You want to come live here with me? Do you? If you do, you will not be the same. You will not live your happy little life of comfort, your suburban dreams of sweet birdsong. You want to crawl inside my mind? Because that's what you're going to do if you want to find the boy. Or should I call him 'the little bird'—that's what our dear Red Angel calls him. And you know what the Devil does to birds? He cuts off their wings. He slices them and he makes pretty little ornaments for angels out of them. Little bloody angels so he can have a choir in Hell. You want to see what I've seen? What I hear from the Devil? What I know? There are other children in the Devil's choir. Some of them never fly away. Some of them go missing, only no one has ever known it because they came from families who didn't care. They were easy for the Devil to take, but they aren't his angels. Do you know what an angel is, Trey? I mean, really, let's talk about it. Do you know?"

Trey nodded. "A messenger of God."

"And who is God?"

Trey hesitated. "According to you, you are God."

"Good boy," Scoleri said. "I am God. And the nature of God is what?"

"To create."

"Not just create. The nature of God is to forgive."

"Is he asking for your forgiveness?" Trey asked.

"He's the Devil. Of course he is."

"Are these children sent out as messages for you?"

"Does God send messages for Himself?"

"You lost me."

"That's because you're not inside my head yet. Once you are, you'll have the key. When you have the key," Scoleri said, turning his head to look out at the snow and the oncoming night, "then maybe

275

you can open the door and get inside me. The way I know you want to be inside me. And then you, and my dear Elise, will find that little angel before it gets all red with blood."

Chapter Forty-four

Jane Laymon was on the cell phone with Tryon.

"Is it Lucas Conroy?"

"It's a girl," Tryon said. "No idea of identity yet. The wings around her neck. Might've been dead just a few hours. Maybe more. We can't quite tell yet."

"Where?"

"In the foothills. Your town. Within four miles of Elise Conroy's house and a mile from the Latimers."

"He's moving fast," Jane said.

"Too fast. And too rough. This one is all torn up, Jane. This one looks like a mountain lion got to her."

"Should we head back?"

"No, go ahead and check out the guy up there, and also go by the Moon Lake offices. They've got night staff, and maybe someone there knows one of these guys well."

"Anything pan out on Pratt?"

"Well, he's nervous. He's got good reason. Today

was his delivery schedule to the Conroys', only he says he didn't deliver because he knew they had plenty of bottles already. We'll keep him occupied. How far are you from Cobble?"

"Maybe another forty. It's slow going. The roads are getting bad up here."

Chapter Forty-five

Duane Cobble heard it clearly, starting with a humming in its head.

Abraxas.

Coming.

Chapter Forty-six

The Volvo continued its climb up the narrow road. Elise was careful on the curves.

Have to get him to say something definite. Something that will tell me. Trey wracked his brain trying to think fast. *Get him to talk, then call the cops and get the hell back to Darden.*

"Did I tell you about my wonderful childhood? I know I told Elise."

"You were raised all over Southern California," Elise said, nodding.

"You lived up here," Trey said. "Big Bear?"

"Let's not get ahead of ourselves. I lived in many places, all of them white trash, state fund-grubbing, fly-traps: Mentone, Barstow, Chino, Cucamonga. Other places. Sometimes for a few weeks, sometimes months, once or twice for a year."

"The year you don't talk about," Trey said.

Scoleri leaned forward toward the back of Elise's neck.

Trey was ready to pull him back fast if he tried anything.

"I guess you shared my files with him, oh doctor my doctor."

"Back," Trey said.

Scoleri briefly flickered a glance at Trey, then leaned back in the seat. "I lived at one house that was more than just a house. It was a regular revival meeting. We were filthy little sinners all set to be saved. In the summer, we worked at the Bible camp for children that this family ran. Servants to children even more fortunate than we. The papa of the house was a minister who had been thrown out of his own church somewhere farther up, maybe Victorville. He'd hightailed it to this place, bought a little land with what he could steal from the little old ladies whose souls needed saving. Ran a little weekend camp in the summers where Jesus Freaks dumped their kids. But it wasn't doing so well, and Papa Bear thought maybe it was because of the little Baby Bears. Me being one of them. At one point, there had been a few other kids at this place, a regular group home without the home. Only those kids had run away or been sent elsewhere. Who knows. But I was stuck there for a year. I found out what I liked, what I enjoyed, right in that little home. Papa Bear, he was good at keeping it secret from Mama Bear. He had this place, this secret little hiding place in the rocks. He called it the Mad Place. It was the part of Hell that leaked through into Heaven, he said. He made all of us children gather

281

'round in it. He told us that God wanted children to suffer. It was right there in the Bible. But you see, I was smarter than my new brother and sister who spent time there with me. I knew I was Abraxas, the God of All, and that Papa Bear was just your average looney tuney. I knew, Trey, that Papa Bear had a kink, and it had something to do with the pain he inflicted on his own children. Sometimes, me, too. But his own kids, he was the worst with them. Little girl named Ruthie, she got it worse than all of us. Papa took a shine to her, I think. He didn't know I knew, but he watched her when she dressed. He didn't touch her. Not in that way. But he knew she had tempted him to terrible, sinful ways. He called her the Whore of Babylon in the Mad Place, and scourged her flesh to drive the demons out of her. He loved doing that. He loved the barbed wire slashing at her pale little back. He loved watching her squirm when he pressed cigarettes against her bare shoulder blades. Truth is, I learned a few tricks from him. And then, my brother, we were bestest friends. We did everything together. We shared our secrets. Papa Bear liked to hit him, too, liked to take little sharp knives from the kitchen and carve words into his back. I'm not even sure of his name right now, because we were supposed to call him 'it.' "

"Must've been awful," Elise said.

"Not in the least. I loved it there. They were my first real family. Some weeks, we'd spend the whole time in the Mad Place. It was dark. It was wonderful. Sometimes we'd be put to the task of writing Bible verses over and over on the walls as punishment."

"For what?"

"Being who we were. Papa Bear didn't know I was God, and he didn't know God's name, but I did. And I knew that he was teaching me about Hell. That's what I needed to learn. Ruthie, she got taught that demons can't get driven out. And it, well, my brother was unfortunate enough to become his father a little too well, I guess. But he always had the Devil in him. In a cage in his mind. I taught him where to put the Devil. How to treat it. How to make it go deep into his tissues. Into a dark part of him that he could lock up for a long time if he wanted."

"Are we headed there?" Trey asked, looking forward, up the road. A sign came up.

MOON LAKE, 5 MI.

BIG BEAR, 27 MILES

"Moon Lake?" Elise said.

"I'm not telling. Not yet. Just keep driving. I love this old road. Look, see how there's a kind of embankment to the left, and to the right, just a little roll space into the woods, and then, down the mountainside? It's so beautiful here. It's not like the main highway. This is where old-timers used to go up. This is how I knew the route when I was little because when the social worker finally took me out, noticing how I had cigarette burns on my stomach, this is the road she took. And I thought, *This is just so beautiful. So secret. Why would anyone take 18 when they could take this lovely loopy road?*"

"There was no investigation," Trey said. "A social

worker got you out of there. But there was no in-vestigation."

"Why should there be?" Scoleri said. "Papa Bear killed himself a few years later. I never talked. I never squealed on people who were good to me. You work at a state hospital for crazy killers. But if you had other jobs, you might understand. Not all social workers are the good kind. Some have prob-lems of their own. This one, the one who really adored me and was worried about me, he was a good family man, he was a good upright man from San Pascal. Probably someone who lives not far from you, Elise. Maybe down the block, for all I know. But he liked the unfortunate little boys who understood him. He got off on our sad little tales. But he didn't like to write them up. He didn't like to take action. Maybe because he had more to hide than anyone knew. I don't know. I never got to know him all that well. But do you know the sad-dest thing about this sad, sad story of Ruthie and my Devil brother?"

Trey hated to admit it, but Scoleri's story fasci-nated him. "What?"

"Ruthie got buried alive in the Mad Place. She never made it out of there. I used to hear her some-times. Just screaming. Screaming. Then she got real quiet. So quiet it was as if she had never existed at all."

Chapter Forty-seven

1

Snow slanted as it fell. Laymon could feel the pressure of the wind on the car in a gentle tugging.

Fasteau was silent all the rest of the way up the mountain, and she enjoyed it, but by not thinking about what a creep Fasteau could be, she started to think about the victims. She wondered who the child was who had just been found. She thought about Elise Conroy, about having met her briefly in a meeting that Tryon had called with her on Friday, soon after the first victim had been found. About the coincidence of a consulting psychiatrist being someone whose child would be kidnapped. She wondered how Conroy might hook up to the Red Angel—why her son? Why that morning? Why just a few days after the first victim? Had someone seen her? Had the killer known that she was consulting? How was she connected to the other parents? She wasn't, really. She was just another unknown neighbor in the nicer parts of San Pascal. If the water-delivery theory was right, she was just another unfortunate customer of the Moon Lake Pure Spring Water company of Moon Lake, California.

How many were there in San Pascal? A thousand households that took Moon Lake Water? Some had to take Arrowhead or one of the other competitors. How many children were potential targets for this guy just because they got that particular brand of bottled water?

She closed her eyes for just a moment, the images of the children's faces going through her mind.

Speak to me.

Tell me what you know.

She felt ridiculous for thinking it. Something in her mind wanted to relax, wanted to listen to the dead children.

Tell me what you saw. Who he is. Where he is.

Is he a friend? Did he grab you? Did he force you? Did he take your hand? Does your mother know him? Were you frightened?

She almost didn't want to know the answers to the questions.

2

Laymon and Fasteau arrived in Moon Lake by dark, and the snow continued to fall. It was not a fierce storm, nor was it a blizzard by any measure, but the snow had begun piling up on the roadside, drifts rose along the fir-lined drive up to Moon Lake itself, and the police car slid now and then on patches of black ice on the pockmarked road up to the small town center.

"Some town," Fasteau said. "Reminds me of *Deliverance*. Squeal like a peeg."

"I think it's cute," she said. "Want a cup of coffee?"

Chapter Forty-eight

"Ruthie died," Trey said. "Were you sad?"

"You're not in my head yet, Trey," Scoleri said. He looked at Trey with a strangely sympathetic expression. If Trey didn't know his record, he would've thought that Scoleri was actually warm-blooded. *He really believes he's Abraxas. Some god of the universe. Some great omnipotent power. Like out of a comic book: the arch-villain. Not the God of Bibles and Korans and Torahs. Not the deities of other religions. He is some kind of amalgam of religious belief and comic books. He had made up his sense of who he was from childhood things: the religion he'd been tortured with, and a child's sense of power over others.*

"I'd like to get into your head more," Trey said.

"Cool, as they say."

"Help me do that."

Trey glanced at Elise. She was listening carefully, but having to be equally careful about the turns in the road. It zig-zagged as it followed the mountain too closely, and the Volvo bounced as it went over one of several bumps in the old road.

"The easiest way to get in my head is for me to read your mind."

"Feel free."

"You don't believe I can do it. That I can hear what people are thinking. What they're about."

"I do believe," Trey said.

"Liar," Scoleri laughed. "That was a half-assed effort to get into my pants, Trey. How do you think I know what our Red Angel is up to?"

"I don't know. Maybe it's because you're Abraxas. God of All."

"Maybe." Scoleri smiled.

"What is he up to right now?"

"This minute?"

"Yes."

"He's trying to keep the Devil in him at bay. He's got him in a chapel of the damned, with an angel and a virgin and me, his God. But it's got bad stuff in it, too. It's the heart of the Mad Place. It's a place in the earth where Papa Bear kept us. Down, down, down. When the world ends, it's the safest place to be. That's what Papa Bear thought. That's what he believed. Some nut had built it before Papa Bear ever owned it. It was a bomb shelter. Under the house, but you couldn't get there from the house anymore. You had to go down this little path to it. We lived down there almost all the time. When Papa Bear got his feeling about the end of the world. Just the kids. He thought we should stay there when the world ended. But it's a place between Heaven and Hell, and Lucas is there. Sweet pure Lucas. The Devil wants to stop little Lucas's breath. He wants to baptize the boy. To sanctify him so that the Devil can't get to him. You see, he hasn't been killing them because he is evil. That's the good in him. He wants to baptize them and then put them to sleep. A gentle sleep. He wants them to go to heaven. Before the Devil in him can come out and devour them whole. The Devil is getting stronger in him. He can't control it anymore. But he wants to change, you see. That's why he's giving me his little angels. He wants me to know. He wants forgiveness."

Without wanting to, Trey let down his guard. He felt as if something was wrong. Something terrible within himself. As if, just staring at Scoleri, he'd begun thinking like him. Imagining some shadow man baptizing Lucas Conroy, wet fingers on the boy's forehead.

Scoleri looked out the window suddenly, as if in the darkness, which had deepened with each minute, he'd see something there. Something on the roadside.

Trey saw it, too. A light in the woods, on a rocky overhang.

So close to Moon Lake. *That's where he is. He lives in Moon Lake.*

Trey had been through it once or twice growing up. Didn't know it well, other than it was a redneck outpost of the San Bernardino Mountains. Friendly, quiet, but not particularly charming. He drank the Moon Lake spring water, sometimes, too.

When Scoleri turned to look at him again, Trey's mind flashed on the gun.

Scoleri's face had changed somehow.

He was a chameleon.

His look had gone from boyish-innocent to something that seemed, in the shadowy light of the car, like a vampire from a horror movie. He had a smile on his face, but it was too broad. Too knowing. His eyes did that trick—of blurred, rapid movement, as if he were not entirely human.

And then, faster than Trey realized, Scoleri's entire face became a blur as it moved too rapidly toward his own.

Chapter Forty-nine

1

Scoleri slammed his head as hard as he could into Trey Campbell's forehead.

Trey flailed backward, the back of his scalp hitting the window of the car door.

In the front seat, Elise Conroy cried out, and Scoleri moved more swiftly than Elise thought possible for a human being.

One thought shot through her mind: *What have I done?*

She felt his teeth tearing at the nape of her neck.

She twisted the steering wheel.

She reached for the glove compartment to the right, but had to get her hand back on the wheel.

The road seemed to shoot out in the opposite direction.

The car spun on the ice and slush.

2

From the road, if you were watching, you'd have seen the Volvo spin on the narrow road, barely missing, going to the right, downward along the mountainside. Instead, it spun to the left, and into the embankment, and then slid down into the woods, along a stream that ran just beneath the next curve of the road above it.

The sound of airbags popping.

No sound at all for a very long time.

The snow was soft and deep along the embankment. It seemed to add a cushion of quiet to the night around it.

3

After several minutes, a man kicked the door open with his feet, which were cuffed. His forehead and scalp were bloody.

He bent his knees, arching his spine as he lay across the backseat. His legs seemed to twist back on themselves like they were made of rubber. He moved his arms down, so far that they seemed to dislocate from his shoulders. His spine continued to arch, and it was as if he would bend over backwards from the lying-down position.

And then, swiftly, his arms rose in front of him. Cuffs remained on.

He slid forward. Got out of the car.

He went around to the driver's side door. Opened it with some difficulty.

A woman was frantically trying to undo her shoulder harness. Her legs were trapped.

The man with the cuffs on his feet and on his hands leaned into her.

Over her face.

Whispered something.

For the barest second, there was a scream, a woman's, but it was muffled, just as the sounds of the forest and mountain were muffled with the heavy coat of snow.

The man appeared to be going to work with his bare hands on the woman's face.

Chapter Fifty

Trey Campbell lay like a broken doll in the backseat. He had an enormous bruise on his forehead, and blood all along his scalp and running along his ears, down his neck.

His eyes were closed, but he was breathing.

In the front seat, Elise Conroy squirmed as Michael Scoleri held her down, using his body weight, holding his hands over her nose and mouth until she was very, very still.

Rummaging through her purse, flung on the other side of the Volvo, Scoleri found a small pair of fingernail scissors.

He returned to the dead woman in the driver's seat.

He wanted something to remember her by.

Chapter Fifty-one

1

When they checked in with the local deputy at the trailer just at the beginning of town, Jane let Fasteau ask all the questions about Duane Cobble because she knew Fasteau's masculinity and ego needed some stroking after her complaints about his driving on the way up the mountain. The cop on duty had nothing but nice things to say about Duane, although one comment stuck in Jane's mind after she and Fasteau went back to their car. "The Cobbles always kept to themselves since Duane's dad died." By itself, it was not a very damning comment, but given the nature of the visit, it planted a warning in Jane's head.

She and Fasteau drove around the rim of the lake, with the snow and ice increasing with each mile. The Cobble place was twelve miles around the lake.

When they arrived at the house, the only one with a front porch light on, Fasteau said, "Holy shit."

2

She glanced through the darkness and falling snow to the small cabins that were off a bit in the woods.

The main house, hardly more than a cabin itself. Lights came from its windows. An old junk heap of a Monte Carlo, which looked like it was at least twenty years old and had never been maintained, sat in the driveway. Out in a clearing, an old truck up on cinderblocks, its doors completely taken off.

Six smaller one-room cabins in a semi-circle in the woods.

Some kind of graying arched sign over the drive, but the darkness obscured it.

"It's the Bates Motel."

"I doubt we can take a guy in just because he looks like he lives like a crazy person," Jane said.

"Yeah, true. Everyone I saw back in that town looks like a loon. Including the deputy."

The headlights cast a beautiful but disturbing brightness across the falling snow, through the pines that edged the property, and the thick woods beyond. They were at the edge of a hillock that went downward right behind the last cabin.

"This really is Bumfuck, Egypt," Fasteau said.

"Looks like this place has been going to the dogs for years."

A light was on in the main house.

They parked on the side of the road, and both got out. "We're going to be stuck here all night," Fasteau said. "We may have to rent one of these cabins. Just the two of us."

"Tell you what, you get a cabin. I'll go back and take my chances with the icy roads."

Chapter Fifty-two

Trey opened his eyes briefly.

Thought he heard a snipping sound.

Fought for consciousness. *Elise?*

We fucked up, he thought.

Then he felt himself drifting back into a cold sleep.

Chapter Fifty-three

1

The guy who opened the door looked to Jane like he had just woken up from a nap.

"Can I help you?"

She got the preliminaries out of the way, just the basics of *show the badge, don't get his suspicions up, and see if he had anything to say,* or if she could notice anything in the house itself.

He made no move toward inviting her in, and she didn't have any legal way to get in unless he invited her. She wondered, briefly, how Sykes and Tryon were doing down in the valley.

"My mother's been sick," he said.

"I'm sorry to hear that, Mr. Cobble."

"Well, it's been a long time coming. She's in her room, but she's sleeping."

"Well, this won't take long."

Jane glanced around the modest home. It was a bit of a mess, and a dog that was so old it practically was dragging its own hindquarters when it got up, came over to her. Fasteau remained behind her, standing by the door.

"We're just checking in with people from the Moon Lake Water company." She knew not to say more. If this was a suspect, or even if this guy might guess who among the other delivery men was the most likely suspect, she was not going to feed him information that would come back and bite her in the ass during a trial.

"Is there a reason?"

"Routine. You've probably seen the news?"

His face betrayed nothing. He was a big man, a little weary looking and frayed about the edges, but he looked like your basic big dumb guy. Nothing felt different around him, she got no sense of weirdness or hesitation in his part.

"I don't watch the news much. We don't got cable. Our reception sucks."

"Well, as you may know, there's a little boy who's missing. We're just talking to anyone who has come in contact with this boy to see if we can learn anything, or if there might be a witness to where he might've gone." She stumbled over her words, but had tried to be careful not to inform too much.

She watched his eyes. Either he was very good at this, or he was completely innocent.

"Geez, that's terrible. Do I know this kid?"

"He's on your Tuesday/Thursday route. His name is Lucas Conroy."

Fasteau drew the photo out of his coat. He passed it to Duane Cobble, who looked at it, nodding. "He's a nice little kid, too. I know the Conroys. I didn't know his name, but that kid was really nice. What a terrible thing. I hope nothing's happened. Maybe it's . . . I mean, I hear a lot about divorced fathers kidnapping their own children."

Small alarm in her head: He mentioned the word "kidnapping" and she had not. She had just said "missing." This might mean nothing. But it might mean something. "Well, we didn't mean to bother you without calling first," she said, a minor-league lie. "But I was over at the distribution plant and thought I might just drop by."

"Three other guys do my route," he said. "But they're all good guys. You think maybe one of them did this? No. No way. None of them could do that kind of thing. I don't think it was one of us."

"I don't think it was either, Mr. Cobble. We're trying to find out if anyone saw anything unusual recently in the Conroys' neighborhood. Any unusual activity. Or cars parked on the street. Anything you might've noticed or heard."

"Nope," he said after a moment. "I can't think of anything. I'm sorry to hear about this. I had no idea. What a terrible world. I hope it turns out happy, like when they found that little girl in Utah a while back. I'll pray for his return."

He stood there, lingering with his hand on the edge of the doorframe. He wanted to close it.

2

Jane felt something click in her head.

Something wasn't right. She wasn't sure what.

She glanced back at Fasteau who stood behind and next to her.

Then she looked back to Duane Cobble.

She wished she could tell Fasteau what she was thinking. She wasn't sure if she should say goodbye, make a retreat to the car, and then just phone this one in or not.

If you do, and it's nothing, you'll have wasted a lot of people's times.

If you want to go, go big.

Aim true.

She went with her instinct.

3

"Would you mind if we came inside, Mr. Cobble? It's freezing out here, and we can probably speak more comfortably . . . you might be able to provide us with some insight into your coworkers." *There,* she thought. *That sounded good.*

If he were innocent, he wouldn't really mind either way.

If he were guilty, he had to invite them in.

He had no choice.

Chapter Fifty-four

It heard something in its head.

Not the Devil. Not the Devil.

It sounded like Abraxas. Just for a second.

Like Abraxas was trying to talk to it.

It watched the two cops. They didn't look much like cops, but it knew cops well.

It watched the woman especially. She was tall and looked like she could beat the shit out of somebody.

The man didn't scare it that much.

It opened the door wider, letting them into its house.

The Devil started to gnash its teeth inside its head, but it kept an even keel.

It would get through this. It was sure it could.

As the woman cop spoke, it could tell she was looking all over the room. Looking for things. For stuff.

Looking for something that would make her know that it held the Beast inside it.

It spoke perfectly normal, like it could sometimes when it needed to mimic the way people talked. It told them about the weather, how bad the snow was for its mother's arthritis, how it always flared up when snow came down. It told them about its girl, Monica, even though it called her its wife just to seem more respectable.

It even made a joke with the man about "women," and it could tell that it had pissed off the woman cop too much, so it made another little joke about how men think they're so smart when in reality women run the world. It mentioned the baby that was coming. It was going to be a father.

But the woman's eyes bothered it. She had sharp eyes, like little scalpels, and she was slicing away at the edge of things when she looked at them.

She's a whore. She's a whore and you can't trust whores.

"Is your mother asleep?" she asked.

"Yes, ma'am. She's sleeping through the night. She has her supper and then pretty much is down for the count."

"I'm sorry to hear about her illness, Duane."

She called it by its first name, and that made it uncomfortable. What else did she know about it?

Did she know God, too? Had she been to see Mikey? Had he talked about it to her?

No. Mikey was Abraxas, the all-powerful. The secret name of God.

He'd never talk to a whore about it.

Never.

Her eyes again. It watched where she looked.

The mantel. The fireplace. Jojo. The sofa. The magazines piled on the floor.

It held its breath for a moment, unsure what to say to get them out.

The Other One began to snarl louder.

The Beast wanted out of its cage in its brain.

The Devil wanted to leap out at them.

Not yet. Not now. They'll leave. It'll be okay.

"My mother was sick for a while," the woman said. "It's rough when it's your mother. It's just very tough to get through."

"Did she die?"

"No. She survived. Breast cancer."

It doesn't like either of those words. The Devil likes them. But it hates them.

"She underwent chemo." She kept talking as if she were pretending she couldn't tell that the Other One was coming out inside it, taking it over bit by bit, rising up in its blood like a tea kettle about to whistle. She pretended not to notice, and so did the other cop. But it knew that they were just pretending. "It was rough. But she pulled through, and she beat it."

Without meaning to, it said, "My mother's got the C word, too."

"Oh," she said. "Well, she'll be in my prayers."

It was getting that biting feeling inside it. Like it wanted to attack. Like a lion.

Like the Devil.

"She's got nurses who come in and see her," it said, wishing it could stop, but something in the woman cop had made it feel almost like it had to talk about this. "But I don't think there's much hope."

"Hospice?"

"Sort of," it said.

"Well, I don't want to waste any more of your time," she said suddenly.

It felt relief at her words.

"Officer Fasteau?" She turned to the man.

"Thank you. We'll be in touch later on," the man cop said.

It returned to the door with them.

When it closed the door, locking it, the Other One took over.

Chapter Fifty-five

Outside, walking through the snow, back to the entry to the dirt driveway, the two of them didn't say a word. Jane felt the excitement inside her, tempered with fear.

"I think we have him," she said as she reached for the passenger door.

"I know," Fasteau said, going around the front of the car, headlights still on, snow coming down. "Once Tryon—"

And that's when Jane heard what seemed like an enormous boom, as if a bomb had been dropped down in the valley.

A rifle's blast.

Fasteau was blown back, first against the hood of the car, and then onto the road.

It happened so fast, she didn't even process it, but acted on instinct.

She reached for her Glock, but as she pulled it up, she felt nervous and scared in a way she never had before.

She ran around the back of the car to use it as some kind of shield.

She shot into the darkness, but could not see Duane Cobble—or anyone. She could only see along the line of the headlights, but beyond that, the house had gone dark.

The snow was affecting her vision, but her fear seemed to intensify—her heart raced—she worked to keep her breathing from becoming too rapid— kept telling herself to slow down, to look, to wait. Her mind went blank, and she wondered if she would get out of this alive. As quickly as she could, she glanced behind her, to the road and lake beyond. Many miles away, across the lake, she could barely see the lights of the small town of Moon Lake.

Someone might've heard the sound.

Surely they would've.

How long would it take for someone to come over here?

Could she get to the radio fast enough?

She ruled that out. She held her gun as steadily as she could.

She shouted, "Duane Cobble! Put down your weapon and put your hands over your head!"

She leaned to her left, putting her weight on her left knee.

Fasteau was still. Dead at the edge of the headlight's beam.

Blood on the snow.

"Shit," she whispered.

Visibility worsened as the snow picked up, and

309

she felt as if she'd been crouching behind the car for several minutes, although she suspected only seconds had passed.

Where was he? Christ. Where the fuck are you, Duane?

She tried to focus on the darkness, but the bright headlights kept her eyes unable to adjust to the dark.

Was that him? The darkness against darkness that moved?

"Put down your weapon right now!" she screamed as loud as she could.

It wasn't him. It was just the fir trees themselves, shaking off clumps of snow.

She could hear each of her own breaths as if she had asthma.

Her heartbeat seemed too loud.

She wanted to hold her breath, but knew that would not make this go any easier for her.

She heard a whooshing sound as if something were moving swiftly toward her.

From the right? She looked to the right and saw a blurred shadow in the dark, and for the barest second thought she saw him—

And then, something heavy hit her hard on the back right side of her scalp.

Chapter Fifty-six

"Whore," it whispered.

It set the hunting rifle on the trunk of the car.

Then it went around to the driver's side of the car to turn off the headlights.

The Mad Place

Chapter Fifty-seven

1

In the Mad Place, it had just finished tying up the cop woman, duct taping her mouth, wrapping it around double and tight, checking ropes behind the chair to make sure she couldn't wriggle out of them.

Then he went over to Lucas, who had been in and out of consciousness for several hours. Its mother's pills helped them sleep. That's what they needed, the little birds. Sleep. When the pills didn't work, it used the syringe. But Lucas didn't need the morphine. The pills were working fine.

Lucas took another little white pill from its hand like a good boy. The boy curled up almost in a ball on the dirty mattress near the statue of the virgin. Lucas no longer needed to be tied. No longer needed tape over his mouth. The Mad Place had sent him into another realm in his mind. He was halfway between Heaven and Hell.

As it meant him to be.

2

It was all going to be okay. Everything was going to work out fine for it.

Brother. It heard the voice in its head.

It turned around.

Someone was in the Mad Place with it.

Someone was scratching around the entryway.

And then it saw Abraxas.

God of All.

Its brother.

3

"Duane," Michael Scoleri said from the flickering shadows at the doorway into the Mad Place.

4

It was shocked, standing there, duct tape in one hand.

"Abraxas," it said.

"I heard your prayers. Your messages." Abraxas's beauty was extreme and frightening. Even though it knew not to fear, it could not help but be afraid. "In you, there is greatness. But you must set it free."

"Free?" it asked.

"The Beast. The Devil. The end of days is at hand," Abraxas said, and came over to embrace him. "Within you, greatness."

"I wasn't sure if you heard me."

"I always will hear you," Abraxas said. "I know all. I see all."

"Why have you come here?"

Abraxas spread his arms out wide.

It trembled slightly at the beauty of its brother.

"You have given me angels. And sacrifice," Abraxas said, in the sweetest voice that it had ever heard. "I can't stay long. You know that. I must return to Heaven. But first, go home. Get your rifle. You will need it. Others are coming. You know they will. I have only a few moments here, before I must leave. But first, I want to spend those moments with this woman. This sacrifice."

It understood. It looked over at the cop woman tied to the chair.

She was still out. It may have hit her too hard. But it didn't care. It should've killed her, but it was glad it hadn't now.

She would be a sacrifice to God.

Chapter Fifty-eight

When Jane woke up, she didn't know how much time had passed. She was in a stone room, bound to a chair. Lights flickered above her. She had to orient herself somehow. She barely remembered what had happened at the Cobble house, but then it came back to her suddenly.

Fasteau's dead.

Rope was wrapped around her. Her hands were cuffed behind her. Duct tape over her mouth.

A man crouched down in front of her. His hands on her knees.

It wasn't Cobble.

This one had a boyish look to him, but was in his late twenties. Cobble had a helper?

He leaned into her, and she felt his coldness as he touched the edge of her face.

He ripped the duct tape from her lips.

"I want to hear you when I take my memento," he said.

Then he kissed her on the lips. Before she had a

chance to bite him, he moved his lips up her cheek.

He whispered, "Your beautiful dark eyes."

He pressed himself against her.

It sickened her.

She felt his tongue across her eyelid.

And she knew.

"Beautiful darkness," he whispered.

She used her weight to pivot back, but his weight held her in place.

He liked the power.

She tried to go somewhere else in her mind.

Tried to prepare for what this madman was about to do to her.

And then she felt the suction of his lips against the eyelid of her left eye.

She could not help it.

She screamed.

And screamed.

The pain shot through her like a knife to the skull.

Chapter Fifty-nine

Jane's body went slack.

Scoleri undid her ropes. He lifted her up, holding her to him. She smelled so wonderful. She smelled like pain itself.

Her mind was free. The pain had driven it away for the moment.

Her suffering was fresh.

He kissed her lips and set her down on the mattress, beside the little boy who stared at him without moving.

"Madonna and child," Scoleri said.

Then he went back up to the house to see if he could borrow Duane's car.

It was time for Abraxas to get out into the world.

Chapter Sixty

1

Trey opened his eyes. Looked up. The interior ceiling of the car.

Then, a rush of air to his lungs and a clutching fear.

He sat up, and as he did so felt a hammering pain in his head.

Instinctively, he touched the top of his scalp.

Wet.

Blood.

He had been crammed into an uncomfortable position.

Mother of all migraines pounding at him.

He collected his thoughts.

Deep breaths.

Remembered going off the road.

He saw Elise's hair falling over the back of the seat.

It took him minutes to find the strength to sit up.

Scoleri, gone.

Shit.

"Elise," he said, but his voice was like a croak.

No answer.

"Elise. Elise."

He felt strength in his arms again, despite the soreness. He could move his legs. He felt circulation come back into his extremities.

He rose completely and slid along the car seat.

He looked over the edge of Elise's scalp.

Blood.

Shit.

He got out of the car on uncertain legs. Had to hold the car door for balance.

The driver's door was open wide.

The deflated airbag.

Elise, the steering column pressing down on her legs.

Her eyes, staring.

"Jesus," he gasped, and fell over into the snow on his hands and knees, retching.

He could not get it out of his head.

Her face.

What had been done to it.

What Scoleri had done.

His handiwork.

The Handyman, he'd been called before he'd been convicted and sent to Darden State.

Of course you didn't get me. Didn't kill me. You only go for women. Only when they're vulnerable. Only when you know they can't fight back.

You wanted me to see this. That's half your fun.

You wanted me to see what a monster you are.
You wanted me to get inside your mind.
Well, I'm there, you sick fuck.
Scoleri had taken both of Elise Conroy's eyes.

2

After clenched fists, tears that would not come, and a terrible feeling of helplessness had seized his gut, and after the feeling passed, Trey knew what he must do.

He checked his wristwatch: 10 P.M.

Too much lost time.

Unconscious a couple of hours.

The cell phone, out. He checked the trunk of the Volvo. Flashlight. That was it.

He checked the glove compartment.

Elise's revolver, still there.

He took it, slipping it into his coat pocket.

Lucas, he thought. *Get help. Get cops. Get Lucas.*

With the flashlight, he looked around the snow-covered woods.

Up the embankment.

Up the curve in the road ahead.

A light emanated from within the trees.

A clearing?

Apprehensive, Trey stumbled over the irregular ground, across rocks, up to the roadside.

Dark as all hell.

He went toward the light in the forest, feeling an urgency and a numbness in his mind that was not from the pain at the front of his forehead where

Scoleri had slammed him, nor from the bitter cold of the high elevation of the mountain road where it turned up toward Moon Lake.

A numbness about life itself.

It took him nearly a half hour to get up the road toward the light, and then just a few minutes as he trudged through the snow.

When he first saw it, he wasn't sure what to make of it.

Shining the light along the entrance.

What Scoleri had said. Scoleri hadn't lied at all. Scoleri knew.

It's a place in the earth where Papa Bear kept us. Down, down, down. When the world ends, it's the safest place to be. That's what Papa Bear thought. That's what he believed. Some nut had built it before Papa Bear ever owned it. It was a bomb shelter. Under the house, but you couldn't get there from the house anymore. You had to go down this little path to it. We lived down there almost all the time. When Papa Bear got his feeling about the end of the world. Just the kids. He thought we should stay there when the world ended.

Chapter Sixty-one

1

It seemed surreal, like something out of a fairy tale such as "Hansel and Gretel."

Through the gap in the trees, a thin path, now simply an indentation of white upon white snow. It led to what seemed to be a rock overhang, a crevasse. Three large lights had been set up in trees to light the rocky area. *He's not hiding. Not in the way you'd think. He's not afraid of anyone. Or else . . . or else he wants to be caught. That's all it is. He wants to be caught.*

Trey had to calm his breathing. He felt as if he were close to Lucas.

Above the crevasse, a thick roof-rock, and above that, perched on the jutting mountainside, a small cabin. But in the indentation of granite was what appeared to be a small door—almost a trap door. Had this once been a mine? He knew that there'd been mining throughout the mountains back in the

nineteenth century, so this didn't strike him as particularly odd, although it was an odd sort of mine,
if it had ever been one.

As he approached the door, he noticed that it
was made of some kind of metal and curved out-
ward at the center, almost like a shield. Someone
had made a bomb shelter out of the crevasse. This
was somewhat unusual, but Trey had seen a bomb
shelter built in the early 1960s during the Cuban
Missile Crisis and the Nuclear War fears of that time
in a friend's backyard as a kid growing up in San
Bernardino.

He had read, in magazines and online, about
bomb shelters built into caves and caverns, but had
never seen one before. He went to the door and
pulled on it. It was not locked.

*He's not afraid. He takes them down here. But he's
not afraid. Of course not. He thinks he knows God.
He thinks he has the Devil in him. He thinks he can
make angels.*

Trey stood over the entrance into the cavern, the
metal door open.

For a moment, he felt the way he had standing
outside Program 28's corridor.

2

He shined the flashlight through the doorway.

The entry area was not flat. It dipped nearly immediately down. It was dark, and he could hear
water splashing from within.

As he positioned the light's beam around the entry, he saw a hanging work lamp—barely more than

a bulb fitted within a protective cup of metal. He reached over to it, switching it on. Immediately, it lit the first several feet of the shelter.

The floor was rough and covered with gravel. Water sluiced across the gravel.

An underground spring.

The ceiling was low and had what were not quite stalactites, but small teats of rock, as if water had been dripping from it over the years, although now it was dry.

A smell came up from within. Not unpleasant, but a kind of gust of humid air.

Some source of heat within the shelter.

He took a step in, but turned and glanced back at the snow as it came down.

No one followed him.

Good.

Inside the entrance, he felt more alone that he ever had in his life.

He took another few steps in. The ground slanted downward, and he took care with his steps because of the thin layer of water that rushed along beneath his shoes.

Strangely, it wasn't as cold inside as he thought it should've been.

Warmth. Some source of warmth.

A gently heated breeze came up from within the shelter.

Instinctively, he reached for the rock wall and crouched down a bit, for the ceiling lowered as it went.

Two more steps and he slipped, falling hard on the ground. He looked at the interior walls. Some kind of limestone along the walls. It was light colored, and had been drawn across as if an ancient cave-painting.

The images were horrific, and he knew that he was in the lair of the killer.

Paintings of demons and angels against a yellow blur of what might've been chalk that was meant to imply fire.

Written on the walls, the words:

SUFFER THE CHILDREN TO COME UNTO ME.

3

Trey remembered those words on Scoleri's stomach.

What the hell are you doing here?

Can't call the police. Can't get out in the snow.

Lucas is here. I know he's here. I have to find him. I have to get him out.

Something within him that felt more instinctual, bypassing his brains and his fears, took over.

He had a gun, after all.

He had a gun.

The killer of these children was going to be easy to subdue. He was sure. He worked around these people. He knew that the ones who went after children were the weakest of all. Were the least powerful. Were scared of adults. Afraid of what a grown man could do to them.

And even if he was wrong . . . even if all his experience was in error . . . all his training . . . he had to get Lucas out. He had to save him.

He had to make it turn out all right.

4

As he went farther down the wet floor, he glanced quickly from one wall to the next, recognizing biblical quotes.

End-of-the-world quotes, scrawled across the limestone.

Then I saw an angel coming down from Heaven, holding in his hand the key of the bottomless pit and a great chain

He was cast out into the earth, and his angels were cast out with him

But every man is tempted, when he is drawn away of his own lust, and enticed

Then when lust hath conceived, it bringeth forth sin: and sin, when it is finished, bringeth forth death

5

At a certain point, far enough in that he could still see the light at the entryway behind him, the floor began rising again. Now he knew what the warm humidity was—somewhere within the shelter, there was a hot springs. He had been up to the Arrowhead Hot Springs before, and knew that the underground springs were usually fed by this warm, often nearly boiling water.

Finally, as he went, flashlight in front of him, Trey had to nearly crawl.

This lasted for just a few feet.

Then, having gone upward with the sandy floor, he came into a room that was large enough for him to stand.

This one was lit with white, blinking Christmas tree lights strung up from its ceiling. Somewhere, there was a generator humming.

On the floor in the corner, piles of cans of tuna, beans, Spam, pineapple slices and peach halves, and large twenty-gallon blue plastic jugs that were probably filled with water.

This was a survivalist's dream.

Or nightmare.

He saw a pile of something that at first looked like feather dusters, until he got closer. Two sets of white duck wings, freshly cut, with brownish blood at the joint where the cut had been made.

You were here, not long ago. You've left. Maybe the snow will keep you out. Maybe you're stuck on the road.

On the wall was a crudely drawn image of Christ on the cross.

Someone has scrawled beneath it: *And the ten horns which thou sawest upon the beast, these shall hate the whore, and shall make her desolate and naked, and shall eat her flesh, and burn her with fire.*

He shined his flashlight in all the curves of the room, and saw something move in one of the dark corners.

"Lucas?" he whispered, not feeling right to raise his voice any higher. "Lucas?"

And as the beam of light hit what was there, he nearly dropped the flashlight from fright.

Chapter Sixty-two

1

It was a woman of an indeterminate age, bone thin, her arms strapped to her sides with thick rope. Where her legs should've been, there were bandages around what could only be described as stumps. She was pale and looked as if she had spent her life in darkness, for when the light hit her eyes, her eyelids fluttered like moths, rapidly, as if the bright light were too sudden for her.

She made a noise, but it seemed like the bleating of a sheep.

Her mouth was blackened, and he didn't see teeth in it at all.

"Jesus," he gasped, and moved toward her.

Her eyes were wide and sunken into their sockets as if she had been kept moments away from death.

For months.

Or years.

You know enough about the patients to know what the predatory mind is capable of.

He knew from Scoleri's words.

He knew.

But he was afraid to say it aloud.

"Ruthie?"

Her mouth went wide as if she wanted to scream, but a rasping sound came out.

"Dear God," Trey said. *Sweet Jesus.*

He went and undid the ropes that kept her in the chair. Her arms fell at her side, as if they were already useless.

You kept her here all these years. Just like Scoleri said your father had kept her when you were kids. She's never seen the light of day since she was twelve. When your mother thought she had died from a beating. When it was all covered up. Closed up.

But it's still an open wound.

Dear God. Please God protect her. Please someone help.

Her scalp was nearly bald, with strands of hair hanging down across her face, which seemed crumpled and misshapen. Her body, what could be seen through the rags that were wrapped around her like a funeary winding cloth, was covered with sores. Her arms seemed twisted, and because of her extreme emaciation, she seemed old, although he was fairly sure she was only in her twenties.

She began bleating again. A word seemed to form in his mind—what she was trying to say.

He knew in the next moment that it was too late.

She was trying to warn him about something.

Someone.
Her brother.

2

Trey heard the footstep echo in the stone chamber.
He turned slightly, not wanting to startle the killer.
But wanting to see him. To face him.

Trey felt for the gun in his coat, but even as he
did, he thought that it might not be enough to have
a gun.

He would have to use it, and use it correctly.
Something he had not done much of.
Always a first time.

Chapter Sixty-three

It stood just outside the light of the Mad Place.

Ruthie was squealing. *She is a whore! She is the Whore of Babylon! Do not let her hurt you!*

It saw the man. Didn't know him. Why was he here? Why was all this happening? All these intruders? All this now? Why now? Why just when the Other One was gaining the upper hand?

When the Beast was out and coursing through its bloodstream?

It hated the man as much as it hated itself, and when it saw the side of the man's face it knew the man must die. Or the man must burn. That was it. The man must burn for his sins. *Burn in the eternal fires of the rivers of Hell.*

Chapter Sixty-four

Trey touched the gun.

Began to draw it from his coat pocket.

A blur of movement behind him as the man rushed him.

Trey felt pressure in his side as the man knocked him down.

Got the revolver out.

Sig Sauer. Elise.

The gun went flying out of his hand.

He felt a crack of bone along his jaw.

Darkness.

A seeping pain.

Then nothing.

Chapter Sixty-five

It stood over the man who had intruded on the Mad Place. It glanced over at the whore. She was trying to lift her arms, but could not. She was weak. She moaned as she watched it go over to her and crouch down.

It began pulling the ropes up again, around her arms.

It said nothing to her, to Ruthie, but it knew that Ruthie was somewhere else in her mind. In Hell. Where all of them would be soon.

Once the Beast was out for good.

Then it went over to tie up the intruder.

Chapter Sixty-six

Trey opened his eyes.

Consciousness came back. He felt like he'd been tackled by an enormous linebacker. He was sore all over. He tasted blood in his mouth.

He saw a slightly overweight man in what looked like a green uniform. The man's back was to him. The jacket he wore had a logo of a lake and trees and read: Moon Lake Pure Spring Water.

Duane. Scoleri's brother in foster care. When they were kids. Here, playing in the mountains. Getting punished in this shelter.

Duane refastened the ropes around the pathetic form of his sister.

Trey felt pains in his back and sides, but managed to roll up to a sitting position.

He looked around for the gun, but he couldn't see it anywhere along the rock floor.

Have to use my body weight. He's a big guy. Maybe if I get him off-balance.

Duane turned, hearing the sound of his movement.

Chapter Sixty-seven

It felt the Other One in the cage. It opened the cage to let the Other One out.

The Beast was coming.

It was coming inside its head.

It was burning through its brain to get out and use its flesh to tear the intruder.

It only felt the Beast inside it now.

Its hands seemed like the claws of a lion.

Its feet seemed to move in a blur of motion, as if it was flying to the intruder.

Chapter Sixty-eight

Trey stayed down as Duane came running at him. *With the patients, you lean forward so they come for your face in front of you. When they're close enough, you pull back quickly. They're off-guard. The way Scoleri did in the car. The way he got you.*

Duane did what Trey expected—went for the face. Having the same delusionary idea that many of the patients at Darden State had—that all power was in the face, in the eyes, in the brain. When Duane did this—his hands outstretched to attack— Trey rocked back, maintaining his balance. Duane's eyes widened as he realized that he was going to tip over Trey instead of hitting him. Trey slid to the left. Duane tumbled to the ground. Trey swiftly moved on top of him, a knee to Duane's back.

From Duane's mouth, growling like a dog.

Trey pressed Duane's face against the rock floor, focusing all his weight into Duane's back, but staying clear of his legs. Duane would probably, in another moment, use his hands and a push from his knees to throw Trey off, but Trey reached and got his flashlight fast and slammed it down as hard as he could on Duane's head.

Duane was out.

For the moment.

Trey breathed too fast. He tried to calm himself from within, with a brief mantra that was little more than *easy, easy.* He dragged the unconscious Duane over toward Ruth. Then he swiftly undid the ropes again around Ruth's arms. She had already begun screaming, and it echoed through the chamber like a high-pitched shriek.

Duane was just coming around. He looked up at Trey.

Chapter Sixty-nine

It will kill him and drink his blood! It will sacrifice him like it did the little angels!

It summoned its Devil strength, and it pushed up, feeling nothing but a redness within its body, a fire-power that came from Hell, and it knew that its daddy was right, that it would be the end of the world, that it and Ruthie would one day be set out on their paths to destroy the world.

It swung its elbow into the intruder's ribs.

Chapter Seventy

1

The force of the blow knocked Trey back. The rope went flying.

Duane was up, and Trey had to dodge him quickly.

Jesus, he's strong.

Trey quickly glanced around for the gun, hoping to see it in the twinkling white Christmas light glow.

He felt a swift kick to his groin. Trey doubled-over in nausea and pain.

Then a kick to his head.

Duane stood over him.

Something in his hand.

What? Trey could not quite make it out because Duane's hands were shaking so much. It looked as if Duane were about to explode if that were humanly possible, as if something were boiling in his blood.

Trey realized what his attacker held and his first thought was: *Lucas, I'm sorry.*

"Cocksucker!" Duane shouted. "You don't mess with the Devil. I am going to send your soul to my homeland! You think you know what Hell is! You don't know what Hell is! Fucking worm, you are going to burn for eternity! And when you feel the fires inside you and the worms in your eyes and the cold darkness around you, you will know that you are an it! You are an it and an it means shit and you live in shit and you will die in shit and you will burn in shit!"

His hands clutched a gun. Not the Sig Sauer. This looked like a Glock.

Then Duane began lowing like a cow, alternating with bellowing and a sound like a child crying from deep within his body. He became racked with coughs, but he kept the gun, unsteady as his hands were, on Trey.

Ruthie made a noise, a keening sound. Trey looked over, and she rocked back and forth. She fell forward with a clattering sound.

Distracted for a moment, Duane glanced at her.

As he did, a shot rang out.

To Trey, it seemed as if a second stretched into a perceptive minute in which he saw a brief flare from the gun that Duane held—Ruth crawling on her hands toward him, dragging her torso along as if it were dead weight—a hole blast into Duane's chest, his jacket spraying open with blood—and a strange steam coming from behind Trey's left ear.

2

Trey felt numb all over his body, but found that he could stand. He wasn't shot.

Duane had missed him.

From behind him, from the narrow corridor of stone, a woman in a police uniform emerged, a gun in her hand. She held it in front of her.

Elise Conroy's Sig Sauer.

Her left eye was bloodied and the eyelid swollen shut. Blood covered half her face. She was shivering nearly as much as Duane had been.

Then she collapsed to the floor.

Trey heard sounds like mewling coming from Ruthie, who went to her brother, laying her body across his.

But Duane was not dead. Wounded. He was down.

But he might be able to get up again.

Before even checking on the collapsed police officer, he grabbed the ropes and crawled over to where Ruthie hugged her brother. As gently as he could, he drew Ruthie back. She fought against him feebly, but moved away from Duane.

Not a lot of blood was coming out of Duane's wound, so he assumed that was good. Duane would be caught. He'd go to jail.

Probably end up in Darden State.

Michael Scoleri, already driving into the valley in Duane Cobble's crappy car, pulled over, feeling an intense headache.

Pounding at him.

He put the truck in park and left the engine idling. He leaned against the wall of a liquor store at the edge of a strip mall.

Something in his head seemed to be triggering a massive headache.

He felt he heard Duane Cobble's voice in his head again.

Just a brief flicker of a voice.

Then it was out.

The words he heard in his mind:

Help me, Abraxas. Mikey. God.

Chapter Seventy-one

1

In the bomb shelter, with Duane safely tied up, and Ruthie lying near him, hardly a threat, Trey went to check on the policewoman.

2

"Thank God," she whispered, her voice raspy. "Thank God. I thought I'd die here." Although she seemed to have been beaten up, and he soon discovered that her eye had been pulled out, there was an unusual optimism in her voice.

"You're going to be fine."

"They're monsters. Those men. Monsters."

Trey couldn't respond. It was too soon.

He was afraid to ask about Lucas. He was afraid to hear from this woman that all of this had been a waste.

"The boy," she said. She pointed back to the narrow space between the walls.

"Alive?"

"Scared. Alive. Maybe drugged."

"It's all right. You don't have to talk anymore. It's all right."

"Go. Go. Tell him. Tell him it's all right. Go." She pushed him weakly. "Up. Up above. On the hillside, a house. Car. Phone. Police radio. We're beneath it. The house."

Just above. The Mad Place was between Heaven and Hell.

"Go. I'm fine. Fine," she repeated.

She was not fine, but because he wanted to make sure Lucas was okay, he leaned her against the wall.

He retrieved his flashlight and went into the narrow, dark stone corridor.

He had to press himself against the rock.

When he arrived on the other side, it was, again, dimly lit with the strung lights. This was more like a room, and even had a metal ladder at its center going up into what looked like a gap in rocks just a few feet above his head.

But the layout of the room made him gasp.

Stone statues, as if for either a chapel or a graveyard, were laid out in three of the roughly sliced corners of the room. The one that drew his eye immediately was of a stone angel; another of the Virgin Mother; and finally, one of Christ, his hands spread out in front of him.

He remembered Scoleri's words: *a chapel of the*

*damned, with an angel and a virgin and a statue of
me, his God. But it's got bad stuff in it, too. It's the
heart of the Mad Place.*

They had been defaced with some dark sub-
stance. He could guess what it might be.

He hoped it wasn't blood.

The room's floor was rougher than the outer
room, and covered with pebbles. At its center, a
small bubbling pool of steamy water. A hot springs.
There must be several in the caverns.

The waters come up from Hell, Scoleri had said.

And there, gone fetal in a corner, his knees
tucked up against his face, his arms wrapped
around his knees, was Lucas Conroy.

"It's all right now," Trey said, softly but firmly.
"Lucas. We're going to get help."

The boy stirred and looked over at him. His eyes
were reddened and surrounded with dark circles.
His look, blank. He was in another world.

He'd been drugged. Trey wasn't sure what it
might be, but he'd seen drugged people before.
Darden State patients.

"Your mother sent me," Trey said, and went to
lift Lucas up in his arms.

As Trey did so, he took in the scrawls on the walls
of the chamber: devil faces and drawings of little
children with angel's wings around their necks.

Chapter Seventy-two

Feeling ragged, Trey cradled the boy in his arms as if he were his own son. He walked the hundred or so yards to the roadside. The crunch of fresh snow under his shoes felt good. Felt pure. He had been feeling the filth of the life that the Red Angel had at his core. He had intuited too much of the killer. It made him feel dirty. But the fresh cold air, the snow, the beautiful trees, and the dawn as it came on.

It gave him a sense of the spiritual. There was more to life than just the here and now. He was meant to help find Lucas. He was meant to do something to stop the man who had killed children.

His thoughts did not center on how he'd probably lose his job now for helping to break Scoleri out.

For setting Scoleri free.

He could not give a damn at the moment.

Elise Conroy was dead.

Children were dead.

But Lucas was safe.

It was all that mattered at the moment. Making sure that little boy got out of Hell.

Somewhere, over the chilly mountains, the sun was coming up from the desert.

The valley below, already warm, its lower elevations probably just reaching 70 degrees, while the mountains were in the high 20s.

From the cave behind him, steam came from the hot springs.

Trey kissed Lucas on the forehead. "It's okay," he said. "We'll get to help."

He took the boy and walked through the snow, following the stone path, where he could find it through the ice, that led up to a house.

Then he went into the house to call the police.

Chapter
Seventy-three

1

After the ambulances, and the plow to help get the ambulances through; after darkness bled into the purple beginnings of dawn; after too much questioning, both in the small trailer in Moon Lake, and then, down the mountain at the San Pascal police deparment; a trip the emergency room to make sure he was okay; an officer drove Trey back to Redlands. The cop told him that Trey's wife had been up most of the night, once the county police were on the horn about Laymon and Fasteau going missing, as well as the disappearance of two staff members and a patient of Darden State.

Trey was numb and had nothing more to say.

Nothing to feel.

All he thought about:
Home.

2

Trey walked into the dark house. He flicked on the hall light. He looked at the living room—the knick-knacks in cubby holes, the Spanish-style fireplace jutting toward the center of the room, the old sofas, the grandfather clock Carly's father had made. He looked out on the garden, the lights near the small reflecting pool hitting the shadows of bird-of-paradise and trumpet vine . . . He heard them.

Breathing.

His children.

He went into his son's room. Messy as it was. He stepped over a basketball left in the middle of the floor, around some plastic track he was building for his Hot Wheels. He sat down gently on the edge of Mark's bed. Mark snored a lot for a kid. Trey put his hand at the back of Mark's scalp and just held it there lightly.

Then, he went to his daughter's room, where he kissed her gently on the cheek. She turned slightly, her eyes still closed. In a dream.

After nearly an hour, he padded as quietly as he could down the hallway.

As he unbuttoned his shirt, Carly said sleepily, "Thank God. I thought . . ." But she didn't finish. "You've been hurt. Trey?"

He went to her and grabbed her, holding her as tightly as he could.

He kissed her and then smelled the faint scent of lavender and baby powder, and felt a tremendous burden lift.

Home.

"You okay?" she asked.

"Completely. Go back to sleep."

"They catch him?" she asked, but he could tell she was already back on the path of sleep.

"They did. I'll tell you the rest when I get up," he said. "Goodnight. I love you."

Even saying the words made him feel safe.

He slipped into bed beside her. They slept together, his arms around her. He felt her warmth, and didn't fall asleep for several minutes while he just listened to her gentle breathing.

It was the most beautiful sound on Earth.

Exhaustion finally took him into dreams.

3

Later that day, after he hugged his kids, after he checked the bandage on his scalp, he went to see two people in the hospital getting treatment. First, Lucas Conroy, whose father had spent the night with him in his hospital room.

Then Trey went to see Jane Laymon.

4

That morning, earlier, when it was still dark out, Monica Scrubb got off her night shift at the Donut Queen and dropped by the doctor's office to pick

353

up a prescription for the witch before she headed back up the mountain to the house on Moon Lake.

It took her longer than usual to get up there, and when she pulled off the road to park the truck, she knew something was wrong when the local deputy, Hank Dollard, was out front with a few folks from town, and there was yellow police tape all around the house.

Instinctively, she touched her stomach. "You're gonna be all right, Matthew-or-Greta, don't worry. The witch probably died."

But she wasn't sure why there'd be the sheriff out there if old Mrs. Cobble had finally kicked off in her sleep. Which Monica had been hoping would happen, along with that damn old dog of Duane's.

5

At the Critical Care section of ICU at San Pascal Valley Hospital, Ruthie Cobble lay in a bed, a ventilator to keep her breathing, on an IV, with monitors all around.

She looked out the half-opened blinds at the clear morning as it came up.

It was the first dawn she had seen in nearly fourteen years.

Ruthie Cobble continued sleeping, waking up now and then and believing that the hospital room was a dream. Although no one predicted that a woman who had been kept for years in a bomb shelter would still be alive, she seemed to show every sign of getting a little better as each minute passed.

5

In a jail cell at the San Pascal County Sheriff's office, it looked up at the ceiling and began praying that God would release it from its torment. After all, God had put the Other One in Hell, and had made the Other One live in the same body as it, the guy named Duane Cobble, who was a sniveling little freak.

No match for the Devil.

Abraxas. Abraxas. I need you. I need you.

Shackles on its ankles, it leaned back against the cold wall.

It closed its eyes and wished it were a little boy again, in the dark of the Mad Place, its father scourging its body with the barbed wire while Ruthie prayed as loud as she could to drown out its cries for help.

To stop the Beast from bringing about the end of the world.

The Other One began fighting for supremacy within its body, and the "it" called Duane receded again, going into the cage in its head to sleep.

Epilogue

1

Day. Sunny. Clear blue skies from the mountains to the sea. The mountains, snow-capped, the valleys, like a vision of heaven with palm trees.

A beautiful Southern California Christmas coming up.

Michael Scoleri rode a bus to downtown Los Angeles, all the while listening to a grandmother in her sixties, who had been a science teacher when she was younger but now was just a grandma, talk about her beautiful grandchildren and her wonderful daughter-in-law and brilliant son. He liked listening to her, and he found it refreshing to have so much noise around him. Wonderful human noise. When he got downtown, he stepped off at Rose Street, then walked up to Santa Monica, where he caught a bus going toward Hollywood.

At Cahuenga, he got off this second bus.

He decided he needed to find someone to take him in, at least for the night.

He'd work out what came next when he had the chance.

First things first.

Have to get a good meal, and find a pretty girl to have some fun with, he thought.

He began walking through the city, taking the wide boulevards, thinking of how beautiful and radiant it all was. No snow here. No rain. Just sun and shining buildings that reminded him of holy places. The shrines of worship. The cathedrals of mankind.

He needed a different kind of girl this time. The kind who understood him. The kind who would take care of him and help make everything all right this time.

He was sure he'd know the right girl when he saw her.

There were lots of pretty women in Los Angeles, nearly on every street corner.

To him, it was just like taking a stroll through paradise.

Pretty girls as far as the eye could see.

2

After a few days had gone by, and the Moon Lake Pure Spring Water company had sent a man to deliver a hundred more bottles to the Darden State Hospital for Criminal Justice in Southern California, to be brought in via the vending machines and the water coolers that were in the offices, including the office of Dr. Elise Conroy, the final message was found by the new delivery guy named Josh Schwartz in Conroy's office, just under where the water cooler rested on its dispenser platform.

From Michael Scoleri to the Red Angel.

On a scrap of paper, Scoleri had written:

Thank you for the beautiful angels, my brother. Love to Ruthie.